PRAISE FOR

A Window Across the River

"From the blank space where the twin towers used to stand to the 'haggard, heavy-bearded air' of Central Park in late summer, Morton paints the city and its denizens with a fine brush.... Nora and Isaac are wonderfully well drawn, an angular, asymmetrical pair whose love has nothing to do with happy endings." —*The New York Times Book Review*

"Some say that love has become too easy, in this era of no-fault divorce and serial monogamy, to make a good subject for novels anymore, but off in his own corner of the literary kingdom, Brian Morton is quietly proving them wrong."
—Laura Miller, *Salon*

"A story at once joyous, funny and bittersweet, told with delicate artistry and an aching regard for human frailty. For some readers, Brian Morton may still be an undiscovered treasure. He won't be for long." —Dan Cryer, *Newsday*

"Morton is particularly skilled at describing the sharp rattle of artistic failure, and at bringing to life the streets and rooms of New York, where the fates of his lonely and desperate characters unfold."
—*The New Yorker*

"The passions of Morton's characters ring true, unlike the hokum in *The Bridges of Madison County*, because the romantic ones conflict with such things as professional ambition and jealousy, or impulses that are not pure or admirable in character but exert equal pressures on the characters' psyches."

—*Chicago Tribune*

"Has both the precision of experience and the integrity of truth." —*The Washington Post Book World*

"The intimacy between Isaac and Nora is fully believable and beautifully realized. From it springs the larger theme of the relationship between intimacy and creativity, and between creativity and betrayal, because Nora, as we soon learn, can only write about people she knows."

—Simone Zelitch, *The Forward*

"Brian Morton is some strange kind of magician; his novels have the luminous transparency of a great city at twilight."

—Scott Eyman, *The Palm Beach Post*

"Terrific... An absolute pleasure... *A Window Across the River* is a very funny novel about a very serious dilemma: How a writer can be true to her writing and true to her loved ones at the same time." —Claire Dederer, *The Seattle Times*

"Portray[s] with fine sensitivity the dilemma of the female writer, who can only clear time and space for her work by refusing the expected role of caretaker."

—Adam Kirsch, *The New York Sun*

"A funny, precise and beautifully written novel. Morton's intelligence shimmers. His perceptions of the conflicts within the human heart are keen. I loved this book."

—Alice Sebold, author of *The Lovely Bones*

"Morton gracefully choreographs the lovers' wary dance, poignantly capturing Nora's ambivalence and Isaac's guarded adoration. . . . The modesty of this novel gracefully offsets the delicacy and insight with which Morton writes about the junction of love and art." —*Publishers Weekly* (starred review)

"There are no easy answers, according to this novel, which digs deep to sift out what people are made of. Recommended for all fiction collections." —*Library Journal*

"An intriguing look at the nature of love and the need for acceptance." —*Booklist*

A WINDOW ACROSS THE RIVER

A WINDOW ACROSS THE RIVER

Brian Morton

A HARVEST BOOK • HARCOURT, INC.
Orlando Austin New York San Diego Toronto London

www.HarcourtBooks.com

The author wishes to thank the John Simon Guggenheim Memorial Foundation for its generous support.

Library of Congress Cataloging-in-Publication Data
Morton, Brian, 1955–
A window across the river/Brian Morton.—1st ed.
p. cm.
ISBN 0-15-100757-8
ISBN 0-15-603012-8 (pbk.)
1. Fiction—Authorship—Fiction. 2. Women authors—Fiction.
3. Photographers—Fiction. I. Title.
PS3563.O88186W56 2003
813'.54—dc21 2003005373

Text set in Fournier
Designed by Cathy Riggs

Printed in the United States of America

First Harvest edition 2004
K J I H G F E D C B A

For Heather

1

SOMETIMES YOU LOSE TOUCH with people for no good reason, even people you love. Nora had lost touch with Isaac five years ago, but he kept coming back to her mind. He would appear to her in dreams (usually looking as if he was disappointed in her); things he'd said to her long ago would bob up into her thoughts; and sometimes when she was in a bookstore she'd drift over to the photography section to see if he'd put out another book. Through year after year of silence, she carried on a conversation with him in her mind.

Every few months she would pick up the phone with the intention of calling him—and then she'd put the phone back down. She wasn't quite sure why they'd finally stopped talking, but something prevented her from reaching out to him again. Maybe there *was* a good reason after all.

2

But tonight she was in a hotel room in the middle of nowhere; it was one in the morning; she'd been trying to get to sleep for hours and she was still bleakly awake; and it was one of those insomniac nights when it seems clear to you that your life has come to nothing, that you've failed at everything that matters and there's no point in trying again, and you know that it might help to talk to someone but you're not sure there's anyone who'd be willing to listen, and you lie there thinking *Is it possible to be any more alone than this?*

And the only person she wanted to talk to was Isaac.

But do you want to get back into that? She didn't know.

It had taken her so long to forget him. Not to forget him—she'd never been able to forget him—but to reach a point where the thought of him wasn't troubling her every day.

It was three in the morning where he was. He'd always been a night owl. He might still be up.

She called Information for the suburb where she'd heard he was living, and she got his phone number.

For all she knew he was married by now. It would be incredibly rude to call him at three in the morning.

It was the kind of thing she used to do all the time. She would call him at midnight, two in the morning, four, and he'd always be happy to hear from her. Once, when she was just getting to know him, she'd called him at midnight when he had another woman there; he was happy to hear from her even then. The other woman hadn't lasted long after that.

But that was a long time ago, when they were psychic twins, sharing every thought. It would be rude to call him now. It would be bratty.

She dialed his number.

After three rings, he picked up the phone. She could tell from his thick hello that he'd been sleeping.

She didn't say anything. Maybe this was all she'd wanted. To hear his voice was enough.

She didn't hang up, though.

"Hello?" he said again.

She just kept breathing.

"Nora?" he said.

After five years.

3

How did you know it was me?"

She heard him laughing softly. "I recognized your silence. It's different from anyone else's."

This might have been the most romantic thing anyone had ever said to her.

"How are you?" he said. "My Nora." His voice—his middle-of-the-night voice, his half-awake voice—was washing over her. He was the only person who'd ever been able to make her name sound poetic.

"Well," she said, "I've been better. Your Nora's been better than she is now."

"What's happening?"

"What's happening is that I've been going down the wrong road."

This sounded pretentious to her, or it would have sounded pretentious, except that talking to him, somehow, freed her to talk in an exalted way. Somehow he lifted her out of daily life.

"And now?" he said. "You're planning to change roads?"

"Yes," she said. "I want to. But I'm not sure I have the strength."

She didn't want to give him any specifics. She didn't know if this phone call was going to be a turning point for her—the inaugurating act of a new life—or if she was just going to burrow under the covers, get to sleep, and go back to the life she'd been living, the old inadequate life. In either case, she didn't want to clutter up the moment with details.

"Of course you do," he said. "I don't know what it is you need to do, but I know that whatever it is, you have the strength to do it."

This was one of the things she had always treasured about him: the faith he had in her.

She didn't say anything. For a minute or two she simply listened to him breathe.

She felt as if she was teetering between love and phoniness. The love was evident in the fact that after five years, they hardly needed to speak: they could just breathe into the phone and be satisfied. The phoniness was evident in the fact that she didn't *want* to speak. The problem with talking in the exalted lyrical mode that was available to them only because it was after midnight and he was half asleep and they hadn't spoken in years—the problem was that if she said something mundane she'd feel like a dope. She didn't want to relinquish her poetic foxiness.

"Maybe we can see each other someday," she finally said.

"That would be beautiful, Ruby," he said. "That would be beautiful."

He'd sometimes called her Ruby in the old days. Neither of them knew why.

There was another long silence, during which she began to feel comfortable again.

When they were younger, they sometimes used to talk late into the night and then fall asleep on the phone. It was one of the most intimate things she knew.

"I want to sleep on the phone with you," she said, "but I'm afraid that would be going too fast."

They both laughed—laughed at the absurdity of this; but at the same time, she meant it.

4

THIS IS WHAT IT'S LIKE to see someone you haven't seen in years. First, you recognize him instantly. Then, a moment later, you realize how much he's changed, and you wonder how you recognized him in the first place. Then, a minute after that, the past and the present begin to cooperate, and he doesn't look very different after all—in fact, he's always looked like this.

Isaac was sitting in a booth in the coffee shop. He stood up as she came toward the table, and they embraced. Isaac was a tall man and Nora was a small woman; he had to fold himself up in sections in order to embrace her.

As she held him, she searched for his scent. He smelled just like he used to: like good, warm, fresh, wholesome bread.

"I see you came straight from the bakery," she said.

She knew he had no idea what she was talking about, but it didn't matter. He was smiling.

She sat across from him. "You're looking well," he said quietly. Which meant he thought she looked beautiful. The more intensely Isaac was feeling something, the more understated he became.

"You are too," she said, although it wasn't true. He looked skinnier than he used to be, skinnier and bonier and balder. And even more frail.

For a minute or so, they didn't say anything. They didn't need to. The flow of information between two people who care for each other can be close to overwhelming. She could tell that his feelings about her hadn't changed.

A waiter appeared—male hipster with earring—and broke the mood. Isaac ordered a salad and a cup of tea, and Nora ordered a cheeseburger and a milkshake. In the olden days, she remembered, waiters always mixed up their orders: they'd put her steak and onion rings in front of Isaac, his pasta salad in front of her.

They were in a coffee shop on the Upper West Side that used to be one of their favorite spots. But it had changed. It used to be called the Argo, and it used to be filled with old people eating alone—people who looked as if they left their homes once a day to have a cup of Sanka and a bowl of soup. But now it was called the New York Diner, and its old shabby friendliness was gone. It was chic now, or retro, or something like that—it had been renovated to look like an imitation of the kind of place that it had once actually been—and it was filled with young people drinking microbrews, and it made Nora feel that the two of them would be foolish if they tried to recapture the past.

Isaac had called her that morning. He had to be in the city for work, and he'd asked if she was free for lunch. She worked at home—she worked as a freelance writer and copy editor for medical journals—so she could make her own hours. If he hadn't caught her off guard like that, she wasn't sure she would have said yes. She wasn't sure it was a good idea to see him.

"So what's going on with you, Nora? You were very mysterious on the phone."

"What's going on with me?" she said. "I guess you could say I want to transform myself."

"You told me that already. From what to what?"

"Back into a writer. From whatever it is I've become."

"Don't tell me you're not writing. I wouldn't believe it."

He actually looked shocked. Which made her happy. No one else in the world would have reacted like this. Hardly anyone else would have cared.

"I *am* still writing. But I'm not getting anywhere. I've been working on things I don't care about and avoiding the things I do. And I'm turning thirty-five this year. I feel like I'm too old. I feel like I'm finished."

"Oh, come on," he said. "Whatever your problem is, it's not that you're too old. A lot of people—"

"I know, I know. George Eliot was forty before she did anything decent, and Wallace Stevens was fifty, and a while ago there was that little granny who published her first novel when she was eighty-eight. I know all that. But I feel like if I don't turn my life around soon, I'm going to lose my chance."

The waiter came back with his tea and her milkshake.

She took a sip. "Midlife milkshake," she said.

"You're not in midlife," he said. "You're just a kid."

That was nice of him to say.

To him, she probably *was* just a kid. He had just turned forty.

Nora had been writing as seriously as she knew how for almost fifteen years now. She wrote short stories—she'd never attempted a novel, never written a poem. Because she was a slow writer, and because the short stories she wrote were actually pretty long, she'd only written about thirty or forty during all that time. Of that number, she'd published only five. But of those five, one had been selected for the annual volume of *The Best American Short Stories* and another for the Pushcart Press anthology *Best of the Small Presses.* As one of her old boyfriends had told her, she was like a ballplayer with a lousy batting average who'd gotten two clutch hits in the World Series.

Lately, though, she'd gotten stalled, in a miserably familiar way. She was a ballplayer in a slump.

Just seeing Isaac was a relief, just seeing his face. He'd always believed in her; he had a faith in her that bordered on the irrational. And even though he wasn't a reliable judge of her prospects, because he was somewhat crazy where she was concerned, seeing him made her feel better.

Isaac wasn't a lover of literature; he was a photographer who knew little about the other arts. But he understood the beauty and the nobility of giving yourself fully to a pure and disinterested pursuit. Even after years of being out of touch with him, she'd felt sure that he was the one person who could understand what she was going through, the one person to whom she could speak freely about the frustration of not being able to give herself to her vocation with the full-heartedness it deserved.

"I'm sorry it's been hard for you," Isaac said. "But look. You're gifted. That's a matter of record. All artists go through difficult patches, and you're going through one now. But you've written some wonderful things already, and if you just keep going, you're going to write a lot more. There's no doubt about that."

It was nice, what he was saying, but it didn't comfort her. He didn't know the whole story.

When she'd left her apartment, on her way to meet him, she thought she'd tell him everything, but now she realized that she wasn't going to be able to. She didn't want to tell him about the other dimension of her unhappiness. She didn't want to talk about Benjamin.

"Excuse me." She got up, went to the women's room (trying to walk gracefully, because she knew that he was watching her), went into a stall, sat down, put her head in her hands, and cried.

She wasn't even sure why she was crying. It wasn't just one thing. It was that she'd started out so strongly but had let her chance slip away, and now she was afraid she was too old. It was that she wasn't happy with Benjamin, but hadn't been able to leave him. It was that she was a weaker creature than she'd ever imagined she was.

She made a fist to punch the side of the stall, but then she decided that that would be melodramatic, and anyway she didn't want to hurt herself. She thought of maybe writing some graffiti on the wall, something as simple as *fuck you.* She searched in her bag for a pen, but she couldn't find one.

There was a spider making his way along the floor. She thought about stepping on him.

She didn't step on him. It isn't the spider's fault—she told herself reasonably—that you don't know if you have the strength to change your life.

She sat there watching the spider proceeding on his solitary mission.

"Hello, Spide," she said sadly.

In one of Chekhov's letters to his brother, who wanted to be a writer, Chekhov suggested that he write a story about a man who "squeezed the slave out of himself drop by drop." The phrase had stayed in Nora's mind; she sometimes used it against herself, when she felt she was living a kind of slave life.

Now, she thought, she had her chance. She had the chance to squeeze the slave out of herself. But she didn't know if she had the strength.

She got out of the stall and washed her face and put on some lipstick.

When she rejoined Isaac, the food was already on the table, but he hadn't started eating. He'd been waiting for her.

Maybe he would have waited for anyone: he was a gentlemanly man. But as he sat there in front of his untouched food, he looked so bony and spectral that she felt that it was a metaphor of his life: she felt as if he hadn't taken any nourishment of any kind since she'd left him. As if he'd been doing little but waiting for her.

Poor Isaac. She saw how selfish she was. She had come here to talk about herself; she'd barely asked about him.

"What's it like working as a photo editor?" she said. "What's it like having a real job?"

He used to make a living as a freelance photographer. He'd taught a little here and there, he'd been on some sort of contract with the *Village Voice,* but mostly he'd kept his time free in order to take the pictures he wanted to take. She'd always thought of him as a model of how to put your art ahead of everything else, and she'd been surprised, a few years back, when she heard that he'd taken on a full-time job.

"It's nice to get a steady paycheck. If I want to buy a pair of shoes now, I don't have to ponder the decision for a month and a half."

"Do you still have time for your own work?"

"Not as much. But it sort of concentrates the mind. If you know you only *have* an hour, you can get as much done in an hour as you used to get done in a day."

"And what's it like living in the suburbs?"

"It's not bad. It's clean. It's quiet. The supermarkets are amazing, if you care for that sort of thing. Everything's just easier out there. It's a semi-perfect life."

Semi-perfect. That seemed like a cue for her to ask a question: What do you mean by that?

But she didn't ask, because she thought she already knew what he meant. He meant that the only thing that was missing in his life was her.

She moved things around on the tabletop, which was composed of large black and white squares. The hot sauce captured the pepper, and then the ketchup put the mustard in check. "Are you still in touch with Meredith?" she said.

"Yeah. She moved to Texas."

"Really? Why?"

Isaac started to explain why she'd moved, and Nora didn't listen. Instead, she wondered why she'd asked. Meredith was a mutual acquaintance of no great importance to either of them.

"And then she decided Austin was more like New York than New York was, or something like that," Isaac was saying. "Austin is what New York was in 1962. I think that's what she said."

Nora reached across the table and put her hand over his. "I'm sorry. I don't really want to know about Meredith. And you probably don't want to talk about her. I'm sorry for asking."

"Then why'd you ask?"

"It was like our conversation was getting too real. I was trying to hide out in small talk. But I don't want to do that with you. If I can't be real with *you*, then I'm finished."

"I'm glad you're not finished," he said.

5

Nora lived on 108th and Broadway. Isaac had parked near there, so they walked together.

"Do you like it up here?"

"I do," she said. "It's exciting."

She used to live in the provinces—in darkest Brooklyn. She'd moved into Manhattan a year ago.

She loved living up here. She was telling Isaac a story about how she'd lucked into her apartment; as she talked, she was reveling in the day. It was a summerlike afternoon in the middle of May; Broadway was crowded with Columbia students, and Nora wondered about each one they passed: two fierce young men who looked as if they'd just been arguing about Trotsky; a woman browsing at the table in front of the art supply store, with a meditative expression and independent-minded hair; a Paul Bunyan type in a flannel shirt and overalls, who looked as if he'd been shipped in a box from New Hampshire. Isaac, though he was a photographer, trained to *see,* had his attention fastened to Nora so closely that he didn't seem to notice any of it. A beautiful young woman on Rollerblades swept by—tall, long-legged, in a halter top and shorts—and Isaac didn't even take a glance.

"Why don't you come with me?" he said. "I only need to work for an hour. Then I can introduce you to the mysteries of New Jersey."

"That sounds like every girl's dream. I wish I could. But I have to see Billie tonight."

Billie was Nora's aunt. Isaac smiled when he heard her name. He'd always liked her; everyone did. Billie was the most lovable person Nora knew. If you didn't love Billie, Nora sometimes thought, you didn't love life.

"How's she doing?"

"Not that great. They found a lump in her breast, and she has to go in for some tests this week."

"I'm sorry to hear that. Please give her my love." He opened the door of his car. "How about tomorrow?"

She felt weird about the idea of spending an evening with him. She *could* do it; Benjamin was at a conference in Berlin. But still.

She sometimes thought that she and Benjamin abided by an unwritten law that held that both could retain the opposite-sex friends they'd had before they met but couldn't make any new ones. Maybe most couples abide by that law.

She hadn't seen Isaac in years. Did he count as an old friend or a new one?

And how about sleeping with him? Did the unwritten law permit her to sleep with guys she'd slept with before she met Benjamin?

"I don't know," she said. "Maybe. Maybe not. I'll call you."

She didn't want to kiss him good-bye. In the old days, they'd never had a kiss that meant nothing. A Saturday-morning kiss on the street corner when he was heading off to do his laundry and she was buying the paper, and they'd be seeing each other again in half an hour—even when it was that kind of kiss, it never felt like a small thing.

But she didn't know if she was prepared for something like that now.

So no kiss.

She took off her watch, dropped it into the heart pocket of his shirt, and patted him there.

6

ISAAC DROVE BACK TO New Jersey, thinking about Muhammad Ali.

He was excited. And upset. And excited.

When Nora had called him last week, out of the blue—but not out of the blue at all, because he was always thinking about her—he'd had a mystical feeling that life was coming full circle. He'd always believed that someday she'd see the mistake she'd made when she left him, and that she'd come back to him.

But she evidently hadn't come back into his life to repair her mistake. It was impossible to tell *why* she'd come back. Or if she'd really come back at all.

He drove to his office, got some coffee, and forced himself to concentrate. He had to choose among sixteen photos of a town council meeting in Leonia; he had to choose all the photos for the sports section; and he had to put together a montage to illustrate an article on Disneyland. All in the next half hour.

He was mad at himself for asking her to get together. He should have let well enough alone.

It was *disturbing* to have Nora back in his life. It had taken him so long to wean himself, so long to let go of the longing. If he ever had. Which he hadn't.

Not too long after Nora left him, Isaac had spent a few months with a woman named Clarissa. She was bright, interested in him, accomplished—she was a cellist—and she was lovely; some people would have considered her far more attractive than Nora. One Saturday night they were in a bookstore on Broadway—he was still living in the city then—and he ran into Nora. Clarissa was upstairs in the poetry section, Isaac was browsing through photography magazines, and Nora floated over to say hello. They didn't say much—just exchanged a few superficialities—and they didn't touch, but he felt as if she'd placed her hand on his skin. When Nora left and he found Clarissa again, leafing through the love poems of Pablo Neruda, he knew he couldn't be with her. He didn't know if he'd ever see Nora again, but he knew he couldn't be with Clarissa.

In 1978, when he was in his teens, he had seen Leon Spinks, a negligible fighter, take the heavyweight title away from Muhammad Ali, who had grown listless and slow-footed with age. After the fight, talking with reporters, Spinks had graciously and accurately said, "He's still the greatest. I'm just the latest."

Nora, Isaac was thinking, was the Muhammad Ali of his romantic life. The women who'd come after her had had their virtues, but each of them had merely been the latest. And because of the memory of Nora, he'd been unable to give himself fully to anyone else. There wasn't room in his heart, it seemed, for more than one person.

And now she was in some sort of crisis of the spirit.

It was hard to listen to her talk about her crisis of the spirit. It was hard to listen to anything that didn't lead to *him*.

He sat at his computer, scrolling through photographs of Daisy Duck. From some angles Daisy was pretty sexy.

While Nora had talked about needing to change her life, needing to rededicate herself to her work, he'd been thinking, Do you really think that's enough? Isn't it fucking *obvious* what you need? Isn't it fucking clear to you that the big thing missing in your life is *me*?

When had men become women and women become men?

It had happened at some point during his lifetime. When he watched movies from the forties and fifties, the men and women struck him as so different from the men and women of today that he sometimes felt as if he was watching science fiction. The wimpiest man of the forties was manlier than the manliest man of today.

Pining after a woman for years, resenting her because she's more interested in her career than in being with you—how had this happened?

He didn't even know *why* he loved her.

Yes he did. He did know.

She excited him. She thrilled him. He'd never felt bored with her. He was always eager to hear what she had to say. In the old days, when they sometimes went to dinner parties where they had to sit apart from each other, the experience itself counted for nothing; what counted for everything was talking about it with her later. In the midst of the party, he'd sometimes watch her from across the room, watch the play of intelligence and humor in her eyes, and feel lucky to know that later that night he'd find out what she'd been thinking.

At the diner, listening to her story, he'd found it hard to believe that she was feeling so defeated. It wasn't the Nora he knew.

Years ago, shortly after he and Nora had started seeing each other, she lent her laptop to her friend Helen, whose four-year-old son got hold of it and zapped out of existence a story

Nora had been working on for six months. Nora hadn't saved it to disk, hadn't printed it out. After a night during which she looked seasick, and in which she watched the entire six-and-a-half-hour *Godfather Saga* on TV because it cheered her to see people blowing one another away, she calmly started afresh on the story the next morning. "This version'll probably be better," she'd said.

That was the Nora he knew.

The Nora he knew had a quietly ferocious tenacity that wouldn't let anything stand in her way.

She was more beautiful than ever, in his eyes. This was maddening; it would have been easier, in a way, if she weren't.

It was funny to think that when he first met her, he wasn't even that attracted to her. He liked her immediately, but she looked too pure to have lustful thoughts about. She looked very *healthy*—that was his first impression. She had the glowing skin of an athlete: a runner or a swimmer or a rock climber. Her nose was slightly, interestingly, crooked—probably, Isaac assumed, from some challenging activity too zealously pursued. A kayaking accident, maybe, or a pole-vaulting mishap. She didn't instantly stir up feelings of desire; she stirred up thoughts of hearty outdoor activities.

When he got to know her, he learned that she wasn't athletic in the least. The freshness of her skin, the subtle muscles of her arms and legs, her swimmer's shoulders—all this was part of her genetic inheritance, entirely unearned. She'd never been on a hike in her life, and she didn't even know *how* to swim. She hardly ever left the city. Once he'd managed to drag her off to a weekend in Maine, and when they got back to Manhattan, after they emerged from Grand Central, as they stood in the twilight with the Empire State Building and the

Chrysler Building blazing above them, she'd spread out her arms and said, "*This* is God's country, my friend!"

She liked to portray herself as a neurotic writer, housebound, averse to natural light, but that wasn't the way he saw her. He still saw her as a mountain climber, or as the moral equivalent. Confident and strong. She was a small slim slight woman, but he thought of her as the person who, if you were pinned beneath a car, would be the most likely to be able to free you.

After she broke up with him, one or two of his friends had suggested that his estimate of her—her brilliance, her beauty, her force—was exaggerated, and that he'd soon be able to see this, soon be able to downsize her in his imagination. But, for better or for worse, he never had.

He wondered whether she was really going to call him again. She'd always been impulsive. She was always getting in touch with people she hadn't spoken to in ages. She'd call up to apologize for something she'd done years earlier, usually something the other person didn't even remember. And then, after that, she might not call again, and if the other person called *her,* she might forget to call back.

He wondered whether he was going to have to wait another five years.

Didn't some guy have to wait seven years for a woman in the Bible—and then have to wait another seven years? The guy who wanted to marry Rachel, but ended up marrying Leah by mistake? He tried to call it up, but he couldn't quite remember the story.

7

NORA STOOD ON THE SIDEWALK, waiting to catch the keys. Her aunt Billie lived in a fourth-floor walk-up on West Fifty-first Street, in the neighborhood that used to be called Hell's Kitchen. Nora couldn't remember what it was called now. Billie couldn't buzz her visitors into the building, so she'd stand at the window and toss them a set of keys.

When Nora was a girl, she and her mother would come to New York to visit Billie two or three times a year, and she was always thrilled by the sight of Billie throwing down her keys. It seemed like something from a fairy tale—Rapunzel letting down her hair. It made her aunt seem magical.

Billie's head appeared in the window.

"Hello, my dovecote," she said. "Could you pick up my mail in the lobby? It's the tiny key."

She lobbed the keys down to the sidewalk. They were on a chain with a lucky rabbit's foot.

Nora let herself into the lobby, got Billie's mail, and made her way up the stairs, thinking she needed to exercise more. The stairwell smelled like boiled potatoes.

As she climbed the stairs, she was thinking about how to cheer Billie up. Two weeks ago, Billie had found a lump in her breast. A biopsy had revealed a cluster of irregularly shaped cells, and she was going in for a lumpectomy in two days.

She'd had breast cancer four years earlier; during the last six months she'd been starting to believe that she might have "beaten" it. But now there was this.

Nora tried to be cheery on the first two flights; on the next two she tried to be resolute. She was telling herself not to cave.

In three days, Nora was leaving for a month-long stay at MacDowell, the artists' colony in New Hampshire. She'd never been to an artists' colony before, but it sounded like paradise. She would get her own private cabin; a silent ghostly butler would leave breakfast and lunch at her door; and she'd have no responsibilities other than to write all day. Nora had applied on a whim—she didn't think she'd have a chance of getting in. But she did get in, and now she couldn't wait. With a month alone, with nothing to do but work, she might finally find her way back to writing short stories.

She'd heard a rumor that Grace Paley was going to be there. Grace Paley, whose stories, when Nora read them in her teens, had made her want to be a writer. A month of writing all day and then having dinner with Grace Paley!

Ever since Billie found out she'd need to have an operation, though, Nora had been thinking of giving up MacDowell. She was thinking she'd rather stay in the city and take care of her aunt. Now, on the stairs, she was telling herself not to do that. She'd be in New York for a couple of days after Billie's operation, and after that she'd be in touch by phone. That was enough. You can take care of your loved ones and still take care of yourself.

Billie was waiting at her door, in sweatpants and a sweatshirt. When Nora came forward to kiss her, she closed her eyes and offered Nora her cheek—receiving the kiss with a childlike intensity, as if she wanted to store it on her skin so she could recollect the sensation later. "I'm so happy to see you," she said.

She put her hands on Nora's shoulders, beaming.

"I always forget how tiny you are," Billie said. "You're like a pocket pal."

She hurried ahead of Nora into the living room, picked up a lint catcher—a plastic rolling pin with a sticky surface—and ran it over the easy chair. She performed the task with great enthusiasm but little craft; when she was done there were still wide patches of cat hair left untouched. Nora sat down anyway.

"Would you like some soda pop?"

"Sure. Thank you."

Billie seemed very excited. It was as if she was so happy to see Nora that she'd forgotten what was in store for her that week. She was humming to herself as she poured Sprite into a glass. She came out of the kitchen with the glass in one hand and a box of prunes in the other.

"Prunes?"

Nora declined the prunes.

"They're all I have to snack on. I tried to order cheese and crackers from the deli but they don't give me credit anymore."

"Do you need some money?"

"No—thank you. I got my Social Security check yesterday. I can cash it this afternoon."

Billie received monthly checks from her pension and from Social Security, and she lived in a rent-controlled apartment, but she was always broke by the end of the month. "I'm not a balance-the-checkbook kind of girl," she'd once explained.

When Nora was little, her aunt seemed to glide above the normal rules of existence. Life treated her generously. If she arrived at the bank at three, just as the guard was locking the door, she'd smile at him with a sort of hopeful helplessness, and he'd let her in. If she didn't have the fare for a cab ride, she could charm the cabbie into taking her for free. When Nora was a girl, Billie's life seemed to offer a glimpse of the magical possibilities of womanhood.

"Do you know they're not called prunes anymore?" Billie said. "They're called dried plums now. The fruit companies think prunes have a bad reputation."

She removed one from the box and drew it toward her. "Don't worry," she whispered. "I'll still call you a prune." Then she kissed it, and then she put it in her mouth.

Billie was the only family Nora had. Nora had no brothers or sisters, and her parents had died when she was still in her teens.

"Are you sure you want to come to the hospital with me?" Billie said.

"Of course I am. Of course."

"You're a state-of-the-art niece," Billie said. She picked up her lint catcher again and ran it affectionately over Nora's knee.

Nora didn't feel state-of-the-art. She was feeling guilty: she hadn't seen Billie in weeks.

"How have you been?" Nora said.

Stupid question, she thought, but Billie didn't treat it as such.

"Fine, except for this dumb lump. Keeping busy. It's about all I can do to keep track of these babies. It's like a full-time job."

The babies were her cats, who were far from babies now. Dolly must have been twenty, and Louie and Edwin weren't much younger.

"What else have you been up to?" Nora said.

"I don't know. Just waiting for the Romance Channel to arrive." She laughed—a self-conscious, embarrassed laugh.

"The Romance Channel?"

"It's a new TV station. They don't have it in Manhattan yet, but they keep running these ads. If enough people vote for it, they might bring it here."

"How do you vote?"

"You call this 800 number. I call it a lot. I put it on speed dial."

The Romance Channel. Billie had gotten married at twenty. When she and Nelson were in each other's presence, they'd always seemed a little giddy, as if they'd each had a glass and a half of champagne. They had a crush on each other for twenty years. To Nora, they had seemed like Zelda and F. Scott Fitzgerald, presiding over their own private Jazz Age.

Nelson died a week before their twenty-first anniversary. Waiting for the downtown E train at Forty-second Street, he'd had a heart attack and died on the platform.

Something stopped working inside Billie after Nelson died. She stopped going to movies and museums; she stopped seeing friends—she just came home from work every evening, double-locked her door, and watched TV. Sometimes, when Nora saw a certain expression on her face, a sort of patient sadness, she got the feeling that Billie was still waiting for Nelson to come home.

When she ventured into the outside world, Billie still relied on the old tools: she was still trying to charm her way through life. But now that she was in her sixties, her charm couldn't take her very far. It didn't keep banks open; it didn't win her free rides. And Nora always found herself wondering—as she never had when she was young—*why* Billie could never get it together to get to the bank on time or pay the cab fare or remember to buy toilet paper or pay her bills.

It was odd. Before her retirement, Billie had been working all her life—first as a dancer, then as a physical therapist at a children's hospital—yet after Nelson died she seemed to be waiting for someone to come along and take care of her. And no one ever had.

For Nora, Billie's life remained a picture of the possibilities of womanhood—but it was a different kind of picture now. As much as she loved her aunt, it was a picture of what to avoid.

Louie, a heavy Persian cat, made his way up to Nora's lap. In his youth he had been a spry thing, but scaling the easy chair was now an undertaking that called upon all his years of hard-won craft.

"Louie still loves you," Billie said. "It's like you haven't missed a day."

Nora ran her hand over his back.

"My community isn't in very good shape," Billie said. "Dolly had a stroke last month." She knelt next to Dolly, who was lying in the corner. "She only eats if you feed her with a spoon. She only eats if you help her." She dipped a spoon into a bowl of water that was sitting on a plastic mat on the floor, and held the spoon near Dolly's mouth. Dolly shifted her head slightly. She hesitantly put out her tongue and touched the water, barely disturbing its surface.

"She's a good girl," Billie murmured. "Good lady."

Maybe, Nora thought, I can call MacDowell and ask if I can get there a few days late.

Except she'd already done this, and they'd told her that if she couldn't come for the full month, she'd have to forfeit her place. They had a long waiting list of people who could put the month to good use.

When Billie sat back down, she looked at the letters Nora had brought up.

She opened one of the envelopes. "Shoot."

"What's the matter?"

"This is from the cable company. They're going to turn off my cable tomorrow."

"Tomorrow? They should give you more notice than that."

"They gave me notice. They called. I just forgot."

"Do you need some money? I can write them a check if you want."

"Thank you. But that's not the problem. I can pay them after I cash my Social Security, but it means I'm not going to be able to tape the Daytime Emmys Thursday night." Again she laughed her embarrassed laugh. "I love the Daytime Emmys. I was planning to tape it and watch when I get back from the hospital. There's this twelve-year-old boy down the hall who comes over and sets the VCR for me."

"I can call them up and pay for it with my credit card."

"Thank you, but they only let me pay them with a certified check. They know me down there by now."

"I can tape it for you."

"Really?" Billie said. She looked astonished, as if Nora had mentioned that she was going to be assisting the surgeon during Billie's operation. "You know how to work those things?"

"Sure," she said. She actually didn't, but Benjamin did. Nora made a mental note to leave him a message.

Billie looked like she couldn't believe her good fortune. It was sad to think that a kindness this small made her aunt this happy.

The Daytime Emmys. The Romance Channel. Nora felt

an obscure shifting, as if every particle of tenderness within her was rising up and streaming toward her aunt.

Don't do it, Nora thought. You can take care of her before you go and after you get back. You don't have to give up MacDowell.

"I hope they don't have to take my breast off," Billie said. "I'm already a fat old bag. That's all I need—to be a fat old Amazon."

"Oh, come on. You're beautiful, Billie." This wasn't true, but she *had* been so beautiful when she was younger, and Nora remembered it so vividly, that it seemed true.

"I don't understand how everything happened," Billie said. "I still feel like the girl who won the jump-rope contest in fifth grade."

Nora took her aunt's hand. At the moment when they touched, Nora knew that she wouldn't be going to MacDowell. Not now, at least. She could reapply later.

"Everything's going to be fine," Nora said. She had to force these words out of her mouth—they sounded completely false to her. But they seemed to comfort her aunt.

I'm too young, Nora thought. *I'm too young for this kind of responsibility.* But as soon as she thought it, she realized that it wasn't true: she wasn't too young at all.

8

After she left Billie's, Nora daydreamed about going out to New Jersey, ringing Isaac's doorbell, and, then, without a word, giving him a long kiss.

What she actually did was more prosaic: she went back to her apartment and soaked her arm. When she was seventeen, two weeks after her mother died, Nora got drunk with a boy whom she knew to be an idiot and persuaded him to drive her to New York and join her in forming an artists' collective, a journey that began in the parking lot of the Lamplighter's Bar in Chicago and ended ten blocks east of there when he ran a red light and hit a stretch limo that was carrying the mother of the former Harlem Globetrotter Meadowlark Lemon. Nora was the only person hurt; she broke her nose, not very badly, and her left arm, badly. She was alone in the world—her father had died two years earlier—and although her parents' friends had arranged to take care of her during her last year of high school, their arrangement, in which she was shuttled from one home to another, meant that no one person was responsible for her, and therefore that no one was responsible for her at all. Her arm, which had been broken in five places, was treated by a not-very-competent doctor, and never healed properly; it hurt more keenly year by year. It looked normal now except for the thin scar that curled around her bicep, but it never felt quite right, and whenever she spent a lot of time at the keyboard it ached the next day—it ached, in other words, almost every day of her life. The pain had its own mysterious rhythms: it usually showed up only for about half an hour a day, but she could never anticipate when that half hour would come. The only things that seemed to help were Advil and ice. Almost every day she soaked her arm in ice water or strapped on a Polar Pack, an ice pack that you could wear like a sleeve.

After she finished soaking, she made herself a cup of tea and checked her answering machine. There were two messages from old friends; a message from someone at a medical journal, reminding her of a copy-editing deadline; and a message from Benjamin. His conference was wrapping up; he'd be home in two days. In her unhappiness she gulped the tea and burned the tip of her tongue.

It was as if she was punishing her tongue for its desire to play around with Isaac's.

She sat down to do some writing. Recently she'd interviewed the songwriter Richard Buckner for a weekly paper in Detroit, and she had to write it up by the end of the week.

Nora kept her laptop computer on a card table near her living-room window. From where she sat, she could see a thin slice of the Hudson River and the cliffs of northern New Jersey. Soon after she moved here, she'd heard that Isaac was living in New Jersey, and she would often look out across the water and think about him. Sometimes at night she'd stand at her window watching the tiny lights of the cars on the other side of the river, imagining that one of the cars was Isaac's. She imagined him coming home, very late at night, to a clean and well-ordered apartment, and watching the news, and getting ready for bed. Thinking of him this way, as she watched the lights, had always given her a mixed feeling of comfort and loneliness.

She thought of what he'd said that afternoon: she'd written wonderful things already, and if she just kept going, she'd write a lot more.

If only it were true. She *had* kept going: she wrote every day; but it had been a long time since she'd written anything she could be proud of. She'd been writing articles and reviews, things she didn't care about much. Though she began her writing session every day by opening a new document on her computer and trying to get a story started, within half an hour she would delete what she had written, if she had managed to write anything, and then she'd turn to some piece of nonfiction—something that interested her less, something that challenged her less.

A year earlier, Benjamin had spent two days in the hospital with symptoms of heart disease. She'd been planning to break up with him, but after he got sick she couldn't do it, and she'd stuck with him, unhappily, from then till now. And during the course of the year, her imagination had closed up shop.

A FRIEND OF NORA'S HAD ONCE summed her up by saying that she couldn't decide whether she wanted to be Virginia Woolf or Florence Nightingale. It was as if she had two needs in life: the need to write and the need to take care of people. The problem was that she couldn't seem to do both at the same time.

In daily life, she was a kind person—at least she hoped she was. But in her stories, she wasn't kind at all. When she sat down at the keyboard, it was as if someone else took over: someone who'd had the same experiences she'd had, but who saw the world with a cold eye.

This wouldn't have been a problem if she wrote about invented people in invented situations. But when she wrote, she became a cannibal, feeding off the lives of acquaintances, friends, and loved ones. The only time she felt excited as a writer was when she was writing about people she knew, and, almost always, she gravitated to their secrets and their frailties. The things they feared about themselves, the things they hoped no one would ever notice—Nora had a gift for divining them. It was a gift she didn't possess at all in her day-to-day life; it was something that emerged only in her fiction. Her fiction was more perceptive than she was, and more ruthless.

In college she'd had a friend named Gina, a brilliant funny charming tender messed-up girl. "Every day is a mountain," she once said to Nora, and if she'd had a coat of arms, that could have been inscribed on it; there was something about her that simply wasn't fit for daily life. When she was in one of what she called her "blue periods," she could go for days without leaving her room, and Nora would visit her every evening, bearing sandwiches and juice and magazines. Nora genuinely cared about her. But at the beginning of their junior year, when Nora found herself writing a story about Gina, a spirit of heartlessness took over her pen, and Gina became a virtuoso of victimhood, a woman whose weakness was her only tool, a tool she loved too much to let go of.

Gina had once told her that she'd been sexually molested by her grandfather. Except for her therapist, she'd never told anyone but Nora. She asked Nora never to talk to anyone about it, and Nora never had...but it made its way into the story.

When Nora was writing fiction, she became so impersonal, such a servant of the story, that although she was writing something based on Gina's life, she barely thought of Gina at all as she worked on it. She gave no thought to the ethics of telling someone else's secrets. The only thing she worried about was that sexual abuse had become such a cliché in fiction that she wasn't sure she could say anything fresh about it. It was only after she finished the story that she remembered it was based on her friend's life.

Nora was taking a writing class that semester. She didn't show the story to the class, because some of the people in it knew Gina and would have recognized her. She did show it to her teacher, however, who told her it was the best piece of student writing he'd read in years and urged her to submit it to *Small Craft Warnings,* the college literary magazine. Nora said she couldn't, but didn't tell him why.

One day at the end of the fall semester, when Nora was in the library, she saw a stack of freshly printed copies of *Small Craft Warnings.* She picked one up and looked idly at the table of contents. She noticed that one of the stories was called "The Mountain"—the same title she'd given hers. Then, next to the title, she saw her name.

She got the number of the editor-in-chief, and after she'd screamed at him for a while, he told her that the story had been submitted by her teacher. She called *him*—a little too cowed by authority to scream at him, but she let him know she was mad—and he told her that he'd thought she was merely "afraid of success."

After this she went straight to Gina's room, to warn her and to apologize.

Gina was in bed, sitting up, with her arms wrapped around her legs. The magazine was on the bed beside her.

"Why did you do this?" she said.

"I'm so sorry. I never meant for it to be published."

She explained what had happened, but Gina didn't look mollified.

"When I told you about my family," she said, "I thought you understood it as an act of trust. I feel like I've been..."

Nora knew her well enough to know what she'd intended to say: that she felt as if she'd been violated all over again. But Gina didn't finish the sentence. She was an honest person, and she didn't want to confuse the issue by exaggerating.

Somehow, knowing this, knowing what Gina had the self-control not to say, made Nora feel worse than she would have felt if Gina had said it.

"My mother's going to read this, you know."

"You don't know that."

"I do know that. They send this thing to everybody's family, because Swarthmore is so proud of all its little student writers. My mother likes you. When she sees your name, she'll read the story. I wanted her to learn about what happened when I was ready to tell her. Now she's going to learn about it because of you." Gina picked up the magazine and tossed it to the floor. "I don't even *care* that you didn't want it to be published. That's not the point. I can't understand why you thought you had the right to put it down on paper in the first place."

"That's what a writer does," Nora said.

"It isn't what a friend does."

Nora couldn't think of a reply, and didn't want to. Gina had the right to the last word.

Gina didn't come back to school for the spring semester. There were rumors that she was in a psychiatric hospital, rumors that she'd tried to harm herself. Nora kept leaving messages for her at her mother's house, but Gina never called her back.

Nora tried not to blame herself for whatever had happened to Gina. She'd always been close to the edge, and Nora couldn't be sure it was her story that had pushed her over. But she could never think of her again without feeling guilty and ashamed.

She tried to change her way of writing: she tried to write about people who didn't exist. She tried the unfamiliar strategy of using her imagination—that was the way she put it to herself in a moment of self-loathing. But she couldn't do it. Rather, she could do it, but the stories that came out were flavorless and flat. The only time the act of writing lit her up was when she was writing about someone she knew.

After her junior year she transferred to NYU, and in the spring she got an internship as a teaching assistant at an elementary school. She became friendly with the head teacher, a woman named Sally. Sally, in her thirties, was unmistakably an adult—she was a capable, confident teacher—but she had a way of letting you know that she still felt baffled by life. Nora couldn't afford to be baffled by life—she'd had to meet life one-on-one, with no guidance, no protection, ever since she was seventeen—but being with Sally softened her up in a way she needed, helped her let her guard down. Nora had dinner with Sally and her family every few weeks; she babysat for Sally's boys; she had long conversations about literature with Sally, who was an ardent reader. Nora felt lucky to know her.

Then Nora wrote a story in which Sally was the main character—not as she was, but as she would be. It was about Sally Burke at sixty. It was a story about a woman who felt she'd never really lived. Nora titled it "What She Wasn't."

Part of the story was about Sally's marriage. Sally's husband was a union organizer: a Good Samaritan, an idealist, a believer in the dignity of labor. He was the Nicest Guy in the World. All of which made him, in twenty-one-year-old Nora's eyes, a bore. The blandness of goodness. He would corner you and tell you that the world should be a place in which no one goes hungry, and that everyone should have health insurance, and that everybody should have the right to a job at a decent wage. All of this was, of course, true, but the calm, thorough manner in which he would elaborate on these insights made Nora feel as if she was visiting one of those dentists who use laser technology. The experience wasn't exactly painful, but she still wanted to get away as quickly as she could.

In the story, the character based on Sally remembers a more passionate relationship she had when she was young (with a character Nora made up; Sally had never talked about anything like this) and wonders what her life would have been like if she'd stayed with him.

Sally had expressed an interest in reading Nora's fiction, and this was the story Nora decided to let her read. She thought Sally would find it amusing to trace the influence of writers they'd talked about—to find herself a character in a story that contained a hint of James's "The Beast in the Jungle," a hint of Joyce's "The Dead." Nora had known that her story about Gina would hurt her, but she was incapable of imagining that she had the power to hurt Sally, a woman in her thirties, an adult.

Nora gave Sally the story on the last day of the school year. Sally said she was eager to read it, but Nora heard nothing from her for two weeks. Finally, Nora called her, and they arranged to meet at a coffee shop. After they ordered, Nora asked her if she'd had a chance to read it yet.

"Yes, I read it. I read it the day you gave it to me."

"What did you think?"

"I can't say it filled me with a fond elation," Sally said. Sometimes she talked like a book. "First of all, it's not exactly flattering to be the main character in a story about someone who hasn't really lived. But the more important thing is, I *trusted* you. Which means that when you were baby-sitting my kids, I didn't expect that you'd be going through my diaries. I don't care that you went snooping. Everybody snoops. But to find my keys and go into the closet and unlock the trunk and read my diaries...and then to write a little fable in which everything is true but everything is taken out of context. How did you expect me to react?"

Nora told her she didn't know what she was talking about.

"Come on, Nora. *Jesse*?"

Jesse was the name of the old flame in the story.

"Holy shit," Nora said. "You mean there *was* a Jesse?"

"Yes," Sally said. "There was a Jesse. His name was Jesse."

"Are you serious?" Nora said.

"Are you saying you came up with the name Jesse out of the blue?"

"Of course I did. God! How weird. Maybe I'm psychic. That's incredible." She was talking too fast. In her own ears she sounded guilty, even though she wasn't. She'd snooped around in Sally's medicine cabinet and in one or two dresser drawers, maybe, but she'd never gone searching for diaries.

Sally finished her coffee and studied Nora as if she was trying to decide about her once and for all. "I'm not sure if I believe you," she said.

They sat there awkwardly for a minute, and then Sally gathered up her things. "Well, good luck," she said. Nora never heard from her again.

The episode left Nora with a confused wash of emotions. She regretted hurting someone she cared about; she was distressed about being suspected of doing something she hadn't done. But she was also filled with a feeling of power. It wasn't the first time she'd seen that her fiction had the power to hurt people—but it *was* the first time she saw that it had the power to root out the truth about people's lives.

She never again had such an uncanny visitation of knowledge; she turned out not to be psychic after all. But time and again, she found that once she started writing about people, she intuited more about them than they wanted anyone to know. It was as if she had a dowsing rod that led her straight to people's psychic frailties.

After she graduated, she started sending stories out to magazines, but she didn't do it often. The stories she did try to publish were those in which she turned the magnifying glass on herself, or on her parents, who were safely dead, beyond the reach of her treachery. She had a fear, perhaps an exaggerated fear, of hurting anyone else with her writing, so although she was writing all the time, most of her stories ended up in a cardboard box in her closet.

When she started to have serious relationships with men, it all got worse. When she was betraying friends, or dead people, even if she never tried to publish the stories, she could at least *write* them. But with her boyfriends, she had trouble doing even that. When she was seeing a man, she would inevitably start to write about him, and inevitably start to explore his weaknesses. And then, in midstory, as soon as she realized what was happening, her imagination would freeze.

The first time it happened was with her first post-college boyfriend, Daryl. Daryl, who worked in a bookstore, struck most people as low-key, unambitious, content. He put in his eight hours at the Strand during the day and then came home and studied the sports page. Nora felt good with him; she'd never been so relaxed with a man before. They had keys to each other's apartments; they wore each other's shirts. But at some point she started writing a story about him, and in the story, the things she knew about him came together in new combinations, and what emerged was a portrait of a someone who was still very young but who had already been defeated by life.

In the story, the central fact about Daryl was a disappointment he'd suffered in his teens. At fourteen, Daryl had won a national chess tournament. He was the best high-school chess player in the country, and he expected to compete for the world championship someday. But that didn't come to pass. He never got any better than he was at fourteen, and, in his freshman year of college, after he tried to enter a national college tournament and didn't even manage to qualify, he got rid of his chessboards and chess books and never touched them again.

Nora had never thought about this consciously—she wasn't even sure she believed it—but if what her story was saying about Daryl was true, he was living the rest of his life in the shadow of this defeat. He worked as a bookstore clerk not because he had no ambition, but because he had world-consumingly vast ambitions that would never be fulfilled. In his own mind, he was an exiled prince, from a country that had been wiped off the map: the country in which his brilliance would be clear to all.

Once she saw where it was going, she felt uneasy about the story, but at the same time she was immersed in it. She didn't want to leave the keyboard. And then one evening she came home from the store to find Daryl sitting in her living room with the light off, the pages of her half-written story scattered on the floor.

She turned on the light.

He didn't look up at her.

"This is me?"

"It's a story," she said.

"Last week, when we were in the park, you said you wanted to be good to me."

She had said that, and she'd meant it.

"Is this what you think it means to be good to me?"

She spent the rest of the night apologizing. It was as if he'd found out that she had another lover. She knew she wouldn't touch the story again. When she saw him sitting there in the dark, when she heard his voice—when she heard the note of need in his voice—it was as if all the cells in her body had rearranged themselves. Taking care of Daryl, shielding him from his sense of himself as a failure, became more important than anything else.

During the rest of her time with him—and when she was thrown against the same wall with her next boyfriend—she backed off from fiction completely. She still wrote: she wrote every day, religiously, for four hours. But instead of writing stories, she wrote book reviews and record reviews. She started to write for the *Village Voice* and the *Boston Phoenix* and the *LA Weekly* and the *San Francisco Bay Guardian*. Her career flourished when she wasn't writing fiction, because she got her name in print much more often with this other stuff. But it was written with her left hand. This wasn't writing that engaged her; this wasn't a vocation she loved; and when she was doing it she felt as if she was turning away from her one true calling. But it felt as if there was a contradiction between writing and taking care of people, and if there was, then she couldn't choose writing.

Her mother had also been afflicted with the caretaking disease. Nora's father, Arthur, after an unsuccessful, throat-clearing career in the classroom and another decade spent sulkily hanging around on the margins of the academic world, had finally become an editor for *Junior Science*, a periodical that was delivered weekly to thousands of middle schools across America and read by no one. Her mother, Margaret, had taught philosophy at the University of Chicago. Margaret was the more accomplished of the two: she was a demanding but popular teacher—her lectures were always boomingly overregistered—who had written three well-regarded books, while Arthur had ended up in a job that meant nothing to him, assigning articles about bacteria. And yet Margaret had a way of putting herself in the background, letting her husband be the star of the show. If the two of them started speaking at once, Margaret would fall silent and let Arthur finish his thought; if anyone asked for their opinion about something, it was always Arthur who answered. It was the oldest story in the world: the woman turns down her light to avoid outshining her man.

So when Nora asked herself why her creative life shut down when she was with a man, she certainly could have put the blame on her parents. But she didn't want to. She didn't want to pass the buck; she didn't want to march in the Great American Victim Parade. If your parents are alcoholics, you might become an alcoholic yourself, or you might become a teetotaler. Or you might become someone who drinks in moderation.

Nora had never written about Benjamin, but she had a sense of the story she would have written if she'd felt free to write it. A few times she'd sat down and made notes, and even the notes disturbed her. What disturbed her was what a satirical character he seemed bent on becoming. Benjamin was a professor of German literature at the City University of New York. In real life he was a serious person, genuinely interested in ideas, but in her notes he became something else: a pompous little pedant with a puffed-out chest, excitedly telling people that he was off to give an "endowed lecture" at the University of Heidelberg (not just a lecture, but an endowed lecture; she wasn't sure what an endowed lecture was, but Benjamin always spoke in an awed tone about the people who gave them). In her notes he became even shorter than he was in real life, a tiny tenured tyrant, browbeating students and departmental secretaries in a high-pitched voice.

What am I? she kept thinking, when she looked over what she wrote. *Is this what I think of him? Is this who I* am—*someone who can write such things about someone who cares for me?*

After Benjamin got sick, her imagination shut down completely. She couldn't even make the notes anymore. Everything about her got heaved overboard—her independence, her need for solitude, her need to pursue her work—everything except the need to take care of him. But the cost to herself had grown too great. She didn't want to take care of him anymore. She needed to change her life.

THE TIP OF HER TONGUE still hurt. She went to the refrigerator, got out an ice-cube tray, held it over the kitchen counter, and cracked it, and four or five ice cubes went hopping over the counter. It was like they were making a break for it.

She put the ice cubes back in the freezer except for one that had skated under the toaster. That one she picked up and pressed against her tongue. No kissing tonight. But maybe tomorrow.

9

SHE WAS WALKING UP a long hill in the soft New Jersey suburb where Isaac lived. It was the height of spring, with wisteria blooming everywhere—maybe; she was a city girl, and she didn't really know what wisteria was. But plant life of some kind was in bloom: mild, inoffensive, uninteresting.

Trees and flowers get a lot of good press, she thought, but what are they good for? They don't provoke; they don't stimulate; they don't have anything to say. How could he have ended up in a place like this?

He'd told her on the phone that he needed to spend most of the day in his darkroom, so she was meeting him there. Later, they were dropping by at a going-away party for one of his co-workers, and then they were having dinner.

That was all they'd planned. She didn't know what would happen after dinner. She didn't know if they were going to kiss.

Her tongue was healed, so she was ready.

Physically ready—but she didn't know if it was the right thing to do. It would be wrong to cheat on Benjamin, and it would be cowardly to use one man as a lever to pry herself free from another.

AFTER HE OPENED THE DOOR to her, he stepped back, looking at her with such happiness that it was almost hard to bear. It was like too much light.

He took her hand and slipped her watch around her wrist. "I've been looking all over for the woman this belonged to," he said.

As he fastened the watchband, his fingers on her wrist felt good.

She followed him into the darkroom.

"This is it," he said.

"It's nice."

"Does it seem familiar?"

It did. It had the same feel as his old darkrooms—the one in Williamsburg, and then, after the building was condemned, the one in Fort Greene. Everything was neatly arranged; everything was clean—gleaming, even in the dark. There was the same easy chair in the corner, the same antique radio on the shelf. On the wall there was the same solitary photo: a tabletop with two pairs of wire-rimmed glasses, an ashtray, and a pipe. She remembered that the pipe and glasses belonged to Piet Mondrian; she couldn't remember who the photographer was.

She used to love to spend time with Isaac in his darkroom, talking with him while he worked. It was a magical place. She felt snug, hidden, safe.

"Happy darkrooms are all alike," she said.

"Can I get you something?" He looked nervous. He picked up a plastic bottle and waved it in the air. "Can I get you some solvent?"

Yes, she thought, I need to be solved, but she didn't say it. She didn't want to seem as self-obsessed as she probably was. Also she couldn't tell if it was witty or not.

Also, she didn't think she *did* need to be solved. She just needed to change her life.

Once again, she had a moment of difficulty putting him together with her memory of him. Over the last year, whenever she was dissatisfied with Benjamin, she'd been able to think, "Isaac wouldn't have done that," or "Isaac wasn't like that." As a figure in the past, he'd seemed infinitely cooperative. But now, as he stood a few feet away from her, she suddenly recalled all the times when he hadn't wanted to do what she'd wanted to do or when they hadn't understood each other's jokes. She'd once written a story called "Things that Don't Fit," and now she remembered that there were many ways in which she and Isaac didn't completely fit, simply because no two people ever do.

She'd never forgotten the big misunderstandings at the end of it all, but she'd forgotten the little ones. He was a real person, someone who could disappoint her, someone she could disappoint.

Christ, she thought. Don't hurt him again.

"Pardon me?" she said.

"I said, 'Can I get you anything.'" He wasn't holding the solvent anymore. "It's an expression."

"You can get back to work," she said. "So we can move on to the social portion of the evening."

"Back to work. Fine."

He tried to get back to work—he took a contact sheet out of a tray and peered at it in the dusky red light—but he still looked nervous. She could feel how much she affected him. He reminded her of the dog in the old RCA ad—ear cocked, listening for his master's voice.

His desire for her made her feel desirable.

She was trembling on the verge of new life, but she didn't know if *this* new life was what she wanted. It was possible that she was getting back in touch with him merely because of the way he saw her. He had cast her, in his mind, as one of the great heroines. That, she thought, feels wonderful, but it's not a reason to get together with him. You have to be the heroine of your own life.

As he worked, they talked about their evening. It turned out that she had it wrong: they weren't going to a party; they were just having a drink with two people who were leaving the newspaper, photography students from Rutgers who'd been working as Isaac's assistants. They'd graduated last week, and they were moving on.

Isaac was pouring something into the sink. The smell of it was sharp and harsh, like paint stripper. It smelled like something that could wipe your brainpan clean.

"Aren't you afraid you'll get brain damage from these fumes?" A question she'd probably asked him before. She worried about him, spending hours and hours and hours with these chemicals.

"Most photographers live to a ripe old age, and they don't get brain damage, usually. I mean, it's probably bad, but it's not like being a boxer."

He pinned a picture to his little clothesline. She was pretty sure he was the only photographer in the world who still had one of those.

He'd told her on the phone that morning that he was making new prints of his work for an exhibit.

"I'm excited about your show," she said. "I can't wait to see your new pictures. I won't ask you to show them to me now. I know how secretive you are. But I can't wait to see them."

He gave her a strange look, which she interpreted as modesty. But she really *was* excited.

A month after she'd met him, she'd gone to one of his shows, on Broome Street. She remembered how thrilled she felt when she got there. Aside from her college writing teachers, Isaac was the first real artist she'd ever met, the first person who was actually doing something rather than just talking about it.

She watched him, for five, ten minutes, working quietly in the Martian dimness, doing whatever it is that photographers do. Witnessing his silent, patient concentration, she felt moved.

"You remind me of that Yeats poem, "Long-Legged Fly." You know that poem?"

"Yah," he said, without looking up. "Like I know any Yeats poems."

She closed her eyes and recited as much as she could:

"There on the scaffolding reclines
Michael Angelo.
Something something something
His hand moves to and fro.
Like a long-legged fly upon the stream
His mind moves upon silence."

Isaac didn't say anything.

"I guess you had to be there," she said.

"Long-legged fly," he said. "Guess so."

She remembered the moment when she realized she was in love with him. It was on a winter Saturday after they'd been together about two months. An old high school in his neighborhood was about to be demolished, and he'd mentioned that he was planning to take pictures of it just before the sun went down. She thought it would be fun to surprise him there.

She saw him from across the street. He had a bulky old

camera with a tripod; he was bent over the contraption, his hands in his pockets in the brittle day, peering into the lens. He looked like a creature of pure attention.

She thought it might be better not to disturb him; she was considering walking away. But then he looked up and saw her, and a look of pure calm happiness transformed his face.

As she walked toward him, she herself felt transformed. People speak of feeling dizzy when they're in love; Nora had never felt more balanced, more clear. She'd finished her devotions for the day—this was how she thought of her writing when it was going well—and now she was joining him while he was still in the midst of his. He was engrossed in what he was doing, fascinated, but she was sure he was equally fascinated by her. And she thought: *This is it. This is everything.*

Now, tonight, in his darkroom, he took a print out of the sink, turned off the red light and switched on a desk lamp, and bent over the print, examining it.

"Through all these years," she said, "I've thought of you as a kind of moral touchstone."

"Oh God," he said. "What does that mean?" He sidled away from her, as if he didn't really want to know.

"The thought of you has been like a lifeline. In all those years we weren't talking, I always felt that if there were maybe ten things I could rely on in the universe, and one of them was that the sun rose in the east, and another was the law of gravity, another of those ten things was that you were out there taking pictures."

"I'm glad to represent something for you," he said. "I'm glad to have a place in your moral constellation."

"It's not only that you were taking pictures. You figured out how to keep going."

"Wow, man," he said. "I'm like your guru."

He didn't look up at her, and he was trying to appear blasé, but she was pretty sure he was interested.

"You're not my guru. But I do admire you. I know plenty of people who dedicated themselves to their art for a few years, but when they didn't become world famous by the age of thirty, they just gave up. I admire it that you found a way to keep going."

Isaac looked up at her with a puzzled expression. "You mean I'm not world famous?" This was a joke.

Like most people, Isaac had trouble accepting compliments; he found it easier to fend them off. But she was telling him the truth.

The truth. The truth was good.

She needed to be honest with him. Everything that followed would be tainted if she wasn't honest from the start. She needed to let him know that she was still involved with another man.

10

SO HE LISTENED AS SHE told him a long story about this Benjamin—this academic peacock, this stuffed shirt. It was hard for Isaac to take it in, because at every turn in the narrative he kept hoping she'd say something like, "And that's when I realized that it's you that I love."

"And then I had to go to a medical writers' convention in Missoula, and I was by myself every night, and I had a lot of time to think. And one night I came back to my room and couldn't sleep, and that's when I called you. And that's my life so far."

She'd skipped the part about realizing he was the one she loved.

"Fine," he said, just to say something. "Very fine."

"So I've told you my story," she said. "What's yours? What have you been doing from then till now?"

"It's a very *long* story," he said. Which it wasn't. He just didn't want to speak. He was still trying to absorb the fact that she was with another man.

He wasn't angry, though he wondered if he should be. Mostly, another man or not, he was glad she was here. It was just that it was hard to take it in.

"If you're not going to tell me anything about your life," she said, "I'll just have to investigate."

His wallet, his keys, and his datebook were on the table not too far from her. She stretched out, swept up the wallet in her hand, and sat up again. Her shirt had come loose from her pants when she'd stretched out.

"Do that again," he said.

"Hush. I'm doing research." She removed his driver's license from his wallet. "You look mean. Were you mad at the picture-taking lady?"

"Not that I can remember."

He wished he had something exotic in his wallet, something that hinted at a Rich Inner Life. In his twenties, after a love affair with a French girl who was working in New York for the Agence France-Presse, he'd kept her farewell note in his wallet for a long time. *Je pars déchirée*... He wished it was still there.

"Credit cards. Library card. Video store card. You're kind of generic. Let's take a look at your datebook."

"That's private," he said. But the truth was that he wanted her to look.

Nora had always been a snoop. Years ago, when he was first getting involved with her, he'd just split up with a woman named Nancy, who began to find him desirable at the moment when he rejected her. One day he left Nora alone in his bedroom and came back to find her sitting at his desk, reading a love letter from Nancy that he'd received the day before. He expected Nora to be flustered and apologetic, but all she said was, "I can't find the second page of this. It was just getting good."

She was nodding at his datebook as if she understood him better now. "New School," she said, and flipped the page. "New School." She looked up at him. "New School?"

"I took a course there last spring."

"A course in what?"

"It was a course about tracing your family roots."

"What did you find out?"

"I was able to trace my mother's side of the family back about a hundred years, in Poland. My father's side is tougher to trace."

"Roots," she said. "The search for roots. You remember that John Berryman line? 'People ask me about my roots...as if I were a plant.' You remember that?"

"Who's John Berryman?"

She turned the page. "Boston," she read. "Very nice. Travel broadens the mind. What's in Boston?"

"I had a job offer from the *Globe*."

"What happened?"

"Turned 'em down."

"Why?"

"Too cold."

"That is the correct answer," she said. "Concert. Concert. Concert. You're a very concert-going man."

"I had season tickets to the Metropolitan Opera."

"Ye gods. All that warbling. Was it any good?"

He thought about this. "No," he said.

He knew that Nora hated the opera: he'd once tried to take her to *La Bohème* and she'd made her feelings clear. He'd always gotten a kick out of this side of her—her unrefined side. She was the only woman he'd ever met who liked Henry Miller. She thought the sex in his books was funny. She liked Steven Seagal movies (on one of their first dates, she'd dragged Isaac to see *Under Siege 2*). She liked W. C. Fields—she even liked the scene where, after checking to make sure no one is watching, he gives Baby LeRoy a kick in the pants.

Most of the women Isaac had dated had been very refined. They were women who didn't watch TV. Women who didn't *own* a TV. Women who never had coffee or tea in the house, except for herbal tea; women who never had sugar in the house, only honey. Women with postcards of Frida Kahlo over their desks. Somehow her little mustache inspired them.

The thing about Nora was that she was a human being. She liked to stay up late and watch Letterman. She drank root beer. Once in a while she'd been known to have a slice of pizza for breakfast.

She was sitting on the long table, her legs crossed at the knee. It would have been nice if she'd been wearing a skirt.

A little-known fact about Nora: she had legs that, if she'd been around during World War II, would have made our boys overseas forget Betty Grable. The only problem was that nobody ever got to see them. She had about twenty pairs of corduroy jeans, which she considered suitable for every occasion. He remembered what it was like during the first few months he knew her, before they got together. When you saw her in a dress you felt lucky, and every other time you saw her, you wondered when was the next time you were going to see her in a dress.

She was still studying his datebook. "Who's Olive?"

He could feel himself blushing. "She was just a mistake I made."

He was hoping she would ask for details, so he could give her mysterious, elusive answers, but she turned the page.

"Cupcake?" she said. "Is she another mistake you made?"

"Cupcakes. It was the last day of work for two college students who were at the paper on a work-study program. What am I talking about?—they're the people we're seeing tonight. Anyway, I was reminding myself to bring in a treat for them."

"You're a good boss."

Isaac was taking intense pleasure in this. Why was it such a pleasure to have someone you love snoop through your stuff?

Now she looked unhappy.

"What are you looking at?" he said.

"Jenny's birthday. You still haven't talked to her, have you?"

He didn't say anything. Jenny was Isaac's sister. Years ago she'd followed a cult leader into a commune in Oregon. Just before she left, he'd had a stupid fight with her, and they hadn't spoken since then.

There was a cordless phone on the table. Nora picked up the receiver and tossed it at him.

"Give her a call. Right now."

"I haven't talked to her in years."

"She'd love it if you called her. You know she would. When's the last time you *tried* to call her?"

"Four years ago. I couldn't reach her. So I gave up."

"That's the old fighting spirit, eh? That's the old bulldog." She shook her head in disappointment, and then she tried again: "Seize the day, man. *Call her.*"

"Maybe I'll call her tomorrow," he said.

There were a million reasons he wasn't going to call his sister. But he loved it that Nora had thrown the phone at him. He loved her generous impulsiveness.

After Isaac's mother died, his father spent three years in anguish. Nora had a dream one night in which Matthew—Isaac's father—was playing with a dog, and in the morning she told Isaac that she wanted to get Matthew a puppy. Isaac thought it was a bad idea. He thought his father was too demoralized to care for an animal. But Nora was insistent; she spent the weekend going to animal shelters until she found a dog that reminded her of the one in the dream. Isaac had to leave town on a freelance assignment, and instead of waiting for him to come back, she took the dog to Matthew's by herself—a three-hour bus ride. She didn't force it on him—she was prepared to keep it herself if he didn't want it—but it turned out that he did want it, and it turned out that her dream was prophetic. Having this tiny feisty needy thing in his care woke him up—delighted him—and helped make the last two years of his life better and lighter than Isaac could have imagined.

He knew that he wasn't going to call his sister—not today; but he was glad that Nora was urging him to, urging him to seize the moment, urging him to do the generous thing. It was the kind of thing he'd always loved about her.

11

NORA NOTICED A HAND-ROLLED cigarette near the phone.

"Isaac Mitchell," she said. "What in the world is this?"

"It's called marijuana."

"Don't tell me you've become a pot smoker."

Isaac had had a drinking problem in his youth and had dealt with it long before they met, and she'd never seen him ingest anything stronger than coffee and tea.

"No. One of those kids I mentioned, Earl, left it here. I think he thought he could shock me. You're welcome to it, if you want it."

She hadn't smoked pot in years. She'd smoked enthusiastically in college, but rarely since then. But now she thought, Why not?

"It might be fun," she said. "Care to have a little?"

"No thanks. High on life."

"Will I blow up anything in the darkroom?"

"Probably better to smoke it outside." He was carefully putting things away. He took meticulous care of his darkroom. "Just give me a minute to shoot up."

He picked up a canvas satchel and got out his insulin kit. Isaac had diabetes. He'd always been very careful: he exercised faithfully, adhered to his diet, monitored his insulin level, and gave himself injections three times a day. Years ago, before he met her, when Isaac was late giving himself his insulin shot one day, he'd passed out. It had never happened again, but sometimes he experienced bouts of the same kind of spaciness that had preceded his fainting fit. Nora used to call those episodes his vastations.

Nora had never known him to complain about his condition, and if he worried about how it might affect him in the future, he'd never spoken of it. She'd always thought there was something heroic about this.

She used to give him his injection every once in a while. It was sad and intimate at the same time.

THEY WERE MEETING ISAAC'S young people in an ice-cream shop about a mile away. They decided to walk there, and Nora lit up the joint on the way.

Their walk took them through an enormous park. Nature in the darkness seemed mysterious, filled with grave intent.

She'd smoked less than half the joint, but that was more than enough. At first she was thinking that pot didn't really do anything, but a minute or two later she found herself reflecting on the idea of how exciting it is to be a person, to be a self, to have a self. To be a person in the middle of a life.

She remembered an afternoon in nursery school when she and a few other kids were building a fort out of cardboard bricks. When she'd handed a brick to a boy named Eugene, he had said, "Okey dokey." It was the first time she'd ever heard the phrase, and she wasn't sure what it meant.

At this moment, it was hard to understand why that memory was even *hers*. What is identity? What knits me together with the little girl who had that experience? What binds the two of us together into a single "I"?

"Isaac?" she said. "Did you ever think about the fact that it's strange that the particular moment you're living is the only moment that exists in the universe? That all the other moments that people have ever lived are gone?"

"You're *my* guru," he said.

The night was awe-inspiring, with an immensity of stars; they looked as if they were sending out messages to one another. She felt as if she were inside the mind of God. She thought of all the trials of her life—the trials that she'd endured already, and the trials ahead—and they all seemed small.

She thought about how strange it was to have a life, to be pursuing your goals—your goal of independence, your goal of self-realization, your goal of helping others, your goal of anything—when the populous night sky provides evidence that none of it matters very much, that the universe has preceded you by billions of years and will outlast you for billions of years. And yet we keep struggling. Apparently we have to.

She saw storefronts in the distance, glowing. She didn't want to arrive. She wanted to keep walking forever, beside her friend Isaac, in the dark.

Isaac. What a name.

"How did you get the name Isaac?" she said. She couldn't believe she'd never asked him that before. "It's really a ridiculous name."

"Nora's not much better."

"I know," she said. "We're both of us absurd."

"I suppose," he said. "I suppose."

And then suddenly they were in the ice-cream shop—it was called "Muffin's"— and the bright loud lights were attacking her. Isaac was talking to the hostess—it was all too much for Nora to deal with—and, thank God, the hostess was leading them through the glaring room into a garden, quieter and darker, and then Isaac was telling her something about the place, and it was hard to keep track of what he was saying, not because he was saying anything complicated, but because every sentence he spoke would open the door to a thought of her own, and then she'd be gone, wandering down long corridors of solitary reflection, and then, when she found her way back to the present, she wouldn't be able to remember what he'd been talking about in the first place.

This was because of the marijuana, but at this moment it seemed to her that normal life wasn't so different. You're always trying to make out other people's words through the static of your own thoughts.

I need to start meditating, she thought, so I'll be able to live in the present.

In the meantime, she could take notes.

Ever since Nora was in high school, she'd carried little memo pads around with her. Generally she used them for the normal purposes—shopping lists, Things to Do—but sometimes she liked to bring them out in the middle of a conversation and take notes. Her friends found the habit half flattering and half annoying. At the moment it felt like a necessity—the only way she might have a shot at keeping track of the conversation. She put her memo pad on the table.

"The little green notebook," Isaac said. "I'd almost forgotten."

"So tell me about these youngsters." She took out a pen. "What merry youngsters doth these be?" she said, and wondered if she'd lost her mind.

"They're both pretty special. Earl has Tourette's syndrome—he once told me that when he was in high school he used to bark like a dog. He's got it under control though, with medication. He's a good young photographer. And Renee—Renee is a wonder."

He pronounced her name in a velvety and tender way, and Nora immediately disliked her.

"What's so wonderful about her?"

"She's on fire. I don't think she ever puts her camera down. I don't think she ever sleeps. She wants to be a crusading photojournalist. She wants to put an end to the world's injustices."

"That's ambitious," Nora said.

"She *is* ambitious," Isaac said. He was so enthralled by the thought of his prize assistant that he hadn't heard the irony in Nora's voice.

A shaggy brown poodle was nosing around leashless, going from table to table.

"Who's that?" Nora said.

"It's Muffin. Muffin himself. He's a celebrity here."

Like a benevolent host, Muffin was making the rounds. The people at the next table were talking to him in baby talk, which he seemed to enjoy.

Isaac was waving to someone, and then the someone was sitting down. A boy. A redheaded boy—too much hair—with a farm-boy face. Earl.

She looked at her memo pad. *Earl: Tourette's. Renee: on fire.* She discreetly put it back in her bag.

Isaac made the introductions.

"I can't believe I'm late," Earl said.

"Not a problem," Isaac said.

"Lateness is the bane of my existence," Earl said to Nora. "My goal in life is to start showing up on time."

Isaac nodded sagely. "The only way to make sure you'll be on time is to be early," he said.

"Wow," Nora said. This seemed profound.

A waitress showed up, name-tagged Priscilla. She had a nose ring, and when she said hello Nora saw the glint of a tongue stud.

Why were so many people stapling holes in their faces these days?

Marijuana, Nora reflected soberly, makes you wise. She had suddenly realized that the young people who wear eyebrow rings and nose rings and lip rings weren't the wild ones, the rebels; they were wallflowers who were trying to escape their wallflowerness but who felt some obscure need to punish themselves for doing so. The self-mutilation was at once the escape and the punishment. Nora understood that poor pierced Priscilla was suffering deeply; the question of what to order seemed trivial by comparison. But Priscilla, who evidently wasn't ready to acknowledge her suffering, was impatient for Nora to order, so Nora asked for a banana split.

"So are you two old friends? How do you know each other?" Earl said after the waitress had left.

"It's a funny story," Nora said. "About ten years ago, I had a job as a hotel detective. One of the guests reported that her necklace was stolen, and when I first looked into it I was pretty sure the culprit was Isaac. It turned out to be the woman he was hooked up with at the time. I had her arrested, she ended up doing twelve months in Leavenworth, and the rest is history."

She liked to make things up once in a while. She'd gotten into the habit after her mother died; lying to strangers was a way of punching a hole in the wall and getting a glimpse of a different life. It no longer served that purpose, but the habit remained. Her inventions were generally harmless, since they were almost always too ridiculous to be believed. The only problem was that they sometimes popped out of her mouth before she could stop them.

"Wow," Earl said. "That's awesome."

And then there was Renee. Nora knew her as soon as she saw her. She was gliding toward the table with a look on her face that seemed to be inviting you to stop what you were doing and admire her.

Renee sat down. She didn't just sit: she seemed to be doing a dance with the chair, which ended with her turning the chair backward, so that when she sat, the back of it was against her stomach. How strange: to be so young that she didn't even sit like a normal person.

She was a sylphlike girl with hennaed hair and alarmingly green eyes. She was insanely skinny—almost painful to behold. Her bones seemed to be pushing against her skin, protesting against their encasement; it was hard to look at her wrists without wincing.

Isaac was obviously enraptured. Renee was sitting next to Earl, across from Isaac, and Isaac pushed his chair back slightly, as if Renee, this thread-thin thing, was such a large presence in his mind that he felt compelled to give her more room.

She'd barely sat down before she started to talk. "I just had some amazing news. At the protests in D.C. last summer I met some people from one of the unions, and to make a long story short, I might be going along on one of their fact-finding trips this fall. Taking pictures of the sweatshops in Indonesia."

"Fantastic," Earl said.

"I'm so excited. Some of these multinational corporations put children to work for five cents a day. They say it's okay because if they weren't giving these people work they'd have no work at all. You could justify slavery on the same grounds. It's horrible."

Nora had an ornery impulse to argue with her. Except that she didn't feel like arguing with her at all, because she agreed with her. It *was* horrible.

Renee was talking about the working conditions of children in China, Indonesia, Thailand. It sounded like she knew what she was talking about, and she genuinely seemed to care, but there was something about her that Nora didn't like: a touch of grandiosity, a touch of mania. She probably *did* think she had a shot at ending the world's injustices.

But Nora understood why Isaac was a little bit in love with her, if he was. Exuberance is beauty, and Renee was beautiful.

"We had a teach-in last month and Renee debated a guy from Nike," Earl said to Nora. "She got him to admit that he wouldn't want his family to be working for fifty cents a day, and then she said, 'I'm sorry you have such a small family.'"

"My finest hour," Renee said, shyly peeking up at Isaac and Nora for their approval.

This won Nora over. She liked this young woman.

The food arrived, and while Nora investigated her banana split, the others drifted off into gossip about people at the newspaper.

Isaac glowed when he listened to Renee. He was looking handsomer moment by moment.

He had a way of making people feel important. This was what he was doing for Earl and Renee—Nora could feel it—

and this was what he'd always done for her. He interpreted her in the largest, the most generous way. He made her feel like a creature with a fascinating destiny. He held her up to the light.

She didn't like to see him appreciating someone else.

She remembered how he'd made her feel during their first year together. She'd been amazed by how fully he accepted her. She'd felt utterly free. Sometimes it seemed that he provided a kind of stage on which she could perform, on which she could put all the different parts of herself in play.

After their first year, she had begun—even with Isaac—to feel the old ache of constraint. When they'd met, Isaac's career seemed to be blossoming; a year later, he was coming off a year of professional defeats. It was around that time that Nora had a story included in *Best American Short Stories.* It took her a week to tell him about it; she felt uncomfortable, almost guilty, about the fact that good things were happening for her when nothing was happening for him. And not too long after that, she stopped writing stories again.

"All things can tempt me from this craft of verse," wrote Yeats. The only thing that could tempt Nora from the craft of fiction was a man in need. If her man was ailing, she dropped everything to take care of him; if her man was insecure, she stooped, morally and emotionally, in order to seem smaller than he was.

During their first year together, she was finishing a group of stories about her mother. During their second year, a new story started to take shape. It was about Isaac, and it wasn't kind. She didn't get very far with it—she had no idea what the story was going to *say* about Isaac, but she knew that it wouldn't be tender.

She never told him about it. She'd told him about her

experiences with other people—with Gina, with Sally, with Daryl—but she didn't tell him that she had begun to write something equally heartless about him.

When she'd talked with him, in a general way, about the fact that her writing always slipped free of her intentions, he'd had a sympathetic response. "You have an artistic demon. You have to respect it." That was kind, but she thought he was glorifying her. It wasn't a demon; it was nothing as noble as that. It was more like a goblin. A fat little goblin that squatted on her keyboard and took delight in sliming her loved ones.

Although he'd counseled her to accept herself, she knew he wouldn't be happy if the goblin put its paws on him. He'd given himself away when he'd once said he thought that if she ever did write about him, she'd write about him lovingly. He was trying to show her that he felt secure in her love, but what he actually showed her was that he didn't understand her. He didn't understand the inevitability of what happened when she sat down to write.

He'd given himself the part of Prince Charming: his kiss would wake her from her spell. But it wouldn't. She knew this.

After she got a hint of where the story was going, she tried to force it in a different direction. First she tried replacing the main character with a man who was nothing like Isaac. But the story wouldn't comply: it *wanted* to be about Isaac. Then, resigning herself to the fact that she was fated to write about him, she tried to make it a story that would show him in a good light—the light in which she actually saw him. But the story refused to emerge.

There was no reason one couldn't write stories about people's virtues—good stories, unsyrupy, unsappy. Grace Paley—her beloved Grace Paley—was always writing about people's generosity, their loyalty, their resilience. It could be done. But as much as Nora valued these qualities in life, they didn't happen to be the themes that unlocked her imagination.

It was as if she was a medium, with no control over the voices that spoke through her. She didn't have a choice between writing about invented characters and writing about people she knew; she didn't have a choice between writing charitably and writing coldly. The only choice she had was between writing the stories she wrote and not writing stories at all.

Unwilling to write about Isaac and unable to write anything else, she finally did the same thing she'd done when she was seeing Daryl. She decided not to write stories at all. Once again, she turned her attention to essays, reviews, and other things that didn't matter to her.

When she got pregnant, she realized that she had to change her life. Isaac was the best man she'd ever known, but their relationship couldn't survive her pregnancy.

Maybe it could have if he hadn't been so insistent. She was clear about not wanting a child, but Isaac wouldn't let it rest; he hectored her about it for two solid weeks while she was waiting to have the abortion.

During those two weeks, she began to shrink away from him. He began to seem terribly old to her: his skin, his hair, his breath, his teeth, his preoccupations. He compared her once to Emma Peel, the heroine from some old TV show she'd never heard of, someone he'd had a crush on since the age of five. He looked as if he'd just given her the greatest compliment in his vocabulary, and she felt as if she was going steady with Methuselah.

Renee was telling Isaac how great it had been to work with him. Nora reached out for Isaac's teacup and took a sip to establish her territorial rights. She did this automatically, while continuing to think about the way things had fallen apart five years ago. She remembered taking his arm when the two of them were standing on the roof of a building—they were in someone's penthouse during a party, and they had ended up on the roof, thirty floors up, looking out at the city—and mischievously asking, "Would you throw yourself off this roof for me?" He had looked at her glumly and said, "Well, I don't think I would. But I'd probably consider it." She remembered the look of resignation on his face, as if his love for her was something that he didn't even want, just something that he'd gotten stuck with, and she remembered that she was at one and the same time full of sympathy, because she didn't really want to make him suffer, and delighted, because she loved being able to think of herself as a woman a man might throw himself off a roof for.

Why had she been so cruel to him that night? Because she knew she was going to leave him, and she was so angry at herself, so sick at heart, that she was seized by a wild desire to treat him monstrously.

He had insisted on accompanying her to the clinic—not taking her seriously when she said she wanted to go alone—and as he sat beside her in the cab, oppressively glum, she wished she had an ejector seat so she could send him popping up into the air and be done with him. While the madman cabbie bolted down Ninth Avenue as if they were in a war zone, she had chattered on about the most foolish things she could think of, knowing that she was hurting him by doing this, and taking pleasure in it.

Even then, on the street outside the clinic, he'd made one last effort to change her mind. He just wouldn't give up. She remembered that she said something that finally silenced him—something he didn't have an answer for. But she couldn't remember what it was.

She didn't make her decision lightly. She knew it was a grave decision; by the time she had the abortion she was eight weeks pregnant, and the being inside her had a heartbeat and the beginnings of a central nervous system. (Nora couldn't stop herself from looking at books that charted the development of the embryo.) It wasn't like lancing a boil. She was prepared to suffer over her choice, and she did suffer—not so much during the day, but at night, while she slept. She kept having dreams in which she was pregnant, though the embryo or fetus was never in her womb: it was growing in her hand, or in her arm—her left arm, her injured arm—or in her brain. The being inside her, in these dreams, was always sleeping—except once, when it was reading a book by Agatha Christie—and always gave off a faint blue glow. She had the dreams once or twice a week, and in the morning she would wake up feeling lost. The dreams had never completely stopped coming, although she didn't have them very often anymore. But as sad as the decision made her, it was one that she never came to regret.

After the abortion, she and Isaac had tried, incredibly, to "be friends," and for three or four months it seemed to be working. She remembered seeing him on his birthday and telling him he was her best friend. Then, the day before she left for a vacation in Canada, she and Isaac took his nephew to the zoo, and, witnessing how joyful it made Isaac to be with him, Nora thought that it would be best to get out of his life—that, mere "friends" though they might be, she was probably holding him back. She didn't exactly decide anything that afternoon, but after she got back from Canada she didn't call him, and he didn't call her either. And that was that.

Isaac and Renee and Earl were talking, but she wasn't even pretending to be listening anymore. She was hoping there was a way for her to atone for hurting Isaac. She was hoping she wouldn't hurt him again.

She felt something cold and wet in her palm: Muffin's nose. He was licking her hand. Then he put his front paws on her thigh and strained toward the table. Apparently he wanted her to feed him.

Nora wanted him to go away. She moved her leg away and Muffin got down and, still hopeful, walked over to Isaac. He nuzzled his head against Isaac's shin, but Isaac, entranced by his young friends, didn't even look down. Nora was the only one paying attention to the dog, so she was the only one who noticed when he got hold of a piece of biscotti that Earl had accidentally dropped on the floor.

"You have to stay open," Renee was saying. "Even when it hurts."

Nora was trying to catch up on the conversation—what had inspired Renee to impart this wisdom?—when she noticed that Muffin was doing some kind of dance near Isaac's feet, taking little leaps backwards. The lambada, Nora thought. The forbidden dance.

Isaac glanced down at him. "Cute dog," Isaac said.

Muffin began to emit a curious sound, as if he was trying to speak.

"I think he's choking," Nora said.

Muffin's front legs were still scuffling, but he wasn't getting any traction anymore; he'd stopped moving backwards. He was still making odd noises, and he was starting to list, like an injured ship.

"Oh my God," Renee said. "Give him some water." Even

stoned, Nora could see that that didn't make sense. Muffin's eyes were going up in his head; you could hardly see his pupils anymore.

A man at the next table stood up abruptly. He was a tall man, somewhere in his fifties. He looked like a take-charge guy. He looked like someone you'd want to have living next door to you, just in case there was ever any trouble. Nora was relieved—he was going to deal with this.

"Jesus Christ," he said, and didn't move.

His wife, a suburban bohemian in a baggy dress, was waving her napkin. "Give the poor thing some room. He needs air."

We're watching this dog die, Nora thought. We're all of us going to sit here and watch.

She was paralyzed by the thought that she didn't know what to do, until she realized that no one around her knew what to do either.

The Heimlich maneuver, she thought. She bent down and picked up the dog, and then she hesitated, because she remembered having read that when an infant is choking you shouldn't give him the Heimlich; you should lay him face down across your knees and tap him sharply on the back, as if you're burping him.

Grown-up or infant—which did Muffin resemble most? She decided that Muffin's air of friendly optimism reminded her of her grandmother, many years gone, so she put her fingers into his abdomen and pressed. A hard chunk of biscotti shot out of his mouth.

I did it, Nora thought.

Before she had time to congratulate herself further, she felt Muffin sinking his teeth into her thigh.

All was well for Nora Howard until that fateful night when she performed the Heimlich maneuver on a dog.

Muffin lifted his head to catch a breath of air and seemed to be ready to bite her again and Nora pushed him and he snorkeled wildly off her lap. Then he went over to the moist piece of biscotti, sniffed it, and wagged off toward the cloakroom.

A stocky woman emerged from the kitchen, drying her hands on a towel. She looked at Nora grimly.

"What's going on here? I heard someone was hurting my dog."

"She saved your dog's life," Isaac said.

The woman looked over at the take-charge guy and the bohemian. The take-charge guy was still standing.

"I don't know *what* was going on," he said. "That dog wasn't happy, I'll tell you that much."

"He was choking on a cookie," Nora said. "I got it out of him and then he bit me."

"Muffin never bites anybody," the woman said, still drying her hands. She seemed to be drying each finger individually.

Muffin had wandered back to the table, as if he wanted to see what all the commotion was about. He looked up at Nora, crouching. He didn't look friendly.

"Your dog was choking," Renee said. "You shouldn't be hassling her. You should be thanking her." She had a light in her eyes, a light of political zeal, as if she'd found a new cause.

"My dog doesn't bite. And nobody should be feeding him cookies."

Nora was afraid that the clean-finger lady was going to call the police. Then the police would find out that she was high on marijuana, and there'd be a trial, and it would be her word against the dog's.

She felt like someone in an Ibsen play, some figure of lonely heroism, reviled by the crowd.

She had a flush of shame after she thought this, because she'd never actually read Ibsen. She'd always meant to, because she wanted to find out what his character Nora, from *A Doll's House,* was all about, but somehow she'd never gotten around to it.

She liked Nora Charles, though, from *The Thin Man.*

"I think you people should finish up and leave," the finger lady said. "Before you do any more damage." She looked them all over slowly, as if she wanted to be able to pick them out in the lineup.

"You can't force us to leave," Renee said.

"Who said anything about forcing you?" the lady said, and then she went back to the kitchen.

Renee seemed disappointed, as if robbed of the chance to have a confrontation.

Nora looked down at her thigh. Muffin's teeth hadn't broken through the fabric of her pants.

Muffin was underneath their table, sniffing listlessly. He looked a little odd, and Nora wondered sympathetically whether the cutoff of oxygen during his choking fit had given him brain damage.

12

RENEE AND EARL WERE HEADED off to a concert in New York. When they said good-bye to Nora, both of them respectfully shook her hand.

"Keep it real," Earl said.

"I liked what you did for that dog," Renee said. "You're a cool lady." Then she gave Isaac a hug, which, Nora thought, lasted too long.

"Are they a couple?" Nora asked after she and Isaac were alone. She wanted them to be.

"I think they may sleep together sometimes, but they don't seem to think of themselves as a couple. I'm baffled by the mating habits of the young."

He took her arm. "Alone at last," he said. "Me and my hotel detective."

They decided to have dinner in Isaac's apartment. They walked there, through quiet suburban streets. They didn't speak. She couldn't speak. She felt as if there was something gathering force between them. As if the kisses they hadn't given each other—yesterday, outside the coffee shop; today, when she met him at his darkroom door—hadn't been given because each of them, without knowing it, had wanted to do nothing to dilute the intensity of the first kiss of this new phase of their lives, the kiss that they were going to give each other tonight, in his apartment, in the dark.

She wished she hadn't smoked the joint. She was still feeling high, still feeling too thinky, and she was afraid that if she and Isaac came together physically, her mind would be wandering hither and yon.

Hither and yon? Was that the expression? She remembered why she'd stopped smoking pot: in a subtle way, it impaired her relationship to the language.

Isaac's apartment was on the twenty-eighth floor of a building near the Hudson River, in Edgewater. There was a long panel of windows in his living room. When he opened the door, the first thing she saw was the city: the entire city, the long, elegant reach of it, alive with light.

It could have been a holy moment. Unfortunately, someone in the next apartment was watching TV. *COPS*. She recognized the theme song. "*Bad boys bad boys...*"

She tried to block it out. She sat on Isaac's couch and looked up at him. "Don't turn on the light." She wanted him to sit next to her and put his arms around her.

He did sit next to her, but didn't touch her, and she was disappointed.

So why not put your arms around *him*? Why not just kiss him?

Because she couldn't. Because she understood her role. Despite Mary Wollstonecraft, Elizabeth Cady Stanton, Emma Goldman, Rosa Luxemburg, Simone de Beauvoir, and Ellen Willis—despite two hundred years of the feminist intellectual tradition—and despite the fact that she was a woman who seized the moment, a woman who could save the life of an ungrateful dog, she couldn't initiate the kiss. That was Isaac's job. Her job was to let Isaac know that she wanted him to kiss her.

He was sitting next to her; they were both looking out at the city, which was burning with a million lights. She looked up at him—she looked at him somethingly. She didn't know *how* she was letting him know, but she was letting him know.

He kissed her, tentatively, and then he pulled back—to check on her, to make sure he'd been invited.

The person next door changed the channel. *NYPD Blue.* She heard the voice of Andy Sipowicz: "I don't care if he gets himself lawyered up with Clarence *Darrow.* He's a low-life skell, and I'm gonna nail his ass to the wall."

Cop shows on every channel. Why? Why do we want to believe what we believed as children: that the police are friendly and wise and good...?

The marijuana had definitely not worn off.

She was upset with herself for letting their first kiss, the first kiss of their new life, if that was what it was, be ruined. She'd barely noticed it as it was happening.

Isaac was still looking at her questioningly.

She leaned forward, determined to put more into it this time, so that she'd stop ruminating and give herself fully to the experience.

At the moment when her lips touched his, however, she was thinking of Wilhelm Reich's theory of fascism. The theory that the mass of humanity craves protection and will do almost anything, submit to any authority, in order to feel protected. That was why cop shows were ever-popular.

Was this why she was kissing Isaac: because she couldn't summon up the strength to leave Benjamin unless she felt she was being protected by another man?

When she thought of Benjamin, the dreadful river of conscience rushed in. She was still *with* Benjamin. She didn't want to be, but she was, and therefore she shouldn't be doing this now.

And then the river of reason. Her task right now was to get back to the life she wanted to live: the life in which she was creating herself through her work. She had sought Isaac out because he, more than anyone else, had encouraged her to go deeper into that life. But if she did finally choose to be with him again, it should be because she *wanted* him, not because she was trying to free herself from Benjamin.

How could she still *be* with Benjamin? How could she be stuck with him a year after she'd realized she had to leave him? She felt like a character in a Chekhov story: not someone who was squeezing the slave out of himself—he actually never wrote stories like that—but someone who knows she's living the wrong life but is powerless to change it. But that wasn't her! Chekhov was her favorite writer, but she didn't *want* to be a character in a Chekhov story! I'm the heroine, damn it, of my own life!

At least I want to be.

While she was thinking about all this, Isaac was somewhere in the room. In fact, his lips were on her lips. How can this be happening? How can I be so deep inside my head? In an episode of *Star Trek: The Next Generation,* Mr. Data, the *Enterprise*'s android science officer, in his never-ending quest to become more like a human being, investigates the experience of love, and becomes involved with a fellow crew member, who, after their first make-out session, sensing that his simulated heart isn't fully into it, asks him what he'd been thinking about while they kissed. He tells her that he was reconfiguring the warp-field parameters, analyzing the collected works of Charles Dickens, calculating the maximum pressure he could safely apply to her lips, and considering a new food supplement for one of the pets aboard the ship. This was supposed to illustrate something about his android nature—his emotional detachment and the capaciousness of his brain. So this is the terrible truth, Nora thought. I too am an android.

This wasn't the way it was supposed to go! She needed to get out of this. She needed to stop.

But how? How could she get out of this without hurting him?

She was at a loss. She was stumped by the difficulty of ending the kissing session.

Where the kissing never stops, she thought. The title of an essay by Joan Didion.

Stop it! she said to her mind. *Stop thinking!*

It would be good, she thought, if an announcer broke in in the middle of *NYPD Blue* with a tragic news flash. If there'd been an earthquake somewhere, whole neighborhoods leveled, that would be good, because they would be shocked into a recognition of how irresponsible it was to be kissing in a world in which people were dying.

That didn't make sense.

But this wasn't right. They had to stop.

She was miserable. Two hours ago she had vowed not to hurt him again, and now she was about to hurt him already.

It would definitely be best if Isaac himself were to end it. Surely he must have sensed that she wasn't giving herself fully to this experience. Although that would probably be more clear to him if she took her hand off his fly.

She had to figure out a way to make *him* end it, so he wouldn't be hurt. Or—what was that plan she'd had a minute ago? Oh, yes: an earthquake. Her shirt was about to come off.

You have to be honest. You have to try to move through this life with integrity, even when you don't want to.

She pulled her head back and put her hands on his face. She hoped it felt loving, but she was restraining him. She hoped it was clear that she was restraining him lovingly.

"Is everything all right?" he said.

"I'm having a lovely time with you, Isaac. But"—she sighed—"I'm still with someone else." She put a hand consolingly on his arm.

He didn't look surprised. Disappointed, but not surprised.

"One life at a time," she said, with a slight inward wince. It was the height of cornball-hood, but she and Isaac talked that way to each other sometimes.

"One life at a time," he said, and she was thankful that she had found a phrase that had the right effect on him. He leaned back on the couch with a half smile.

13

NORA WAS SLEEPING IN HIS BED. She'd asked if they could just lie together all night with their clothes on; he'd said yes, but after she fell asleep he realized he couldn't stand it. He got up and went into the kitchen.

It was amazing how his desire for her had only grown.

One night after he'd been with her for about a year, they were having dinner at midnight in a dark little bar in the East Village and she mentioned that she'd seen *Body Heat*—William Hurt and Kathleen Turner—on TV the day before. "Their sex was hot," she said. She took a sip of her drink, smiling, looking him straight in the eye. "But ours is hotter."

He hadn't even gotten to see her legs tonight. She hadn't taken her damn pants off.

He hadn't even gotten to see her *scar*. She hadn't even rolled up her sleeves.

He was maddened by the fact that she didn't want to sleep with him.

He wondered whether she'd ever make a life with someone—with him or with anyone else. Even though she'd almost always been in relationships, there was something essentially solitary about her. Growing up an only child and being orphaned in her teens; her early life might have left an indelible mark.

He paced around his kitchen, not knowing what to do. He felt all jangly and insulted. "Blue balls," a term from his youth, came into his mind. Sexual insult: they'd gotten started, and then she wanted to stop.

He felt inept. He wondered if the real reason she'd wanted to stop was that he hadn't been touching her right. Their sex used to be hot, yes, but he'd always secretly worried that eventually he'd start to bore her. He thought of himself as the kind of person who, when he cooked a meal, always followed the recipe. He worried that he lacked the improvisational spirit without which one can never hope to achieve greatness in any field that matters, be it sex, jazz, or basketball.

And he was worried for another reason. He felt as if he was wooing Nora under false pretenses. A few of the things she'd said that evening—how he was her moral touchstone, how excited she was about his show—had unnerved him.

Nora, without knowing it, was talking about the person he used to be. He didn't know how she'd feel about the person he'd become.

Sometimes he thought he had made his way in life through a series of nervous breakdowns. The problem was that Nora didn't know about the most recent of them, the one she'd helped bring about.

When he was a boy, when his friends were thinking about nothing except sports or cars, he was thinking about nothing except God. Just after Isaac's tenth birthday, his grandfather died, and he started thinking about the mysteries of life and death, casting his mind out over these mysteries with a small boy's great capacity for wonder. He decided that he wanted to become a student of the Talmud, and he spent seven years in solemn preparation for a lifetime of worshiping God.

When he was in high school, he began to find his history

classes fascinating, and the study of history undid him. The steady record of human barbarity, reaching its awful blossoming in the twentieth century—progress, it seemed, meant little more than the development of ever more efficient ways to slaughter people—swept away his belief that we were fashioned by a divine intelligence. He was too honest to try to pull the covers of faith back over his head, no matter how much he might have wanted to. He was still little more than a boy, but his rejection of religion—a body of thought that had given a shape to every day of his life and freed him from anxiety about the future—left him feeling like a spent old man.

In his senior year of high school he took a photography class and immediately became obsessed. Photography took the place of prayer. He'd lost his belief in God; he'd come to believe that nothing existed except this world: the fleeting world, the disappearing world. But he hadn't lost his sense of reverence, his sense of wonder before the mysteries of life. And now he believed that the best way to express his reverence was to try to capture the object of it with his camera: this world of appearances, this world that is all we have.

He majored in photography at Cooper Union. When he graduated, he barely noticed the event, because nothing essential changed in his life. He was obsessed with taking pictures the day before he graduated and obsessed with taking pictures the day after.

Until his early thirties he lived in the heroic mode, putting photography before everything else. He picked up freelance work to pay the bills, but as little as possible; he lived like someone who'd taken a vow of poverty. He was sustained not by external rewards—there *were* no external rewards—but by the pure love of taking pictures.

Gradually, as the years went on, it got harder. Standing on a corner for hours waiting for the light to fall in the right way—it was one thing when he was young. When he was young it was worth it: there was grandeur to the activity of waiting—waiting for the moment when the texture of the light altered subtly and everything was transformed. But as he grew older, it became harder to sustain that level of devotion. His legs began to give out. His will began to give out.

By his middle thirties, he'd had a few moments of recognition—the Boston Museum of Fine Arts had bought one of his pictures for its permanent collection; he was showing his work in galleries about once a year; he'd put out a book of photographs, which had come into the world unheralded and then gone demurely out of print—but they hadn't cohered into anything approaching a reputation. When he was younger he wouldn't have thought this would matter. He'd thought that you do the thing solely because you love it, and the idea of needing to be rewarded for it seemed absurd. But it had come to matter somehow.

Just after Isaac's thirty-fifth birthday, he suffered a series of misfortunes, large and small. A gallery owner who liked his work died suddenly, and the hipsters who took over the place never even returned his calls; his sister, his beloved little sister, followed her guru to Oregon and cut off all contact with the family; an editor at Aperture, the best publisher of photography books in the country, turned down his proposal for a new volume of photographs by telling him that his work was "unoriginal." And Nora left him. All this within a few months.

The confluence of bummers sent him reeling. His way of working through his unhappiness was to take pictures. Without meaning to change his approach, he found that his approach had changed. He stopped focusing; he stopped worrying about how much light to let in. He stopped trying to play matchmaker between the camera and the world; he let them work out their relationship on their own. All he did was press the button. These new photographs were blurry, unfocused, uncomposed, yet he thought there was more feeling in them than in anything he'd ever done before.

He had no idea whether these photographs would mean anything to anyone else. It turned out that they didn't—not, at any rate, to anyone who mattered in the wider world. Some of his friends liked them, or said they did. But he couldn't get them into any of the galleries or magazines that occasionally welcomed his work.

He took his time figuring out his next move. If anyone had asked him, he would have said that he'd persevere. He wouldn't have considered himself someone who could be thrown off course by a few rejections; he thought he'd developed an immunity to all that.

And then he heard about the job at the paper ("deputy photo editor," which seemed vaguely humiliating, reminding him of the tin deputy sheriff's star he used to wear pinned to his pajama top when he played Cowboys and Indians before bed, but which, on the other hand, paid fifty thousand a year, more than twice what he'd ever earned in any year till then), and he thought, What the hell, I'll apply for it and see what happens. He didn't think they'd offer it to him, and he didn't know if he'd take it if they did.

But they did, and he did—and he found, to his amazement, that he liked it. The work was absorbing, it was sort of creative, and it was a little different every day.

It was strange to live like a normal person. It was a blow to his ego, in a way. He'd been telling himself for more than ten years that he simply wasn't built for the office-going life, yet here he was, not only enduring but enjoying it.

Just as much as he liked the work, he liked the rituals that surrounded it. He liked waking up early; he liked getting coffee from the guy who came around with the cart at break time; he liked standing around bullshitting with the other people who worked there. And he liked getting a regular paycheck. By the standards of friends who'd been solidly in the work world for decades, his salary was measly, but by his own standards, it was unbelievable. He liked having a decent health plan; he liked not having to pay for insulin and syringes.

At first he told himself that he wasn't going to keep doing it—he was just taking a rest for a few months and putting some money in the bank before going back to the freelance life. And then he wasn't sure. He agonized for months about whether to keep the job or rededicate himself to taking pictures. You spend a lot of time worrying about what choice you're going to make, until one day you take a look at your life and realize you've already chosen.

Sometimes he felt as if he'd been cured of a disease. It was as if he'd been carrying a parasite—a worm that used to gnaw away in his brain, and that had finally stopped gnawing. When you devote your whole life to taking pictures, it never lets you rest, because whenever you're not doing it you feel as if you should be doing it, and whenever you're doing it you feel as if you should be doing it better. Whenever you pick up your camera, you know that if André Kertész or Berenice Abbott could stroll up and take it from your hands, they could produce an unforgettable image of the scene in front of you, no matter how flat and unpromising it looks to you. They could make the moment live forever. The parasite of art, the virus of art, never ceases to gnaw away at your brain, never ceases to torture you with the knowledge that whatever you're doing could be done more beautifully, more powerfully, more stirringly, more disturbingly, more deeply.

But now he was living in a different world. If he decided to shoot a roll of film on the weekend, he was no longer haunted by impossible standards. And when he chose the photographs that ran in the paper, simple clarity was enough. After years of beating his head against the unbreakable wall of beauty, it was a relief to be living in a world in which it was possible, even easy, to be good enough.

And yet... He'd never been able to get rid of the idea, somewhere in the back of his mind, that he was going to make his way back to photography someday, and that these last few years of office-going life would finally turn out to be an invisible seedtime, during which, inside him, new powers and new approaches to his art had been taking form.

About two months ago he'd met someone who owned a gallery in New Jersey, and she'd said she'd like to put up a show of his recent work. In fact, he had no recent work—he hadn't taken pictures in over a year—but he didn't tell her that.

The show was still months away, but he was starting to feel more and more excited. He was hoping that it would jump-start his career, jump-start his desire to take pictures again. If he got some good reviews; if he could parlay the show into another, splashier exhibit in Manhattan; if he could get the attention of a younger crowd of curators and gallery owners... There was no telling what might happen. People get rediscovered all the time.

When he was young, he took pictures for the sheer love of it, just to bow down before the fleeting loveliness of the world, but that kind of purity had become impossible to sustain. He just didn't have the strength to get back into photography unless he could be sure of a payoff.

The man he used to be—the man who was Nora's moral touchstone—would have had nothing but scorn for this. The man he used to be would have said that the very fact that he was cautiously testing the waters proved that he wasn't serious about art at all.

And he was afraid that this was what Nora would believe. He knew the outlines of Nora's story; he knew about her struggles. He knew about the way she followed her own aesthetic demon, even when it led her to places where she desperately wanted not to go. Nora was alarmingly pure—as pure as he used to be.

If he'd been approaching his future with a different spirit, he might have told her that the two of them were in the same situation, both of them wanting to rededicate themselves to their calling. But they were animated by such different reasons that he couldn't say it. It was better to let her believe, for now, that he was the same man he used to be, driven by a pure love of taking pictures. Maybe he'd rediscover it. She wouldn't have to know he'd ever lost it.

If she knew about all this, he wondered, would she be less interested in me? Would she be here at all?

HE WENT BACK TO THE BEDROOM and watched her sleep. She was a small woman who slept big: with her arms and legs flung out as if she were making angels in the snow, she took up the entire bed. He thought of taking her picture, but he didn't.

He'd never taken Nora's picture, and he didn't think he ever would. She was the great uncapturable.

In novels and songs, people often sit up watching their lovers sleep. But in real life, it was kind of boring. So he didn't stay there very long; he went into the living room and lay down on the couch.

14

WHEN NORA WOKE UP, ISAAC had already left for work. He'd left her a note telling her to help herself to breakfast. She found some leftover Chinese food in his fridge, ate a cold veggie egg roll and two scallion pancakes, and tossed a few darts at a dartboard on his kitchen wall. She felt virtuous about the fact that she'd cut short their encounter, but also sad.

She would have liked to hang around his house and do some snooping, but she had too many things to do that day.

Waiting at the bus stop, she copyedited an article for a journal of cardiology. Nora wasn't a hypochondriac—she usually felt like the healthiest person in the room—but when she read about a disease, she often spent an hour or two thinking she had it. According to the article she was reading now, open-heart surgery, even when it went without a hitch, could have delayed complications, the most disturbing of which was subtle mental impairment. Evidently this was such a frequent occurrence that doctors had given it a nickname: "pump head." She spent the ride to the city certain that she herself was destined, someday, to end up suffering from pump head. For a few minutes she was convinced she had pump head already, until she remembered that she hadn't actually had open-heart surgery.

She went home and listened to the messages on her phone machine. There was another message from Benjamin, who'd returned from his conference that morning. He was calling to remind her that they were getting together later that night, and to say that he'd be able to tape the Daytime Emmys for Billie.

She copyedited an article about lupus, briefly contracted lupus herself, and then sat down to write. She was just about done with the Richard Buckner article, but she didn't turn to it immediately. As on every other day, she began her writing session by trying to write fiction and seeing if anything would come.

Today, for the first time in almost a year, something *did* come. She couldn't believe it. It was hard to keep herself in her seat—she was so excited she wanted to leap around the room.

It wasn't a story; maybe it was only a character. Maybe it wasn't even a character; maybe it was just a name. But at least she had a name.

She was writing about someone named Gabriel. She didn't know where he had come from; he'd just turned up. The only things she could sense about him at first were that he was older than she was, he was unpretentious, and he was a good listener. She didn't know what he looked like or what he did for a living. But she thought she had the seed of a story. She had a picture in her mind of him meeting a woman at a train station. Nora didn't know much about him, didn't know anything about the woman. But she wanted to find out.

She couldn't write for long, because she had to meet Billie, who was having her operation later that day. But she didn't *need* to write for a long time. She'd finally stumbled into the beginning of a story, and that was enough for one day.

Nora took the subway downtown and met Billie at her apartment.

"How are you doing?" Nora said.

"I'm not scared. I trust the doctor. Dr. Buffalo."

Buffalino was his name. "It's nice to have a surgeon you can trust," Nora said.

"I like it that he takes the time to explain things. I wish he could be my regular doctor. I can't really talk to Dr. Cyclops."

Billie's internist was named Skyler. For a while she'd referred to him as Dr. Skylab; after she grew familiar with his habit of rushing into the room and dashing back out before you had a chance to ask him any questions, he had become Dr. Cyclone; and finally, for no particular reason, he became Dr. Cyclops.

Billie was putting things into her overnight bag: toothbrush, toothpaste, liquid soap, shampoo, lipstick, a pocket-sized photo album, a novel with an Oprah's Book Club seal, and a little book of puzzles and jumbles.

"You'll be able to tape my show for me?"

"Already taken care of."

She didn't tell Billie that it was Benjamin who was doing the taping. She knew Billie would be embarrassed at the thought of Benjamin, the professor, knowing that she watched the Daytime Emmys.

Billie was silent.

"What is it?" Nora said.

"You're nice to me," Billie said.

Edwin was standing by the door, meowing. Billie let him out into the hall and waited patiently at the door until he came back in.

"He has dandruff. He likes to go outside and scratch his back on the banister."

Billie's apartment smelled heavily of cat. Nora tried to ignore this. To be more precise, she tried not to let the smell lead her to the all-too-obvious equation: older woman with cats equals sadness.

One of our tasks in life, Nora was thinking, is to peel away the clichés. TV and movies had touched upon every conceivable situation, and had banalized them all, so that it was difficult to see things clearly. Every situation you encountered had a cliché stuck to it, a label—so that Billie's cats, for example, weren't just cats; they were symbols of how sad it was for an older woman to be living alone.

It *was* sad that the cats were her closest companions. But there was more to Billie's life than that. She'd brought joy into the lives of many people: into Nora's life, into Nelson's, into the lives of the children she'd worked with at the hospital. She had a thick file of letters and cards, from the children and their parents, telling her how much she'd meant to them.

So her life hadn't been so sad. The only sad thing was that she'd ended up alone and uncared for. She had no one to care for her except Nora.

Billie handed Nora a set of her house keys.

"You remember what to feed the little aardvarks?"

Nora closed her eyes, to remember. "Louie and Edwin get the chicken and seafood combo. Dolly gets the gourmet tuna fish."

"And you have to make sure she eats."

"I know," Nora said. "You have to feed her with a spoon."

Billie was having her operation at Mount Sinai. They didn't have to be there until the late afternoon, so they decided to take the subway up to Central Park West and walk across the park.

There was a hot-dog cart in front of the Museum of Natural History, just across from the park. "I think it's time for a snack," Billie said. She walked to the cart—she walked slowly, with her heavy body bent forward. Billie, who used to be a dancer. She ordered a pretzel and a Diet Coke. "How's business?" she said to the vendor, a guy in his twenties, as he passed her a large soft pretzel with a pair of tongs. "Are things going swimmingly today?" She liked to flirt—she always had; but whereas, years ago, when she made these light remarks, people would respond eagerly—men and women alike used to glow with pleasure when she paid attention to them—now they usually ignored her. The guy didn't even bother answering. Nora felt like slapping him. She felt like saying, "A few years ago, if this woman had smiled at you, you would have fallen over yourself, you little shit."

Across the street, just inside the park, there was a huge sealed tent. The museum was sponsoring a special outdoor exhibit: the World of Butterflies.

They went inside. The space, about the size of a football field, was filled with plants and climbing vines and man-sized trees, and, everywhere, butterflies: thousands of brightly colored butterflies, resting on every surface, fluttering in the air with a nervous grace. Fluttering, freckled, stippled, swimming slowly in the air—it was too much beauty to take in.

There was a contingent of New York City schoolchildren in the tent, but instead of being the kind of insane mob Nora usually encountered when she saw kids on class trips—the girls taunting one another, the boys crazily chasing one another, punching—they seemed filled with a sort of awed solemnity. The butterfly world had transformed them into philosophers.

A large and brilliant blue butterfly approached her—dancing toward her and backing away at the same time—and she was filled, not only with joy, but with gratitude. The sheer trustfulness of the people who'd put this exhibit together nearly brought tears to her eyes—their faith that the young people who visited this tent wouldn't be inclined to maul the butterflies, to tear their wings off; their faith that the experience itself would be civilizing.

Some of the butterflies seemed to float through the air without moving their wings. It was like being in a summer shower, a shower of pure beauty. It was like being in some utopian jungle, the tenderest and calmest jungle that could possibly be.

They left the exhibit and walked through the park. They walked around the reservoir, a part of the park that Billie loved. It was a sparkling day; braids of sunlight rippled across the water.

At Mount Sinai, they waited for two hours until Billie was given a room. The other bed was empty, which was nice. The first thing she did was take out her photo album and put it on the night table. It unfolded accordion-style, so you could look at all the pictures at once. There was a picture of Billie's parents—Nora's grandparents; one of Nora with her mother—Nora, at the age of three, standing on Margaret's lectern at the University of Chicago; one of the cats—all three of them sandwiched together on the couch, sleeping; and one of Billie with Nelson, more than twenty years ago, in a paddle boat, laughing.

"Home sweet home," Billie said.

Nora looked around the bare room. "There's just one more thing this room needs," Nora said. She took a bottle of bubbles from her bag—she'd bought it in a party store on Broadway that morning. She opened the bottle, dipped the wand in the liquid, held the wand in front of her lips, and blew.

Ten or fifteen bubbles shot up toward the ceiling and settled slowly in the air: glistening, iridescent, slippery, circling, trembling, wavery, gone.

Nora gave her the bottle and Billie, with a soft breath, sent four small bubbles into the air.

"You're good to me," she said.

"You're easy to be good to."

WHILE NORA WAS IN THE waiting room, a nurse came in to tell her she had a phone call. She took the call at the nurses' station. It was Isaac.

"I was just calling to find out how Billie's doing."

Nora told him that she was still in surgery.

"How did you find me? How'd you get the number here?"

"You don't spend the night with a hotel detective without picking up a thing or two," he said.

She stayed at the hospital until Dr. Buffalo came out to tell her that the operation was over, that everything had gone smoothly, and that they wouldn't know the results for a few days. Billie was in the recovery room; she was under sedation, and would probably just sleep all night.

After leaving the hospital, Nora took the subway downtown to meet Benjamin.

She was meeting him at a restaurant where a group of writers he knew got together for dinner once a month. After that the two of them were going to a book party near Battery Park City.

While she rode the subway, her arm began to throb. It was hard to understand why no one else was aware of it. It seemed to be calling out.

Three different doctors had told her that she needed an

operation: her bones had knitted together in the wrong way, and they needed to be broken again and reset. She didn't *want* to go through an operation, and anyway she had no faith that just one operation would do the trick. She had tried physical therapy, acupuncture, acupressure, yoga, Swedish massage, Chinese herbal medicine, magnets, and prescription painkillers (some of them made the pain go away, but they made her stupid), and nothing helped. So she'd finally decided just to live with the pain. The only problem was that it sometimes affected her mood. Pain can make you less generous, less patient.

A couple of days earlier, Nora had read an article in the *Nation* by someone who had been a longtime member of the American Communist Party. He said he understood why he'd joined the party (idealism), and why he'd left (it had corrupted every ideal it claimed to stand for). What he couldn't understand was why he'd stayed with the party for so long.

Sitting on the subway train, awkwardly massaging her arm, Nora asked herself the same thing about her relationship with Benjamin. Why have I stayed with *this* party for so long?

She'd met Benjamin a year and a half ago. For the first few months, he intrigued her. She thought he was the most serious person, the most touchingly serious person, she'd ever met. He taught in the comparative literature department at the City University of New York; he was a specialist in German literature and philosophy. He was always reading people like Windelband and Dilthey, whoever they were. Dilthey! When she first knew him, she thought of his reading habits as heroic. He was rescuing people from oblivion—because if he didn't read Dilthey, who would? He was like a fireman of intellectual life, rescuing frail forgotten thinkers from the burning building of time.

When she was getting to know him, she'd sometimes drop

in on him at his haunt at the Hungarian Pastry Shop near Columbia—he'd spend hours there, reading and drinking coffee—and when she'd sit down across from him he'd look up, smiling kindly but vaguely, as if unable to place her; and she was charmed by this. It was as if he belonged in another century. She always had the feeling that if she'd arrived ten minutes earlier, she would have seen him chatting with Freud or Wittgenstein or Karl Kraus.

Her unhappiness arrived quietly, almost without announcing itself. One afternoon a few months after they got together, she was in his apartment when he got a call from someone from Rutgers University Press. Benjamin was publishing a book, a beefed-up version of his dissertation—a study of the later work of the Austrian novelist Hermann Broch—and he needed to do some last-minute revisions. She picked up something to read and went to the kitchen, and after he got off the phone she went back to the living room and asked him if the revisions were done.

"No. I still have to have one more conversation with Alex"—his editor. "I was talking to some lowly assistant just now."

After he said this, she realized she'd already known it. Even from another room, even without hearing his words, she'd been able to tell that he was talking to some lowly assistant. If he'd been talking to someone he considered important, he would have had a different tone of voice.

She began to be bothered by the way he spoke to people: waiters, receptionists, his students when they called on the phone. Unless they could help him or impede him in some way—unless they were important to his career—just about everyone was a lowly assistant to him.

She could pinpoint the moment when she realized she needed to leave him. It was on the day the new phone books arrived. She picked one up in her lobby and took it upstairs and looked herself up—not to make sure her listing was accurate, but because finding your name in the new phone book is a small and slightly startling confirmation that you exist. Then she looked Benjamin up. She'd never looked him up in the phone book before.

He existed too: Benjamin Mandelbaum, Ph.D.

Ph.D.?

The funny thing was, it didn't really surprise her. It didn't surprise her that he felt the need to inform the readership of the Verizon Manhattan SuperPages of the fact that he had a Ph.D.

When you're bothered by your boyfriend's listing in the phone book, it's probably a sign that you're not really meant for each other.

It wasn't that he was a bad person. He *did* have a passion for learning, like few people she had ever known. There *was* something moving about his devotion to old dead thinkers. He wasn't a bad person, but he wasn't the person for her. There was nothing left to do but leave him.

But before you leave someone, you have to have The Talk. How she dreaded The Talk! She'd once heard that the essayist Lionel Abel had left his first wife by going out to buy a pack of cigarettes and never coming back, and she kept wondering if this was an option for her. In order to do it, of course, she'd have to start smoking, but it might be worth it, if The Talk was the only alternative.

When you tell someone that you're leaving him, he will ask why, and then you'll have to give your reasons, and then he'll dispute them—when our lovers try to leave us, we suddenly become lawyers—and the two of you will debate about whether your reasons for leaving are good enough, when all along what you really want to say is simply, "I don't love you anymore. I'm not happy."

Maybe there were people who could just come out and say this, but Nora wasn't one of them. Many of her friends, down through the years, had referred to her as impulsive, and she didn't think they were wrong. But this wasn't true in every sphere of life. When she was unhappily involved with a man, she got stuck.

She kept reviewing the possibilities. There was The Talk. There was the Lionel Abel option. And best of all was the *Superman II* option. After Lois (Margot Kidder) discovers that Clark (Christopher Reeve) is really Superman, they have a love affair, which ends when Superman, fearing that her knowledge of his true identity would put her in danger, gives her a hypnotic kiss, erasing both her memory of his identity and her memory of their affair. What wouldn't she give to be able to kiss Benjamin with a kiss of forgetfulness!

Benjamin had once said that if a woman he was seeing ever cheated on him, he'd leave her instantly. "Infidelity," he had told her, "is the only unforgivable." But she didn't want to cheat on him.

The difficulty of breaking up with him had nothing to do with a fear of being alone. She was sure about that. She never thought of herself as an orphan—the term seemed too self-pitying—but she was used to being alone, schooled in it. She'd once read an essay by Michael Ventura called "The Talent of the Room," in which he said that if you want to be a writer, the most important piece of equipment you need is the ability to be alone—to spend your best hours by yourself at the keyboard. If that's the most important thing, Nora had thought, I've got it made.

Finally she decided there was no way around it. As much as she dreaded The Talk, she knew she had to go through with it.

There couldn't have been a better time to leave him. Benjamin's book was being published; he was on a tenure track; everything was falling into place for him. No one could accuse her of kicking him when he was down.

She decided to have The Talk the next time she saw him. Benjamin had no idea what was coming. She thought it was best that way. She would dispose of the matter quickly and efficiently. She felt like a hit man.

On the appointed night, a Friday, she paced around her apartment, tidying, waiting for him, thinking about all the movies about hit men she'd seen in the last few years, wondering why the hit man had become a cultural hero. Then she ate two Mars bars to give herself a jolt of sugar for her task.

Benjamin showed up precisely at nine, and as soon as she opened the door she could tell that something was wrong. People carry their own climates with them, their own ecosystems; Benjamin's, lately, had been perpetually sunny. With his book out and his tenure imminent, he'd seemed, during the last few months, to be walking around inside a golden bubble; at times she felt she could have reached out and given it a squeeze. But tonight something was different. His golden bubble was gone.

He even smelled different. He smelled meaty. Unpleasantly so, like liverwurst.

"What's wrong?"

He dropped a copy of the *New York Review of Books* on the kitchen table.

She turned to the table of contents. His book had been reviewed.

"Go ahead," he said. "Read it. You read it, and I'll weep."

The review had been written by somebody from Harvard, evidently a big shot in the field. It was a long review, and it wasn't nice. The reviewer made a distinction between intellectuals (people who put ideas to use in interesting ways) and scholars (people who merely amass facts, with no idea of what to do with them). "Sadly," the reviewer concluded, "this is the work of a scholar."

While she read the review, Benjamin sat beside her at the kitchen table, reading it over her shoulder. He'd probably already read it more than once, but he couldn't stop himself from reading it again. He was thrusting his chin in the air, working the muscles of his throat, as if he'd forgotten how to swallow. He looked like a frightened little boy.

After she finished, he began to explain why the review was unfair. "It's a joke. It's worse than a joke: it's a scandal. This is going to destroy his reputation. Look at this. He writes that Broch sold his family business to devote himself to literature—as if I didn't spend an entire chapter on the fact that he sold it to devote himself to *philosophy.* He only turned to literature *after* he studied philosophy. If you can mix up something that basic, how can you think you have the credentials to review a book on Hermann Broch?" He talked for five or ten minutes, citing the reviewer's many errors. Every once in a while he leaned over and made notes for a letter to the editor—a letter she hoped he wouldn't send, because it would convict him more thoroughly than the review had. Accused of being an arid scholar, Benjamin wanted to refute the charge with the tools of arid scholarship.

She didn't have the heart to have The Talk that night. It would be too cruel.

Benjamin was still working his throat muscles oddly, still thrusting his face forward.

"Are you okay?"

"I feel weird. I think I must have eaten something bad. I feel like I have a stomachache all the way up to my jaw."

"Benjamin?"

"I'm all right. Just let me lie down for a second."

He lay down, but it didn't help. After a few minutes he said he couldn't breathe. "I feel like I have something stuck in my throat."

"Do you think we should call your doctor?"

"It's Friday night. My doctor's home bleaching his teeth."

Benjamin's doctor was famous for his wondrous teeth.

"Maybe we should go to the hospital," Nora said.

"That's ridiculous. I'm just upset that that charlatan got his hands all over my book."

But after half an hour on the couch he didn't feel better, and he let her take him to the hospital. In the emergency room—overweight male with chest pain—he moved quickly to the front of the line. He sat on the examining table in a paper gown, his plump white hairless legs dangling. "I have an anomalous sensation in my chest," he said to one of the doctors, and Nora was touched by this. Who talked this way? Nobody but Benjamin.

After twelve hours of testing, the doctors concluded that he'd had a mild "coronary event," and they kept him in for observation.

He sat in his hospital bed, stiff with fright; when his brothers came by the next day, they made jokes to cheer him up, but Benjamin just sat there, nodding tightly. Later, after his brothers had left, Benjamin's doctor stopped in, and Benjamin asked him, in a small voice, whether it was all right to laugh.

"Of course," the doctor said. "Laughter's the best medicine," he added predictably.

"It won't put a strain on my heart?"

Sitting in the corner, Nora felt ashamed of her own mind. Because at the same time that she was genuinely concerned about Benjamin, she was also wishing that she'd broken up with him a month ago. She didn't know when she'd be able to break up with him now.

ALL THIS HAD HAPPENED more than a year earlier. Benjamin was as good as new: he'd lost weight; he'd gotten tenure; his book had been well reviewed in the scholarly journals. His golden bubble had long since reappeared. But still she hadn't left him. She hadn't been able to.

Her inability to leave him was stunning—and yet it wasn't stunning at all. Anytime she thought about it, she remembered him as he was that night in her kitchen: the frightened boy who'd forgotten how to swallow; or as he was the next day in the hospital: the timid boy asking his doctor if it was okay to laugh.

She didn't love him, but she stayed. And two days after he was discharged from the hospital, she'd put away the notes she'd been making for a story about him, and she'd written barely a word of fiction from that day until this morning.

During the past year, she'd become an amateur authority on coronary health. She'd subscribed to *Nutrition Action* and the *Harvard Heart Letter*; she'd read half a shelf of books about "heart-healthy lifestyles." She was trying to keep him on something approximating the Dean Ornish diet. She'd nudged him into an exercise program (he finally acquiesced when she explained that he could read while he exercised, and now he was dutifully spending half an hour a day on the treadmill, a copy of Schopenhauer's *The World as Will and Idea* propped up on the instrument panel). And without his really being aware of it, she'd begun to oversee his schedule, trying to make sure that his afternoons were free for reading and writing so that he was no longer staying up till two in the morning and getting by on five hours' sleep.

Sometimes she told herself that it made perfect sense that she hadn't been writing any fiction: the creative energy that she normally poured into her stories had been diverted into the effort to take care of him. But she knew that wasn't the real reason. She wasn't writing fiction because she was afraid of where it would lead her.

THE RESTAURANT WAS ON Third Avenue and Thirteenth Street. It was one of those places that make you feel like you're back in the 1940s—it had a neon sign outside that said "Steaks and Chops." It was a comfortable place, where you could sit as long as you liked.

She knew this was a big night for Benjamin. During the last six months, he'd grown restless with the confines of being an academic scholar, writing only for other academics. He wanted to write for *Harper's* and the *Atlantic*; he dreamed of writing for the *New Yorker* someday. He wanted, he once told her solemnly, to become a "public intellectual." He valued these monthly get-togethers, because many of the people who attended them wrote for the magazines he dreamed about writing for.

At the back of the restaurant, ten or fifteen people were sitting around a long table. Nora knew about half of them—not well, but well enough to consider sneaking away. But then Benjamin spotted her. Too late.

The people at the table, in Nora's view, could have posed for a collective portrait illustrating the varieties of self-glorification in literary life.

Sitting next to Benjamin was Marty Rubin, whose zeal for self-promotion took innovative forms. Two years ago, after he'd published his first book, a political novel about the drug war, he'd hired a team of college-age "assistants" to read the book for a few hours a day while riding the subway. Last year, after the death of a mutual friend of theirs, he'd sent Benjamin a packet in the mail. It contained a note that read, "I was so sorry to hear about Paul's death. I want you to know that only an unbreakable obligation like the one described in the enclosed flyers could prevent me from attending the memorial service. If you get a chance, perhaps you could distribute them after the service, so that if any of our friends happen to be traveling to the West Coast they can attend the second or third lecture." The note was accompanied by twenty copies of a flyer advertising a lecture series he was giving at UCLA; it featured a color photograph of him, standing shirt-sleeved in a blighted barrio in East L.A., looking both compassionate and streetwise.

There was Peter Anderson, who in his early thirties had written two books in quick succession: an authorized biography of Giorgio Armani and a slim study of foot fetishes. After the foot-fetish book flopped commercially, Peter had spent a few months engaged in anguished introspection, a period that culminated in a trip to the Middle East, where, during a tour of the West Bank, he had discovered that the Palestinians were possessed by irrational furies and an inability to let go of their grievances. He had expanded on this insight in a series of articles, which had led to a contract for a book about world trouble spots; the thesis of the book, *The Limits of the Liberal Mind,* was that the conflicts in places like Ireland, Rwanda, the former Yugoslavia, and the Middle East were beyond the reach and even beyond the comprehension of idealists, humanitarians, and peacemakers. He now appeared regularly on *Charlie Rose,* offering deeply pessimistic reflections about global politics in a voice that was stricken, burdened, weary, weighed down by all he had witnessed.

And then there was Frank Millstein, an investigative reporter who in recent years had taken to referring to himself in the third person: "When people see Frank Millstein's name at the top of the page, they know they'd better sit down. They know they're about to read something that's gonna pack a punch." And why, Nora thought, shouldn't he? If you consider yourself a figure of major importance, you *should* refer to yourself in the third person. Anything else would be false modesty.

All these forms of self-aggrandizement seemed peculiarly male. But *why* were men like this? And was it *only* men who were like this? Of course not. But it was much easier for men to be like this. She found a chair at an empty table and slid it next to Benjamin, who kissed her hello, but who was so absorbed in the discussion that he barely looked at her.

They were talking about an article that had recently appeared in *Harper's.* Nora hadn't read it, so it was hard for her to follow the conversation.

Just before she'd entered the restaurant, Nora had noticed a judo school next door. Now, after ordering a drink, she glanced up and saw a man who must have been one of the teachers. A small, compact Asian man in his late fifties or early sixties, he was standing near the door, waiting to be seated. He was dressed simply, in a white shirt and khaki pants; he was carrying a gym bag that bore the school's emblem. His hair was wet and neatly combed, as if he'd just showered after his class. A busboy went hurrying by, holding up a tray of plates and glasses, and the man turned aside to let him pass; it was a tiny movement, a half step, but it was a study in economy of motion.

The hostess led the man to a table and a waiter immediately brought him a pot of tea. Evidently he was a regular.

Nora, watching him thank the waiter and pour himself a cup of tea, his movements elegant and precise, felt as if she could learn more of value from him than from any of the people at her table. Maybe he could even fix my arm, she thought.

She didn't want to be reductive; she didn't want to exalt the life of the body over the life of the mind. She didn't want to engage in some implicitly racist assumption that as a representative of the Ancient East, he was in tune with the unchanging verities. But he *did* have a quiet grace—in the calm simplicity of his gestures, in the way he'd thanked the waiter who'd brought him his tea. He had the air of someone who had tended his life wisely.

But of course the people at her table, heaving their abstractions around, had tended their lives as well. Some of them were ardent readers; some of them were gifted and careful writers; almost all of them, she was sure, genuinely cared about the ideas they were discussing. Even if their interest in these ideas was tied up with their own ego-strivings, their obsessive concern for their careers, they were serious people.

And even if they *were* to some extent full of shit, who wasn't? What about the judo guy? Maybe if she knew him she'd discover that he was full of shit himself. She might find out that he spent all his waking hours boiling with envy of some other judo guy who was more famous than he was.

And what about me? Nora thought. Maybe the biggest fool at this table is the person who sees the foolishness in everyone else, the small hypocrisies, when the significant thing about them is that they're trying, through their writing, to keep some sort of intelligent cultural conversation alive. Why was the transformation of Peter Anderson, the foot fetishist turned prophet, any less admirable than the transformation that Nora was trying to bring about in her own life? If there's a joke here, it's probably on me.

The discussion broke up; people were standing. Benjamin fell into conversation with a woman Nora had never met. She was almost as small as Nora, and she wasn't much younger, but Nora felt as if they could have been from different planets. This little thing, you could somehow tell from the quickest glance, had a motor of ambition inside her that never stopped working. Even as she spoke to Benjamin she was scanning the room, making sure she could get rid of him before any of the heavy hitters left.

She was wearing a tight dress, short and sleeveless, so you could admire her arms and legs, which were, indeed, admirable: you could tell she worked out.

I should start working out too, Nora thought. That girl over there will never get pump head.

Nora talked for a minute with one of the few people she felt comfortable with there: Ilya Kaplan, a stooped, gentle guy who worked for an arts foundation.

"Are you still writing?" he said.

"Always."

"Fiction, I mean. You tend to go back and forth, right?"

She thought of the thing she'd written that morning: her two or three pages about Gabriel.

"Right now I'm somewhere in the middle."

"Well, I hope you get back to writing fiction soon. I shouldn't be telling you this, but I've always loved your stuff—I guess I've only read two or three of your stories, but I loved them."

"Why shouldn't you be telling me that? Everybody should be telling me that."

"What I shouldn't be telling you is that I'm going to be judging a short-story competition this year for the *Atlantic.* It's limited to writers who've published, I think, at least two stories, but who haven't put out a book yet. So you'd qualify. The winner gets five thousand dollars, and the story runs in the *Atlantic,* of course. So if you have anything you haven't published yet that you feel good about, think about it. The deadline's pretty far off, so you have some time."

"Wow. Thank you." She'd never published in a magazine with a circulation approaching that of the *Atlantic.*

"I can't guarantee anything, obviously. They'll probably get about a million submissions, and they only send the thirty finalists on to me. And even if you *are* one of the finalists, I might end up liking somebody else's story better. But I've loved everything I've read of yours, so...give it a shot."

Nora kept thanking him until he asked her to stop. It

would have been a very happy moment, except that she was still suffering in her arm.

"You're funny," he said. "You seem like such a sweetheart—you *are* such a sweetheart. I'll never forget the way you were with my daughter when she got that bee sting." Something that happened at a barbecue a year ago—Nora barely remembered it. "But in your stories, you're like some—I don't know what you're like. But you're no sweetheart."

"I know. When I pick up my pen I become a monster. I don't really write with a pen. But."

"Not a monster. I wouldn't say a monster." He was thinking about this seriously. "That story of yours that was in *Boulevard* a couple of years ago—that had a touch of Adam Halliday in it, didn't it?"

"I can't believe you saw that."

"*Was* it Adam?"

"I'm not at liberty to say."

"Well, if it wasn't, it was an interesting coincidence. How well do you know him?"

"I only really met him once or twice."

"That's what I thought. He's a good friend of mine, and I was amazed at how much of him you got right."

"Lucky guess," Nora said. "Not that I'm admitting it was about him." Adam was an English writer who'd come to New York to become the fiction editor of the *Atlantic*—promising to turn the staid old magazine around, to make it brilliant and edgy and snarky and all that—and had slunk back to London in obscure circumstances six months later. Nora had met him a couple of times—he'd rejected two of her stories, but kindly, and they'd met for coffee—and something about him had intrigued her.

"What did he think of the story?" she said.

"I don't think he saw it. I never told him about it. I didn't think he'd be too pleased."

"That's what I mean. Everything I write turns into a poison-pen letter."

"I wouldn't say that. You had some pretty harsh things in that story...but you took him seriously. I thought about that story for a long time. You were pitiless, but you didn't make him a joke—and after he went back to England, *everybody* was taking him as a joke. I remember thinking that you gave his life the dignity of the tragic." He smiled what seemed to be a self-deprecating smile, as if he was apologizing for the fancy phrase.

"I'm glad you think so," Nora said.

"On the other hand," he said, putting on his coat, "I would never, ever, *ever* want you to write about me."

Benjamin was eager to move on to the next event. Nora said good-bye to Ilya Kaplan, and then she said good-bye to the judo guy, though only in her mind, and she and Benjamin left the restaurant.

The tips of his ears were red; he'd perhaps had too much to drink.

"Did you have a good time?" Nora said.

"Fantastic. Did you see that woman I was talking to?"

"I noticed her."

"That was Heather Wolfe. She used to work for Tina Brown at *Talk* magazine. I asked her what she's up to now, and she said she's helping launch a new magazine. But she was very mysterious about it. She told me to send her some clips. Maybe Tina's starting something new. Wouldn't that be amazing—to be writing for Tina?"

He'd never met Tina Brown, but like everyone else in the publishing world, he referred to her by her first name. She was like Madonna for intellectuals.

Benjamin had his hand on Nora's elbow—he was half dragging her down the block. It was her left arm, the damaged one, but the pressure was a welcome distraction.

"That would be great," she said. "Did you set the VCR, by the way?"

"What?"

"The VCR. For my aunt's TV show."

"No. Sorry. I forgot."

"You're kidding, right?"

"No, I wish I were. I'm not."

She stopped walking. "But you said you would."

He raised his eyebrows, a sort of eyebrow-shrug. "Sorry. I was about to. But then I got a call from Marty telling me that Heather was going to be there, and I got so excited I forgot all about it."

She should have figured out how to do it herself.

You can never rely on anybody else. Never.

It was almost ten. The show had started at nine; it was supposed to end at 11:30.

"I'm sorry—really," he said. "But Christ—the Daytime Emmys?"

"She wanted to *watch* the Daytime Emmys. She asked me to *tape* the Daytime Emmys. You mean you would have remembered if she'd wanted us to tape a special about Fritz Lang?"

Benjamin was an enthusiast of pre-war German cinema. She tried to get in a good sneer as she pronounced the name.

"Well," he said, "it's too late now. We'll make it up to her.

We'll go to the video store tomorrow and buy her a classic tearjerker. You can pick it out."

Benjamin raised his hand for a cab and in a moment they were traveling farther downtown.

"Shoot," Nora said.

The party was being held for a woman Benjamin knew slightly, who'd written a book about her experiences traveling around the world alone in a boat. She was a regular contributor to *Vanity Fair*, and Benjamin thought he could make some useful contacts at the party.

The party was being held on a yacht off Battery Park. It had started at eight; at ten, the yacht was going to circle Manhattan.

Benjamin was probably right: they could make it up to Billie easily. They could get her something that she'd appreciate even more than a tape of the show. Nevertheless, she was counting on having the Daytime Emmys to watch when she got home, and Nora hated the thought of letting her down.

Nora was heading off to a party that she didn't even want to go to, when she had a clear responsibility to go home and figure out how to tape the rest of the show.

Go with the one who needs you.

They were streaking through the streets in the wrong direction. They arrived at Battery Park City and made their way to the dock. The yacht was easy to find: it was all lit up. You could hear music and laughter and voices in the cool spring night.

Battery Park City without the World Trade towers. She couldn't get used to it. She'd never liked those buildings—they'd always reminded her of supermodels, awesome in their way, but blank—but without their vapid glamour it was impossible to be in the area without the feeling that something was happening to your heart.

She didn't know what to do.

There was a clutch of people just behind them, heading for the yacht; an equal number of people, not wanting to be part of the midnight cruise, were streaming off.

She and Benjamin walked onto the yacht. Everybody there was about three yards taller than Nora. Normally she didn't mind being small; she thought she owed some of whatever strength of character she had to the fact that she needed to battle for things that other people took for granted. But it could be frustrating in crowds. Benjamin spotted someone he knew, an enormous young man in a black suit and a black T-shirt. Benjamin hurried over to talk to him, and Nora was alone.

I could just leave, she thought. *I don't even have to say good-bye to Benjamin. He won't even notice—he's already networking away!*

But she couldn't do it.

It was ten o'clock, and one of the tuxedoed young men who was working at the party—obviously an aspiring actor, so handsome he was like a hologram—was moving toward the gate, about to close it so the yacht could start off on its cutesy cruise.

Last chance to leave. Benjamin was back at her side. As though he knew what she was thinking, though of course he didn't, he took her by the hand.

"I want you to meet Tom," he said, introducing her to the huge guy.

"Are you a literary giant?" Nora said, stupid joke, as somewhere inside her a miniature Nora, a Nora homunculus, was stamping its feet in frustration and self-hatred, for not having the guts to get off the yacht and get home and figure out her VCR.

The only way for her to escape at this point would be to make a scene—break free of Benjamin and make a run for it—and she was too old for that, too old too old too old.

Someone tossed a bunch of red roses on the water, in the light of the dock you could see them clearly, it was beautiful to see them scattered on the black, but Billie was in the hospital, and she was expecting that when she got home the next day there would be comfort there, comfort and familiarity, in the form of a video, and Nora was trying not to see Benjamin as a villain, it wasn't that he'd lied, he'd just been too excited to keep his word.

This is your last chance, she thought. *This is your last chance to do what you need to do.*

And it seemed to her that at every moment of your life you know what you need to do; you know, in your deepest heart, what you should choose.

Go with the one who needs you.

But that was ridiculous! If you were guided by that idea, you were just making yourself a hostage to other people's weaknesses.

"This is great," Benjamin said, referring to she-didn't-know-what.

What to do? Her arm was hurting so much that it was hard to think.

If only something would happen to stop the boat. If only—

The day before, at Isaac's, she'd been wishing for an earthquake.

You can't go through life hoping for earthquakes, she thought. You have to be your own earthquake.

"Excuse me," she said to Benjamin.

She walked toward the back end, toward the stern, whatever it was called. Young Mr. Handsome was latching the gate.

"Excuse me," Nora said.

She put her leg over the gate.

"No, no, no," the man said. "You can't leave now. Not on my watch, Ma'am."

I'm a Ma'am, am I? Fuck you, she thought. But the boat was moving. There was a yard-long gap between the boat and the dock. Well, here goes. She felt like a detective on TV. *Spenser: For Hire*, she thought.

The ledge she was standing on was too narrow for her to make a running start, so she just crouched, readying herself to make a standing broad jump, the way her fourth-grade gym teacher, Mrs. Applebaum, had taught her.

She landed clean and true, and she thought *Things work out in life after all*, and she was balanced perfectly on the edge of the dock—*She nailed it! Nadia Comaneci!*—and then the sky was in front of her, and she was slamming backwards into the water, shit!, she was actually in the Hudson River, the Hudson River was over her head, she gulped a mouthful of the Hudson River, this is how she died. Shit! Shit! Shit! Shit! Shit! I'm dying!

Everything was dark, and she had taken the river into her mouth, and she was clawing at the water, not knowing whether she was going up or down, and her head was out of the water but it was horrible there too, the air was water too, murky and wet, and this is how you die, when you drink too much air and it explodes you, and there was a railing or something, something hard, and she was clutching it more tightly than she'd ever clutched a lover, she loved this railing more than she'd ever known she could love, and her eyes were clear of the river, her eyes were clear of the murk, she was going to live.

She was able to pull herself back up to the dock, and she lay there, sprawled out, spent. She felt no need to rise. Just lying on the dock was the most beautiful thing she had ever done—the most intelligent, witty, graceful, generous thing she'd ever done.

But she was happy only for a moment. She'd swallowed the river, all five hundred miles of it. She'd taken the river in her mouth. She'd given the horrible river a blow job. Now she was on her knees, sopping wet and shivering and spitting, spitting convulsively, because who knew what she'd ingested in that horrible moment. PCBs, fecal matter, detergent, toe snot, snot snot, human corpse jelly, parasites, worms, evil worms from unsanitary countries, rat hairs, rat vomit, pus, pus pudding, penis juice, scabs scrubbed off the scrota of syphilitic Slavic seamen: yes, you will die now; your time is up. She'd gulped up mouthfuls of death from the river. Death was in her belly now, strutting off into her bloodstream, smug about having conquered her so soon. She had given death a gift. Death was in ecstasy.

The yacht was fifty feet away. It sat unmoving in the water. *All because of me.*

Everyone, it seemed, had gathered against the railing to look at her. She could see Benjamin in the crowd, but he was too far away for her to make out his expression. She was shivering, sopping, stringy-haired, humiliated, in the cool and clear spring night.

15

She went home on the subway. The train was crowded. A girl-mob of Barnard students was making a lot of noise—they were standing in a circle, singing "Like a Virgin"—so nobody looked twice at Nora. She was just another New York City madwoman making her way uptown.

When she reached her building, Arthur, the doorman, nodded, taking her in. He had a perpetual air of having seen it all before. You would have thought that Nora was the third stinking and dripping person he'd seen that night.

"There's probably a pretty interesting story here," he said, "but I'm not going to ask what it is."

Back in her apartment, she took a quick shower, and then she tried to figure out her VCR. She couldn't do it, and soon it was too late: the Daytime Emmys were over. She took another shower, much longer, and she was strapping her Polar Pack on her arm when the intercom sounded. Arthur told her that Benjamin was in the lobby. Nora asked Arthur to send him up.

She hadn't even considered the possibility that he'd follow her home. It didn't fit the script. The way the script went, in her mind, was that after the heroine makes the big leap from the yacht, she never sees the man again. He goes back to his mother, in Albany.

That would have been a movie with Ralph Bellamy. Apparently she'd gotten the genre wrong. This wasn't a screwball comedy; this was a horror movie, where, at the end, after you think the heroine has killed the mutant, it jumps back out and she has to kill it again.

The mutant wasn't Benjamin; it was her life with him.

She put her ice pack in the freezer and went to the door. She expected Benjamin to look downcast, stricken, but instead he looked purely enraged.

He walked in quickly. "Are you crazy?"

"Maybe. I don't think so."

"Then what were you doing back there? Did you have any goal, other than to make us both look like idiots?"

He had a right to be angry, and, on reflection, she was *glad* that he was angry. If he'd seemed devastated by the thought of losing her, it might have made things harder. It might have awakened her protective instincts. But because he was angry, she felt free. She wasn't afraid of having The Talk anymore. If he'd come for a fight, she could fight him.

"I'm sorry, Benjamin. But I needed to get out. I needed to leave."

"Why? Was it because of the VCR thing? Was that it?"

"That wasn't it. It was, but it wasn't. I just...this isn't working. I need a different life."

"That's a cliché," he said.

This hurt her. She wouldn't have thought that he had the power to hurt her.

"Well, whatever," she said, which didn't exactly refute him, but she didn't care.

"I don't understand you. Five days ago, when I called you from Berlin, you said you loved me. Has something changed in the last five days? Or is this the way you think you should *treat* someone you love?"

She'd often told him she loved him. But did she? Had she ever? She'd first used the words a few days after his Coronary Event, when she was overcome by pity and tenderness. You tell someone you love him, because you think you do—or because you want to, and you hope that saying it will make it become true—and then, when you begin to see that you never have, never will, you can't quite take it back.

She'd once read a book by C. S. Lewis called *The Four Loves*, which distinguished among erotic love, charitable love, something love, and something else love—she couldn't remember. Spiritual and amicable love, maybe, the last referring to the love we feel for our friends? Maybe she could tell Benjamin, "I love you in the amicable sense, but no longer in the erotic or spiritual senses, and the category of the charitable doesn't apply."

"If you want to be with me," Benjamin said, "this is a crazy way to show it."

"I'm sorry, Benjamin. I *don't* want to be with you."

He looked as if he hadn't considered this possibility before. Which was surprising. It would seem to be axiomatic that when your lover leaps off a boat to get away from you, she's probably unhappy with the relationship.

He sat down on the couch. "So you really *don't* love me. You probably never did."

She was about to answer this, but then she realized that she had no answer. No answer that wouldn't hurt him more than she was hurting him already.

He put his head in his hands, and instantly she wanted to walk over and comfort him, and she had to force herself to stay put. Then he lifted his head, and he was smiling. His smile was a little scary. He looked like a madman in a James Bond movie, who'd just hatched a plan for world domination.

"I'm not going to let you do it," he said.

"What?"

"I don't think you know what you want right now. It's pretty obvious that you're not thinking clearly. Some people down there thought you were trying to commit suicide. I know you weren't, but I do think you're not well. We're not breaking up. I'm sticking with you until you come to your senses."

This was something she hadn't anticipated: that he might not *allow* her to break up with him. She didn't know what to do. And then she did.

"There's something I haven't told you," she said. "I've been seeing someone."

Cheating on him, as he'd once told her, was the one unforgivable.

The mad confidence of a moment ago shrank away. He seemed to get swallowed up by the couch.

"Who is he?"

"You don't know him."

"Who is he? I want to know his name."

"Why?"

"I just want to know his name. He has a name, doesn't he?"

"His name," she said slowly, "is Gabriel."

"How long have you known him?"

"Not very long."

"What's so great about *Gabriel*?" He said this as if the bearer of such a name must self-evidently be a stupid man.

Well, Nora thought, he fits onto a floppy disk. That's pretty great.

"He listens to people," she said. "He listens to me."

He had no response to this. He sat on her couch, nodding, looking down. It was as if he knew that listening to people was not one of his strong points.

Finally she said, "I think it's time for you to leave."

"So it is," he said, and stood up. She put her hand on his back and steered him toward the door. Tamely, he allowed himself to be steered.

At the door he turned around, and they looked at each other: the first full, frank look they'd exchanged in months. She felt as if she was seeing him, really seeing him, for the first time. He was a baffled creature, just as she was, groping his way through life.

"Take care of yourself," she said, and touched his arm, and then she closed the door.

She put her ice pack back on, sat down at her keyboard, and starting banging away. The Gabriel story.

There was a knock on her door. It was Benjamin.

"I forgot my glasses." She stepped aside and he retrieved his glasses from the coffee table. He stopped for a moment, looking at her computer. She wished she hadn't started writing so quickly after he left. She wished that he'd found her sitting in a contemplative silence.

After he left again, she waited until she heard the elevator going down, and then she went back to the keyboard.

16

IT'S NICE TO BELIEVE THAT each of us has one true love. This is a story we all enjoy. When Ingrid Bergman asks Dooley Wilson—Sam—to play "As Time Goes By," and Humphrey Bogart, hearing the song, turns pale, we know it's because the only woman he's ever loved has just come back into his life. We don't want to think that there might have been three or four other women who could have laid him even lower by strolling in after her and asking Sam to play something else—"Begin the Beguine," say, or "Struttin' with Some Barbecue."

Isaac believed in the idea of true love more than anyone else he knew—anyone his age, at least. He believed that Nora was his mate.

But at the same time, he sometimes felt that if he'd been much, much younger, he might have believed it of Renee.

He tried not to think about her this way. He wasn't her boss anymore, but that made no difference; he had only one role to play in her life, the role of a fatherly friend.

"You're such a throwback," Renee said. "You're like a doctor who's still treating people with leeches."

She was visiting him in his darkroom. She'd never been there before. She was teasing him because he still used a darkroom.

"Or, you know what you're like? Really? You're like one of those people who don't buy CDs because they say vinyl sounds warmer."

"I'm a phony, in other words?"

"I wasn't going to say that."

He was glad she'd stayed in touch after she'd stopped working at the paper.

She was dressed absurdly, in a Hawaiian shirt, extra-large, that went all the way down to her knees, and blocky, cloddish shoes, shoes that might have been designed for Frankenstein.

"How are you?" he said. "How's your noggin?"

Two weeks ago, while she was taking pictures of police breaking up a demonstration of squatters in the East Village, one of the cops had clipped her on the side of the head with his billy club. He'd tried to grab her camera, but Renee had refused to relinquish her grip.

"He cleaned my clock," Renee said proudly. "It still hurts. But I'm getting the last laugh. One of the pictures is going to be published in the *Tenants' Rights Newsletter*."

Had Nora ever put her body on the line for a cause? Never. Renee, he thought, was a better person. She gets slammed with a billy club, but if she gets a good picture out of the experience, she has no regrets.

He was angry at Nora for neglecting him, so he ran Renee against her in his mind. He wanted to place Renee and Nora on the scales of human merit, and to conclude that Renee was a superior person.

Nora had disappeared. It had been a month since she'd broken up with Whatshisface, and although they'd been speaking on the phone since then, and she always sounded as if she missed him, she was keeping her distance. The one time she'd been willing to make a date to get together, she'd cancelled it at the last minute. Isaac wouldn't have predicted that she would leave the other guy yet not come hurtling into his arms.

Oh well.

Before Nora had come back into his life, he'd sometimes had romantic daydreams about Renee. He never would have tried to make them a reality, but he didn't think there was any harm in dreaming. He didn't dream about the two of them as they were now; rather, he imagined some *Star Trek* time warp that made them the same age.

When he'd thought Nora was coming back into his life, he'd instantly stopped daydreaming about Renee. But now Nora was out of reach again.

"What have you been up to?" he said.

"I'm mostly just waiting around for the fact-finding trip. Gotta go find them facts." She hoisted herself up onto a table and, sitting there, kicked her legs idly in the air. She looked like she was about nine. "And I've been sending my pictures out to magazines and stuff."

"Where?"

"Everywhere. The *Village Voice, DoubleTake,* the *Democratic Socialist,* the *New Yorker.*"

There was something incredibly pure-minded about her, or about her stage of life—that stage of life in which you can believe that getting a picture into the *Democratic Socialist,* circulation 408, is as much of a triumph as getting one into the *New Yorker.* More of a triumph.

"You should use me as a reference. I still know some people at the *Voice.* I can call them for you if you want."

"Thanks. That's really nice of you."

"I'd be happy to."

"When I get back from Asia, maybe you can teach me the mysteries of the darkroom," Renee said. "You can teach me how to spend three hours developing a picture that doesn't end up looking quite as good as if you'd done it on a Mac."

Renee didn't have the same pure passion for taking pictures that he'd had when he was her age. For Renee, photography wasn't an end in itself; it was a tool in the struggle for social justice. If she'd been a writer, she would have been a crusading journalist; if she'd been good with a guitar, she would have been a protest singer, if there was such a thing anymore. She had no special attachment to photography.

And yet she was gifted. Isaac didn't think she'd realized it yet, but she was a far more gifted photographer than he was. He was sure of this.

"How's your girlfriend?" Renee said.

"How's that?"

"The woman I met last month. Norma. Isn't that your girlfriend?"

"Nora. No, she's just a friend."

"It sure looked like she was your girlfriend. As my five-year-old niece would say, it looked like you two were crushed on each other."

Talking in the darkroom was good, because if you were blushing, no one could see. "We used to be."

"What's her story? She looks like she has an interesting story."

"Why do you say that?"

"She has a certain look. She looks like she has a tragic past."

Isaac found this surprising. She'd never looked that way to him.

"She does have a tragic past," he said.

"Really?"

"Both her parents died when she was still in high school. She was an orphan when she was still in her teens."

"God. That's rough."

Renee was trying to seem respectful, but she sounded unimpressed.

She was probably thinking that the death of your parents was small potatoes. She had spent the previous summer, after all, in Peru, where the government was dynamiting the homes of peasants who were suspected of sympathizing with the rebels. Compared to the political horrors that Renee had heard about or even witnessed, Nora's life probably seemed peachy.

Losing your parents early might not be such a terrible thing. A month ago Isaac had had dinner with an old friend, Eric, who spent a good part of the evening talking about his conflicts with his father, a high-octane businessman who disapproved of the career choices Eric had made. Listening to Eric, who seemed to have been rendered stoop-shouldered by the weight of his father's disapproval, Isaac realized that he himself felt like an adult, like a man, in a way that Eric did not. Isaac had loved his father, but, listening to his friend, he found himself thinking that he was glad his father was gone.

Thinking about this now, he decided that Nora hadn't had such a bad fate after all. She'd had parents who loved her, who steered her through her formative years, who left her with enough resources to get through college, and who were considerate enough to die young.

"How'd they die?" Renee said.

Isaac didn't actually know. Nora had told him about her

parents' deaths soon after they met, but he'd forgotten the details, and it was the kind of story you can't ask to hear a second time. "Tell me how your parents died again...?"

"Car accident," he said. He didn't want to admit he had no idea.

"Is she afraid of cars now?"

"No. She's a good driver."

"Earl told me she's a hotel detective?" Renee said.

It took him a second to figure that one out. Nora *had* said that to Earl.

"She used to be." For some reason he felt he had to be loyal to Nora's lie.

Nora, then, was a former hotel detective whose parents had died in a car crash.

"I have to pee," Renee said, and walked off toward the bathroom. This casual bit of crudeness struck him as unpleasant—he *was* a throwback—and he wondered how he ever could have been infatuated with her. The two of them were from different centuries.

He was finished working; he turned the red light off and the white light on. And then she came back into the room, and for some reason she'd taken her Hawaiian shirt off and was wearing only a leotard and shorts, and her shoulders and her legs were golden, and he felt confused again.

"Hi," he said.

"Hi."

Sometimes he suspected that he wasn't daydreaming at all—that whatever he was feeling, she was feeling as well. Earlier that spring she'd been reading a book called *Half a Life*, by Jill Ciment, which she said she liked a lot. He leafed through it one day and found that it was a memoir, which ended with a chapter describing how the author, when she was in her early twenties, fell in love with a painter, a man more than twice her age. From the "About the Author" paragraph he saw that she was still with him, more than twenty years later. Maybe Renee had a thing for older men...?

One night about a month ago, Renee had accompanied him to a reception the paper was sponsoring in New York. They were in a cab on Broadway; when they stopped at a light, she'd taken a tube of lipstick from her bag.

"This is my new toy," she'd said. "It's not very feminist, but it's fun." She'd carefully applied the lipstick and then turned toward him. "What do you think?"

He'd wanted to kiss her—he'd wanted it badly. And he couldn't believe that she didn't know it.

"Looks nice," he'd said. "Looks great." And then he'd forced himself to look away, and the moment had passed.

He still wondered about that moment, still replayed it in his mind. Had she been disappointed? Or relieved? Was it possible that without even knowing it, she'd been testing him—making sure she could trust him? And that by not responding, he'd passed the test? He'd probably never know.

Now, in his darkroom, Renee was searching around in her backpack. "Tangerine?"

"No thanks."

"It's my vegan anniversary," she said. "As of today I haven't had any dairy in a year."

"Quite an accomplishment," he said, although what he was feeling was concern. Was she getting enough protein?

"I decided to give up dairy because I realized it was already ten years since I became a vegetarian. I thought it was time for a burst of self-improvement."

"What do you think you'll be doing for self-improvement ten years from now? What do you want to *be* in ten years?"

He liked asking her questions like this, big what-do-you-want-from-life questions. He didn't quite know if she liked this habit of his or thought it was corny.

"I have no idea," she said. "I feel like I'm open to anything. The only thing I'm sure of is that I don't want to get trapped in the meantime."

"That sounds very deep, but I have no idea what you're talking about."

"So many people think they want to be writers or musicians or painters, or they want to work for the Peace Corps or something. But they're worried about security, and they think they need something to fall back on, and they decide to do something else in the meantime. So they go to law school or business school or they become copy editors instead of writers. And then five years go by, and then ten years, and they never end up doing what they wanted to do. They just end up stuck in the meantime."

Isaac nodded at this, and didn't say anything, and felt hurt. Suddenly he wanted her to be gone.

It's impossible to know what young people think of you. When Isaac was a photography student, he went through wild opinion swings about his teachers. In his freshman year, he had a teacher he worshiped: the teacher was a man of small gifts, but his encouragement meant so much to Isaac that Isaac thought he was the most important photographer since Mathew Brady. When Isaac was a senior, he was one of only five students admitted to a "master class" with Robert Frank. Deep into a season of arrogance, Isaac regarded Frank with a sort of benevolent amusement; he was so sure of the hugeness of his future accomplishments that he couldn't help but look down on what Frank had actually accomplished.

So it was impossible to tell whether Renee respected him, because he'd had a respectable career as a photographer, or pitied him, because he didn't really do it anymore. It was impossible to tell whether she thought he'd gotten stuck in the meantime.

"I hope I'll still be taking pictures," she said, "but not for the sake of just taking pictures. If the pictures I take aren't about exposing something that's wrong or celebrating something that's right, then they really don't mean much to me. I couldn't do what you do. I'm, like, an agitator. You're an artist."

He liked her again.

"What do you hope to get from your exhibit?" Renee said. "In your heart of hearts."

"Fame. Fortune. Immortality."

"Okay, now give me the real answer, instead of the joking-around answer."

He didn't want to give her the real answer. He didn't want to tell her how much was riding on this show.

He wasn't dreaming about impossibilities. When he was just starting out, in his twenties, whenever he had an exhibit he used to imagine that it would change everything, that it would lead to a life in which he would be paid just for taking the pictures he wanted to take—some no-show professorship, say, with a college that would be honored just to be able to use his name in their ads. That was back in the days when his ambitions were endless, when he thought he had a shot at taking his place among the greats: Atget, Weston, Cartier-Bresson. It was embarrassing even to remember those days.

Now he dreamed modest dreams. Now he was simply thinking that if he could get some grain of genuine recognition from this exhibit, some affirmation that his work meant anything—if he could get one or two good reviews from people who knew what they were talking about, or if someone from one of the first-rank galleries showed some interest—it would reawaken his confidence, reawaken his desire to take pictures.

Though he hadn't actually started taking pictures again, he'd been spending a lot of time in the darkroom, making new prints of his old work. The show was going to consist of pictures he'd taken during his first two years at the paper, when he sometimes filled in for staff photographers who were ill or on vacation, plus a few other things he'd taken around that time. He was sending out invitations to dozens of people, including the reviewers and curators who'd been kind to his work in the past.

The exhibit was more than two months away, but he was beginning to think that things were changing in his life already. Last week he'd received a note from a woman who was curating a photojournalism exhibit at the New York Public Library. She wanted to include one of his old photographs, something he'd taken for the *Village Voice* fifteen years ago.

"You never tell me anything, you know," Renee said. "Do you *try* to be mysterious? Is that your thing?"

"No," he said.

But maybe it *was* his thing. He was dying to let her know about the library exhibit, but he'd restrained himself. He hadn't said a word. Sometimes Isaac thought that all he really wanted to do was talk about himself, and that the reason he talked about himself so rarely was that the urge was so powerful that he had to keep it violently repressed.

Don't boast, he was telling himself. Think Clark Kent. If you have to boast, it's a sign that you don't have anything to boast about.

Renee finished her tangerine, they chatted for a few more minutes, and then she had to go. She was heading off to get a left-wing tattoo: a fist holding a rose. "See ya later, Pops," she said.

Isaac puttered around in the darkroom for another hour.

Renee, my daughter.

Renee, my not-quite-daughter.

It was hard to get comfortable with the mix of feelings he had for her.

He wouldn't be feeling any of this confusion if Nora were around.

To hell with Nora.

He shouldn't have been surprised by Nora's vanishing act. It was as though he'd forgotten what she was like, forgotten the essence of Nora. The essence of Nora was that she bowled you over, and then she disappeared. It was the Nora Howard Two-Step.

Isaac's uncle had met Nora once and had later summed her up as "a slippery little thing." Isaac normally thought of him as a moron, but this time his uncle was right.

Isaac always loved to remember the way she'd insisted on getting that dog for his father. What he thought about less often was that six months later, his father came down to New York for a visit, and Nora was supposed to meet the two of them for lunch but didn't show: she was writing, and she lost track of the time. On the phone that night she talked about meeting them for breakfast before his father took the train back upstate, but she called the next morning to say that she'd been writing all night and was too zonked out to make it. His father tried to act as if it didn't matter, but it was clear that he was hurt. He was in poor health and never made it back to the city, so that turned out to have been his last chance to see her.

To hell with Nora, Isaac thought, and then called home to pick up his messages, but she hadn't called.

17

YOU WAKE BEFORE DAWN. You shower, dress, and make coffee, and then, without letting anything else intervene, you sit down at the keyboard.

If every morning begins in this fashion, Nora thought, then the rest of the day will be blessed.

"God," Tolstoy once said, "is the name of my desire." Writing was the name of Nora's. Isaac had once told her that photography had taken the place of prayer in his life, and she knew what he meant. It wasn't writing she worshiped; writing, rather, was a way of worshiping. It was the best way she had ever found to express her fascination with life, her quarrels with life, her questions. She sometimes thought that even if what she wrote every day was doomed to disappear during the night, she would keep writing stories, just to make a daily pilgrimage to the realm of mystery and reverence and play. She didn't always reach that realm when she was writing stories, but merely to turn toward it was a kind of nourishment unlike any other.

It had been a month since she'd left Benjamin, and she still hadn't seen Isaac. They talked on the phone, conversations in which there was tenderness and longing in every word, but she didn't want to get together with him yet. She didn't want to leap from one man to the next, like someone who crosses a river by stepping from stone to stone. She didn't want to use him. Her first task in life was to find her way back into her writing, and this was a river she wanted to cross without help.

She'd kept writing about Gabriel, whom she'd been finding more and more intriguing. He wasn't such a fantasy figure now; he had flaws.

The story was still murky—she still barely knew what it was about—but she was writing with an excitement that she hadn't felt in years. For the first time in years, she wasn't afraid to follow her imagination; she was eager to see where it would lead her.

She'd put a Post-it note next to her computer, with the deadline of the contest that Ilya Kaplan had told her about. She was trying to use it as an incentive to keep working quickly.

There were times when she found Gabriel in situations in which she didn't know what he'd do. When Gabriel made his decisions—she experienced it as him making his own decisions—she kept realizing that he'd done what Isaac would have done. Gabriel was starting, not to merge with Isaac, but to borrow a few of his qualities.

And this was another reason why she hadn't seen him. She wanted to let her story breathe; she wanted to give it room and air and light. She was afraid that if she got involved with Isaac now, the old walls of constraint would rise up around her again.

She was as unhappy as ever that her imagination worked this way—that she had to feed off the lives of her loved ones—but she wasn't trying to fight it.

Years ago she had spent six months in therapy, primarily in an effort to change the way she wrote. She wanted to uncouple her imagination from her real life, and she wanted to stop writing stories that were so pitiless. The therapist was an intelligent man who respected artists—his wife was a painter—and he didn't disagree when Nora finally concluded that she had to accept the unhappy terms and conditions that guided her creative life. She came to think that you can no more change the terms of your creative life than you can change your sexual preferences. Her goblin couldn't be dislodged.

During their last session, the therapist said, "Let me tell you a story about Rilke. You know Rilke? *Letters to a Young Poet*? Like most artists—like most people, I suppose—he was a tortured soul, and he thought psychoanalysis might help him. He was in treatment for a while, but he finally broke it off: he said that he feared that if the treatment took away his devils, it would take away his angels too."

She was surprised she hadn't heard this before. She'd already been compiling a little library of quotations and anecdotes, designed to reassure her that her own case wasn't unique. D. H. Lawrence had said that "one sheds one's sicknesses in books," which she took to mean that if you let your dark side into your fiction, you won't have to live it. Norman Mailer had said that writers who are sunny in their work are crabbed and curdled in real life, whereas writers who let the most wicked, vicious impulses into their work are usually sweet and generous people. Philip Roth had compared his misanthropic fiction to the comedy of Jack Benny, who always presented himself as a miser, not because he actually was one, but because it happened to be the role that set his comic energies free. And Joan Didion had simply said that a writer is always selling somebody out.

All of this helped, within limits. It helped her come to

terms with herself in theory, but not in practice. It didn't, for example, make it easier for her to contemplate the thought that the story she was writing, which hadn't even begun to take shape yet, was going to turn into something that would cause Isaac pain.

There had been times when she wished she didn't need to write at all. But she did. She'd needed it ever since she was a girl.

Nora could date the birth of that need. She'd been writing stories all through junior high school, but it became a need only after her mother died. Margaret died suddenly of a stroke when Nora was seventeen. Arthur, Nora's father, had died two years earlier, of cancer, so Nora was alone. During the next few months, while she was being shuttled among the homes of her parents' friends, her diary was the only thing that kept her sane. Every night she would write for an hour in the black-and-white marbled composition book she used for a diary. Everything else about her life was in doubt: she didn't know if she'd be going to college in a year; she didn't even know where she'd be staying from week to week. The diary gave her a way to link each day to the days that had come before, to link her life with the life she'd had when her mother was alive. Writing was the only way to join the days.

When Nora met Isaac, she saw how he carefully monitored his blood-sugar levels and injected himself with insulin three times a day. When Nora thought back to the months after her mother died, when she'd found sanctuary every night in her diary, she thought that she'd been driven by a physical need, not too different from Isaac's need for insulin. And ever since then, ever since those diary days, her need to write had felt just as ungovernable, just as urgent.

Kafka once said that a writer should cling to his desk as if it were a life raft. Nora felt like she knew what he meant. And maybe, she thought, a woman writer has to cling to it with a special ferocity. Swarthmore had had a busy creative writing program, and every semester three or four visiting writers came in to give readings, lead daylong seminars, and be picturesquely literary in the coffee bar and the cafeteria. Nora tried to observe them closely. All of the successful male writers, she'd noticed, were carried through their lives by a sort of rapture of egotism. Most of them were married, or had been—most had burned quickly through several wives—and many of them had children, but she got the feeling that none of them had ever let anything come between them and their work. The women were different. Most of them seemed nicer than the men—more modest, more approachable—but less obsessed; Nora found it easy to believe that their devotion to writing had always had to compete with the many varieties of caretaking with which women fill their lives. Some of the older women had long gaps in their writing lives, ten-year periods in which they'd published nothing. The single women were the only ones who seemed as fantastically devoted to writing as the men. "Them lady poets must not marry, pal," wrote John Berryman in one of his *Dream Songs*; more than forty years later, it still seemed to be true.

Sometimes she daydreamed that writing might be enough. She could become one of those odd women, one of those abrupt, withdrawn, eccentric women who did nothing but write.

Part of her was even excited by the thought of turning her back on the world. It was like taking holy orders, like becoming a monk or a nun. This is all I need in life, she sometimes thought. This desk, this keyboard, these imaginary people, this bare white room.

She could just stop worrying about hurting people. She didn't have to take care of anyone anymore.

Except, of course, for Billie.

Billie had recovered quickly from her surgery. The lump that had been removed was "precancerous," and she'd have to go in for tests every month, but she didn't need radiation or chemo. Within days of getting out of the hospital, she'd gone folk dancing again. Supposedly she went folk dancing to meet men, but she never met any. Billie said it was because she was too fat and too old, but Nora suspected that the real reason was that she didn't really want to. The truth, Nora thought, was that Billie was still married to Nelson.

Nora and Billie would meet for dinner once or twice a week. One night in the middle of June they met at a restaurant in Riverside Park, near the Hudson River. It would have been Nelson's seventieth birthday. Billie and Nelson always used to do something in the park on his birthday, and since his death Billie had faithfully returned there every year.

As they ate, Billie barely spoke. Finally Nora said, "You still miss him a lot, don't you?"

"I do," Billie said. "But most of the time I can manage it. Most of the time I just feel happy about what we had. I only feel sad when I think about the things we didn't do. I feel sad about all the places we wanted to see together. We wanted to see Stonehenge. We wanted to see the Nile. For a couple of years after he died, I thought I'd see them by myself. I thought it would be like seeing them together. But I don't think I ever will."

"You might," Nora said. She hoped that she would. She hated the idea that Billie's life had stopped after Nelson died.

In some ways Billie was the image of what Nora didn't want to become. And yet she loved Billie with a love that was unbendable and complete.

Nora looked out across the river, trying to find Isaac's building. She wondered what he was doing.

As the evening went on, Billie shed her sadness and started to joke around. She was good at putting her sadness aside. Nora felt more relaxed than she had in a long time.

This is what Billie had always given Nora: a zone of ease. When Nora was a girl, growing up in Illinois, she used to talk on the phone with Billie twice a week; she loved being able to talk with her about horses and the Olympics and Joni Mitchell and Bruce Springsteen, subjects her mother considered unworthy of a serious person's attention.

It was hard to imagine two sisters less alike than Nora's mother and aunt. Margaret once told Nora that when they were growing up, she'd been known as the smart one and Billie as the pretty one. She was the capable one, Billie the fragile one. That was their family mythology.

When Nora heard this, she got mad; she was fiercely loyal to Billie, and she thought her mother was putting her down. But a few years later she experienced Billie's fragility for herself.

The day after Margaret died, Billie flew out to Lake Forest. There were several couples in Illinois who had offered to take Nora in—Margaret's University of Chicago friends—but Nora assumed she'd go to New York with Billie and live with her. This was just after Nelson died, and Billie was living alone.

When they embraced at the airport, Billie put her lips near Nora's ear and whispered, "I'll take care of you."

Later that day they went to arrange for the disposal of Margaret's body. The funeral home was a beautiful building, a mansion, on a large tract of land. It looked like the main building of a campus, a school for the dead. They parked in the lot and walked across the long green lawn. Nora was wearing a gray dress; Billie was wearing a sleeveless sundress—pink and orange flowers—and a floppy straw hat. She looked all wrong; she looked as if she was on her way to a dance.

In the middle of the lawn, Billie, wobbly on platform sandals, turned her ankle. She took her shoes off and held them in one hand, and with her other hand, to steady herself, she held on to Nora's arm. She glanced up at the funeral home. "The Scary House," she murmured.

After a few more steps, Billie began to have trouble catching her breath.

"I think I'm hyperventilating," she said. "I feel a little panicky."

"It's okay," Nora said. "We just have to take care of a few details."

As they drew closer to the building, Billie grew more and more distraught. She was biting her lips in agitation. She was limping, supporting herself on Nora's arm; after every two or three steps she'd pause, bend over at the waist, and take long creaky breaths through her mouth.

There was a bench in the middle of the lawn. "Let's sit here for a minute," Nora said.

They sat on the bench. Billie still couldn't breathe. "I'm sorry," she said. "The harder I try to breathe the more I feel like I'm not breathing." She lowered her head between her knees, apparently thinking this would help; her straw hat fell to the ground.

"Maybe I should go by myself," Nora said.

"Are you sure?" Billie said. She had bitten herself so hard that there was blood on her lips.

"I'll be fine," Nora said. "I think I might prefer to do it alone, really."

She squeezed Billie's hand, stood up, and walked toward the Scary House. When she reached the door she looked back, hoping that Billie might have changed her mind—might be hurrying forward, half limping half trotting, to catch up with her.

Billie was still on the bench. Her arms were wrapped around her body; she was shivering, in the baking sun.

Nora met the funeral director, a dark-jowled man named Mr. Tenzi—he looked as if he needed to shave five times a day—and made the arrangements. His office was filled with flowers. Nora asked if she could take a violet.

She emerged into the bright day. Billie was still on the bench. She looked renewed; she'd put her straw hat back on, and she was smiling.

As Nora walked toward her, she realized that she wouldn't be going to New York with her. As much as she loved her aunt, she couldn't rely on her.

Nora stood over Billie and held out the flower. Billie reached for it hesitantly, squinting in the sun, smiling up at Nora shyly from under the brim of her hat.

For the next few years, Nora barely spoke to her. Billie had failed to take care of her. In Nora's sophomore year of college she came across a line from T. S. Eliot: "After such knowledge, what forgiveness?" This passage not only justified her anger; it gave it a glow of stern nobility.

But as time went on, Nora missed her aunt's tenderness, her playfulness, her generosity—she just missed her. During her senior year of college, after she transferred to NYU, she finally called her, and soon they were getting together for dinner almost every week.

Forgiveness brings knowledge of its own. Nora came to

see the past differently. She came to understand that Billie had wanted to take care of her; she just wasn't strong enough. And in time her memory of Billie on the bench—distraught, shivering, biting her lips—became transformed. It was no longer a memory of someone who had failed her, but of someone who'd wanted to help her, wanted it with all her heart.

18

NORA HAD BREAKFAST WITH HER friends Robert and Judy, who lived in Toronto and were making their annual trip to New York. Robert had been one of Nora's pot-smoking buddies in college; he'd turned respectable in his old age but he hadn't lost his anarchist spirit. When Nora tried to talk about her problem—that she couldn't write without writing about people she knew, and she couldn't write about people she knew without hurting them—he let out a huge laugh. "Put *me* into your stories! You wouldn't hurt *me*! Write about my sexual fantasies! Better yet, try them out!"

Judy patted him on the hand. "Back down, Rob. She's not interested in writing porno."

"That's the problem. She's been writing that literary shit long enough. If she spilled some of *my* secrets, she'd be on the bestseller list."

Nora was sorry to say good-bye. It was good to be around friends who didn't take her problems very seriously.

After breakfast, she picked up a rental car and drove to Connecticut. It was July second, the day before her birthday. Nora had been planning to spend the day working on the Gabriel story, but a company that made dental products had offered her a deranged amount of money to go up to Connecticut and help them with a last-minute rewrite of their brochure.

She spent the afternoon and early evening doing the job. They put her to work at a computer with a fancy new ergonomic keyboard, which was the most awkward thing she'd ever laid her hands on, and as she drove back to New York her arm was keening in distress. She couldn't wait to get home and strap on an ice pack. She'd bought a new model a few days before, a Freeze Wrap, and she had high hopes for it. It was filled with space-age goo.

What she wanted to do after that was spend the evening playing around with the Gabriel story. Which, in truth, although the main character was still named Gabriel, was becoming a story about Isaac.

It still wouldn't have been accurate to refer to it as a story. At this point it was still just notes toward a story. This was how it always went for Nora: she had to write for months, getting to know her characters, before she could begin to find her way into the story. Sometimes she felt like a private eye, spending months following up false leads until she stumbled upon the one that provided the key. She wasn't always sure the effort was worth it—she found it embarrassing that it took her six months to write a story—but this was the way the process always went for her, and she had come to trust it.

It seemed to be turning into a story about Isaac and his sister, though she didn't know much more about it than that. She wasn't thinking about Isaac's feelings or his sister's feelings; she felt responsible to no one, responsible only to the story itself. So although Isaac called her faithfully every week, she was still keeping him at arm's length. If she started seeing him again, she wouldn't be able to write freely anymore.

She was driving down the highway, listening to a Tanya Donelly tape, when the car started to shudder. It felt like it was having a seizure. She managed to guide it onto the shoulder just before it died.

What are you supposed to do when your car dies on the highway? Do you get out and flag somebody down? Do you walk to a service station? Do you just sit there?

She thought of the writer Andre Dubus, and concluded that she should just sit there. Dubus once stopped on the highway to give a hand to somebody whose car had broken down, and another car slammed into him, and he was rendered paralyzed and lived out the rest of his life in physical anguish.

A literary anecdote for every occasion, Nora thought.

For the first time in her life, she wished she had a cell phone. She realized she was at a bridge moment in history—or maybe just in the history of the telephone. Two years ago, it had seemed pretentious to have a cell phone; in two years, it would seem pretentious not to.

Trucks were blasting by her, trucks so huge that her two-door Chevy trembled as they passed. She put on her emergency blinkers, but no one stopped to help. An SUV slowed down, and the woman in the passenger seat, who seemed to be wearing a cowl—maybe she was a nun—leaned out the window and held up her middle finger and shouted, "Fuck you!"

Nora rested her head on the steering wheel. All she had wanted from the evening was to sit at her keyboard working on the Gabriel story, and here she was, stuck on the highway, being given the finger by nuns.

Clinging to your desk, as Kafka recommended, is not enough. It's not solitary enough. I should live in a shack in Montana, she thought, with just a typewriter and some paper. No phone, no fax, no e-mail. Off the grid. Maybe the Unabomber's place is still available.

After half an hour a police car pulled up behind her. The police officer was a woman. She walked slowly to Nora's window.

After Nora explained what had happened, the officer looked under the hood and told her that her alternator was shot. Her name tag said "Officer Lundquist."

"I suppose you don't know anything about alternators," Officer Lundquist said.

"Not really."

"Figures. You think you don't have to know anything about your car—you just drive it."

Nora didn't know what to say to this.

"I can give you a lift back to town," Officer Lundquist said. "Then you can call Avis or whatever and demand your rights."

Nora didn't know why this woman was being so hostile. Maybe it was the eternal conflict between the pretty team and the not-so-pretty team. Nora didn't overestimate her own appeal—whenever she looked in the mirror the first thing she saw was her nose, which meandered slightly off course—but she knew that men usually found her easy on the eyes. Officer Lundquist, on the other hand, had not been smiled upon by nature. She looked a little like the guy who played Carole Lombard's father in *My Man Godfrey.* Or maybe it had nothing to do with prettiness. Maybe she was just having a bad day.

When they got into the police car, Officer Lundquist offered Nora a toothpick. Nora didn't want it, but she took it, because she was scared of the police.

Her arm felt twenty degrees hotter than the rest of her. Her arm wanted to get this over with and get the hell home. It was like having a bad-natured cousin who accompanies you and poisons your own mood.

"You wouldn't be from around here, of course," Officer Lundquist said. "Where you from?"

"Montana," Nora said. She said this just to take her attention off her arm. And also because Officer Lundquist was being so rude.

"Montana. Never been there."

"It's a beautiful state," said Nora, who hadn't either. "It might be the most beautiful state in the union."

"What do you do there?" Officer Lundquist said.

"I'm a psychiatrist."

Officer Lundquist nodded reflectively. "I wouldn't have thought there'd be many psychiatrists in Montana."

Nora forced a "you've got my number" chuckle out of herself. "It's true. I have a lot of free time."

Officer Lundquist was examining her out of the corner of her eye. Nora was staring straight ahead, but she could feel it.

"Got any kids?" Officer Lundquist finally said.

"Sure do. A girl named Billie and a boy named...Steve."

Officer Lundquist eyed Nora slyly, as if she had proof that she was lying. "I thought psychiatrists aren't supposed to talk about their personal lives. I thought you get in trouble if you do."

"We don't tell our patients. But we can tell other people. Just like anybody else."

They drove along in silence for a while. Nora was hoping that Officer Lundquist wouldn't ask her any more questions.

"Can I talk to you about something?" Officer Lundquist said. Her voice sounded odd. It sounded wet.

"Sure," Nora said. *How can I get out of this?*

"I have a new baby. My first. He's eight months old."

Nora was about to say "Congratulations," but then she

realized that, as a psychiatrist, she should say nothing of the kind. It was the psychiatric equivalent of leading the witness. Maybe Officer Lundquist wanted to confide that she didn't really *like* her baby, and if Nora congratulated her, it would make it hard for her to own up to this distressing truth. Nora hadn't been a psychiatrist for long, but she had her professional ethics.

"He's a charmer. Really a charmer. Gregory. He takes center stage, I'll tell you that much. He owns the whole show. I can tell he's going to be a preacher someday, just like his grandpa."

Nora smiled understandingly. You can always tell when your boy's going to grow up to be a preacher. It's one of the true joys of motherhood.

"He's got the cutest little feet. You'd love 'em. But here's the thing. Here's my question. Sometimes, when I'm with him, I feel so crazy about him that I just want to give him a kiss on the lips. You ever feel like that with—what was your boy's name?"

What *was* his name? Nora couldn't remember. She smiled and said, "Well, I've got my professional hat on now, so no more talk about me."

Officer Lundquist grinned, one canny old pro to another. "I knew you'd say that." She grew more serious. "But really. When I'm with him, you know, I just want to cover him with kisses. I *do* cover him with kisses. Just like a mother should. Kisses on his belly, on the top of his head, on his knees. I never want to kiss him, you know—I never want to kiss him down *there*." She looked at Nora meaningfully, and Nora understood that she wasn't referring to his feet, the feet that Nora would love. "When I give him kisses on the cheeks I'm always careful not to put my lips on his mouth. But I *want* to. I really want to. I want to kiss that little baby on the mouth. And I don't want to do it just once. Do you think that's sick?"

How did I get into this?

You can't avoid it. You can't stop it from coming. If you so much as walk outside your home, you find yourself with someone's life in your hands.

Officer Lundquist was looking at Nora zestfully, as if it exhilarated her to talk about this. This was alarming.

Nora spoke slowly, trying to think the question through. "We all have urges that disturb us. The difference between being a responsible human being and not being one isn't whether you *think* about doing disturbing things. It's whether you actually *do* them. Listen. I don't think you're sick at all. But I do think you should get some therapy. Real therapy. Not just a chat on the Connecticut Turnpike."

Officer Lundquist nodded thoughtfully, but then, as they got off the highway, she took on a different expression, shaking her head slowly as if Nora had said something stupid. "Well, that's quite an opinion," she said. "Straight from the honcho's mouth."

They drove on in silence. Nora was thinking about poor little Gregory. She heard a voice in her mind—she couldn't identify it—saying, *It turns out you can't save anyone.*

Someone had said this to her, but she couldn't remember who, or when, or why.

Officer Lundquist dropped Nora off at a pay phone, and Nora called the rental car company and demanded her rights. They arranged for a cab to take her back to New York. When she got home she strapped on her Freeze Wrap, and, although it didn't quite live up to the hype, her arm felt better after a while.

Later she tried to work on the Gabriel story, but she couldn't concentrate. She couldn't stop thinking of Officer Lundquist and her son. Poor Gregory! She hoped that Officer Lundquist would find a way to beat back the craziness inside her.

She decided to stop writing for the night; she saved her work onto a floppy disk and lay down on the couch.

It turns out you can't save anyone.

She still couldn't remember who'd said that.

It bugged her. Not because the remark itself meant much to her. She didn't think it was profound; she didn't even think it was true. You may not be able to save anyone's soul, but a heart surgeon can save someone whose arteries are blocked, and a lifeguard can save someone who's drowning. People save each other all the time. But it still bugged her that she couldn't remember, because of the feeling she had when she thought of the words.

Nora knew of one infallible way to find out what she really thought of someone, but it wasn't an operation she could perform at will. Occasionally she'd remember some remark without being able to remember who'd said it, and when she tried to figure out who it was, before she could conjure up a face or a name, she would get a *feeling* about the person, and this feeling represented the truth of her emotions. Shorn of any of the tags of circumstance—of the context in which she knew the person, of their mutual history or lack of mutual history, of her superego's decrees about what she *should* think of the person—it was the bare, pure essence of what the person meant to her.

Now, turning the simple sentence over in her mind, she had a strong warm feeling, a feeling of connection: whoever had said it was someone she cared for and respected and trusted. It was, she realized after a moment, Isaac. Of course.

She remembered now. He hadn't presented the idea as a general rule; he'd been talking about something specific. He'd been telling her, years ago, about the week he'd spent taking pictures in Haiti during the last days of the Duvalier regime. He'd been sent there by *Rolling Stone*. He told Nora that the experience had cured him of his romantic ideas about the power of photojournalism. He'd seen men and women who'd had their arms hacked off; he'd seen children hunting for food in garbage dumps. "Some people go into photography because they think it can save lives," he told her. "But it turns out you can't save anyone. You can only bear witness to their suffering."

She remembered what she'd been feeling as he'd said this. She had felt an intense respect for him; she had had a deep sense of his seriousness, his compassion, his sadness at being unable to do more. Remembering this, she felt a bond with him that was so strong that it seemed to be something she ignored or disregarded at her peril. She decided to change her plans for the next day. She'd give herself a birthday present, by seeing him.

19

HER BIRTHDAY FELL ON A SATURDAY. On the phone a few weeks earlier, Isaac had mentioned that he was playing in a summer softball league in Central Park. He could have found a league in New Jersey, but this was a way of keeping in touch with old friends from his *Village Voice* days. She remembered him saying that he played on Saturday afternoons.

She wrote during the morning, performed her birthday devotions in the early afternoon, and then walked to the park. It was a warm, welcoming day. There were five or six baseball fields on the Great Lawn, all of them with games in progress. On the fringes of the lawn, at a safe distance from batted balls, families were picnicking, couples were lying in the grass, a small group of elderly men and women was doing t'ai chi. New York felt almost like a family.

She walked from one softball game to another until she saw him. He was playing first base. She watched him for a while without trying to catch his eye. The second batter hit a pop-up to the right side of the field; she watched Isaac ranging over to the foul line to catch it. Relaxed and confident, he caught the ball in a basket catch, a little show-offy, and tossed it back to the pitcher, a tall woman with thick dark slightly graying hair. Isaac moved nicely.

Nora hadn't been looking forward to her birthday—thirty-five seemed old. But now, on a beautiful summer day, having sought out and found the man she cared for, she felt young.

The inning was over. Isaac was the second person to bat for his team. Nora felt very old-fashioned: Teresa Wright in *Pride of the Yankees*, watching with love and awe as Lou Gehrig hits a home run. Isaac didn't hit a home run, though, but a grounder to the third baseman. He was thrown out by fifteen feet.

When he was walking back off the field, he saw her.

"You must have put the jinx on me," he said. "I never hit ground balls."

He stopped about two feet away from her. He looked happy to see her, but wary.

The sun was behind him; she had to put up her hand to shield her eyes as she looked up at him.

"You've got a little halo thing going there, Tall Man."

"It's good to see you," he said quietly. "Did you give blood this morning?"

He'd remembered it was her birthday. Her birthday devotions: she gave blood once a year.

She held out her arm for him to see the bruise.

"You're remarkable."

"I do it for the cookies."

The inning was over; he had to get back on the field. She sat on the grass and watched the rest of the game, and then the two of them walked through the park.

"Did you get the invitation to my exhibit?"

"Yes. Thank you. It's exciting. Are you excited?"

"I am. Were you planning to come?"

"I think so."

"I'm glad." He looked, though, as if he wasn't sure he believed her.

She knew he was happy to see her, but his energy was different. He was wary. He even *moved* differently: he was walking more rigidly, as if he wanted to be sure to stay two feet away from her.

This was good. He wasn't going to allow himself to wait for her forever. If she kept opening the door and closing it again, the time would finally come when she'd open it and he wouldn't be there. She felt glad about this, not for herself, but for him. He had better things to do than wait for her.

"How were you planning to celebrate your birthday?" he said.

"Like this."

Isaac walked her back to her building, and without their discussing it, he accompanied her to her apartment. She realized he'd never been there before.

After she closed the door she pointed toward her window. Her view wasn't as magnificent as his, but it was a view. "Someday when you're in your place and I'm here, we should blink our lights on and off and find out if we can see each other. We could have a conversation in Morse code."

He walked over to the card table on which she kept her laptop computer. The computer was on, humming quietly.

"The holy of holies," he said. "Here's where the stories get written."

"Or don't."

"Do you always leave it on? So when a bolt of genius strikes, you can be sure to get it all down?"

"Well, that's just a nice by-product. I never do miss those

bolts of genius. But the reason I keep it on is that it's dying. When I turn it off I can never be sure it'll come on again. It's like my grandparents' TV. When I was eight years old I was over their house and I wanted to watch the *Brady Bunch* reunion and the TV wouldn't come on. I could get the sound but not the picture."

"What a sad, sad story," Isaac said.

"What would you like to do for dinner? Would you like to just eat here?"

"It's your day. Would you?"

"I think so. It's cozier."

"Coziness is important."

"The purpose of life is to be cozy." This was something that had once been said by her old friend Sally Burke—another person who'd ended up feeling violated by her writing. "What do you feel like?" She opened up her filing cabinet and pulled out a folder stuffed with take-out menus. Then she noticed another folder and handed it to Isaac.

"This is for you. You probably know it all, but maybe there's something you haven't seen."

The folder was filled with articles about diabetes, from newspapers, from magazines, and from some of the medical publications she'd worked for. He looked through them quickly.

"These are, like, from the last five years."

"I know," she said. "Sorry. Most of them must be out of date. The newer ones are toward the back."

"That's not what I meant. I meant: you've been clipping these things for me over the last five years?"

"Yes. So?"

"I didn't know if we'd ever see each other again."

"I didn't either. But that didn't mean I wasn't thinking about you."

They sat at her kitchen table and talked for a while—he was telling her about a philosophy class he was taking in the general studies program at a college in New Jersey—and then the teakettle was whistling. In the old days, she used to put the kettle on whenever they came back to her apartment, so Isaac could have a cup of tea. This evening she'd done it without even realizing.

After Isaac finished his tea he went to the sink to wash the cup, and then, while they continued to talk, he started washing the rest of her dishes. She felt moved by this. He always used to wash her dishes; he claimed to enjoy it. They were falling effortlessly into old habits, and this struck her as beautiful. Her making the tea; his washing her dishes: what was beautiful was that the habits they'd slipped back into were the small habits of daily caring.

He had rolled up his shirt-sleeves before starting on the dishes, and the sight of his arms—bony, soapy—and the flexing of his muscles, or tendons, or whatever they were, as he rotated a bowl under the hot stream, sent a slithery scrill of desire down her spine.

"Come sit with me on the couch," she said, and he did, but once they were there she didn't know what to do with him.

She knew she wanted to let him into her life, but she didn't know how far. A voice in her mind was saying: Stay back. Don't jump into anything. You know what happens to you when you get enmeshed. Treasure your freedom.

If you get back together with him, you won't be able to write about him. The same old thing is going to happen. Them lady poets must not marry, pal.

But on the other hand, she wanted to kiss him.

She leaned forward, all the way, and kissed him—a long, slow kiss—on the mouth. She thought about kissing him again, but she didn't have to, because this first kiss didn't stop.

She wasn't thinking about Wilhelm Reich this time, or Joan Didion, or Mr. Data.

There was no one in her thoughts but Isaac, she was nowhere but in this room, but, being Nora, she was still thinking. She was thinking that what she had always loved about their physical life was that there was no break in continuity when they went from the world to the bed. Isaac pulled back his head and smiled at her, and his eyes were beautifully warm, but they'd been just as warm fifteen minutes ago, when she'd been asking him questions about his philosophy class. Their sex wasn't sealed off from the rest of their lives. Everything in the world was in this kiss.

She loved the strange way they fit: she loved the fact that he was half a world taller than she was, yet somehow made her feel like the most formidable woman on earth. He was lying back on the couch, and she was climbing him, and there was a tangle of hair below his throat that she'd been thinking about for years—*there*—and the buttons of his shirt were clicking on the hardwood floor because she seemed to have ripped his shirt off.

His shirt was off, and she was touching him in a way she knew he liked.

Isaac unbuttoned her shirt, and took it off, and kissed her palm, and her wrist, and the scar that ran around her bicep.

Isaac had once told her she was a genius in bed. She wasn't a genius in bed; it was just that he was so open about what he liked, so refreshingly easy to read. He was like the little red diary she used to write in when she was ten. It had a tiny lock on the cover, but if you lost your key you could open it up with a bobby pin.

Lying on top of him on her couch, she took his head in her hands and brought her mouth to his ear and whispered, "Dear diary," and this, she could tell, excited him, even though he couldn't have known what she meant by it.

20

AFTER HE LEFT THE NEXT MORNING, she wrote all day, and in the evening she went out to New Jersey and they walked to the Hudson River to watch the fireworks over Manhattan. It was nicer than it would have been in the city: a crowd was gathered by the river, but no one was pushing, no one was bellowing, no one seemed to be drunk. She could see why he liked it out here. She wouldn't want to live here herself—it was too tame—but she enjoyed partaking of its calm.

They lay on a blanket, watching the fireworks bloom in the night sky. The sight reminded her of videos from junior high school science class: the life cycle of a flower, from bloom to graceful dying.

After the display was over, as they stood up, she reached over to retrieve a book that had slipped out of her bag. *The Sportswriter*, by Richard Ford.

"I read that," Isaac said. "What do you think of it?"

She started to answer, and then, instead, she grabbed his arm and pulled him toward her and hugged him.

"What's that for?"

"Nothing," she said.

But it wasn't for nothing. She'd hugged him because the previous boyfriend wouldn't have asked. The previous boyfriend, if he was familiar with the book she was reading, would have launched into a lecture about it.

The pleasure of being asked questions: a pleasure she hadn't even known she'd missed.

SHE STARTED TO LIKE NEW JERSEY. Astonishing. On the one hand, it made her nervous to spend the night in a place where you couldn't walk to the corner at two in the morning and get some fried dumplings or the *New York Review of Books.* She wasn't used to frontier life. But on the other hand, if you did go out at two in the morning, you could see stars in the sky, the moon walking in brightness, and at moments like this she thought that Isaac hadn't made such a bad trade.

One night when she was telling Isaac a story about her college years, the phone rang and he had to take the call. He talked for about ten minutes, and when he hung up he said, "So what were you saying? You thought Shakespeare was important because he led to Bob Dylan?"

She hadn't even remembered she was telling this story. And she thought of how rare it was that when you get cut off in the middle of a story, the person you're talking to will remember that you were talking, much less what you were talking about.

One weekend they spent Friday night lounging around his apartment, he in jeans and she in sweatpants, watching two movies they'd rented (Cocteau's *Orpheus,* which was one of his favorites, and *The Terminator,* one of hers), and then they spent Saturday night at a party in the city for a friend of his who'd just put out a book of photographs, a party for which Isaac wore a suit and Nora wore a tight black dress.

She'd had boyfriends she loved to be cozy with, lounging

around in sweatpants, and boyfriends she loved to be out in the world with, wearing a tight black dress. Isaac was the only man with whom she loved both.

One day she was having lunch with Helen and Laura, two old friends from high school, and Helen turned to Laura and said, "Doesn't Nora look *great* since she and Benjamin broke up?"

She did look great; she could feel it. Men were looking at her in a way they hadn't in years. A guy would look at her as he passed her, then look again; and then, she sometimes noticed, he'd steal another look from across the street, as if he wanted to keep a picture of her in his mind. She was a three-look woman again.

An idiot saying vulgar things to you on the street was one thing, but walking past a sweet-looking, unintrusive guy who looks like he's about to get hit by a truck because you're so beautiful—this is one of the great pleasures of life. As long as he doesn't get hit by the truck, of course.

As nice as it felt to be noticed, she didn't feel the least hint of interest in any of these sweet-looking, unintrusive guys on the street. The reason she looked beautiful was that she was in love.

Isaac's nephew, Sam, was learning to play the bass; Isaac saw a beautiful upright bass at an auction and bought it for him. He told Nora that if she weren't in his life, it never would have occurred to him to buy it. "You make me more generous."

Isaac was planning to give Sam the bass as a birthday present, but his birthday was months away. Since Isaac's brother and his family lived in the city, Nora suggested that they keep it in her apartment so Isaac wouldn't have to drag it out to New Jersey and drag it back in again. They propped it in a corner of her living room, where, darkly shining, it was like a piece of sculpture. She liked having it there, both because it was beautiful and because of what Isaac had told her after he bought it. Being with him made her feel like a better person, and she was happy to learn that he felt the same way about being with her.

One night she took the subway downtown to meet him in the Village. The subway at rush hour is a kingdom of bad smells: an awful intimacy of sweat and breath. Everyone was cramped, everyone was pushing; everyone was somehow damaged. A legless beggar jerked angrily through the car, propelling himself with his elbows. A man peering at the subway map looked as if half his face had been frozen by a stroke. A woman with no nose sat reading the *Weekly World News*. ("Bin Laden Clones Plot Worldwide Terror." There were photos of a French bin Laden in a beret, a Bronx bin Laden in a baseball cap, and a British bin Laden in a bowler.) A young mother held the hand of her blind son. It was the casualty show. But Nora was on the way to see her lover, and neither of them were casualties yet, and everything inside her felt light and lit and lifted. She got off the train and waited for him at an outdoor café on Cornelia Street, and when she caught sight of him coming down the block, her soul was lifted.

There was more liftedness to come. Isaac had a friend at the newspaper, a woman named Velma, who'd just gotten her pilot's license, and on a cloudless scary Saturday—scary because Nora had been half hoping it would rain and the outing would be called off—Nora and Isaac met her at Teterboro Airport and she helped them into the back of a four-seater plane for what she ominously called a test drive. After she squeezed into the cockpit and closed the door, Nora and Isaac were alone. They held hands as the plane lurched slowly up the runway with a horrendous accompaniment of knocking and grinding and banging. Nora was sure she was going to die, and then they were tearing down the runway, terrifyingly picking up speed, so that she felt as if her heart had been hurled against her spine, there was no way a machine this rickety could fly, and then the plane took a nervous jump, as if it wasn't sure it could manage this, and they were in the air, and man wasn't meant to fly, but they were flying, and then they were rising, and they took a sharp sickening turn and headed for the city, and after a few minutes they met the Hudson River near the Empire State Building, and they proceeded north, skimming the air a mile or so above the river, and passed over the glorious George Washington Bridge—glittering in the sunlight, it looked like the Eiffel Tower at rest. As they shot beyond the bridge it was like being ripped backward through the time barrier: the buildings fell away, and out her window, on the west side of the river, she saw nothing but lush green cliffs, everything looking as it must have looked a thousand years ago. She was thankful for her life. She had the thought that she didn't regret anything she'd ever done, because the course of her life had taken her to this moment. She was grateful for everything, even grateful for her mistakes.

That night they went back to her place and ate Chinese food and rented a movie and turned it off in the middle because they needed to touch each other, and this, all of this, was happiness.

The only problem was that she was starting to feel her story slipping away. She was still sitting down at her keyboard every day, but Gabriel was eluding her. A few weeks ago she thought she'd been on the verge of understanding him; now he was more of a mystery than ever. She was trying to blame it on the fact that she had so little time these days: she was seeing Isaac every night, she was spending time with Billie, and she'd had an unusually large amount of medical writing to do. But the truth was that none of these reasons sufficed. She was backing away from her story because she didn't want to know where it would take her.

21

On the night of Isaac's opening, Nora put on a black dress and, splurging wildly, took a taxi out to New Jersey. There was a lot of traffic on the highway, and she realized she was going to be late. She was mad at herself: Isaac was going to be disappointed.

When she got there, she saw that she needn't have hurried. The gallery was crowded, and he was surrounded by people. Some of them she recognized from the old days—his brother, a few of his college friends. Most were people she'd never met.

When she'd thought about this event, she'd imagined herself examining Isaac's photographs while he hovered at her shoulder, anxiously awaiting her verdict. But he was surrounded by well-wishers; he was looking the picture of contentment and success; so she was free to look at the pictures by herself, and to have her own unmonitored reactions.

She walked from room to room, looking at his photographs.

Although she'd known him for years, and although he liked to talk about his work, she still had no vocabulary to understand what he was doing. She could tell, however, that these pictures had been lovingly crafted. She could tell, even without knowing anything about photography, that each of these pictures had behind it a wealth of care.

He had a distinctive style in these new pictures, a distinctive way of seeing people. In all of these photographs, his subjects, his people, seemed strong.

It was a curious thing: even the children he photographed seemed heroic. He had photographed his nephew, eight years old, struggling to open up a present on Christmas Day. There was a look of utter intentness on the boy's face. He seemed ready to meet any challenge life might offer.

People, she was thinking, have handles, and different artists grasp people by different handles. Dostoevsky grasped people by their feverishness, their intensity. Yeats grasped people by their nobility of character. Whitman grasped people by their sexuality, or by whatever it is in us—something that includes but is larger than sexuality—that makes us want to merge with others.

She wasn't placing Isaac in this company. But he had his own distinctive way of seeing people, and it seemed to her that what he saw in people was their strength.

She was feeling an immense relief. She realized now that she'd been preparing a litany of euphemisms; she'd been preparing to lie to him. But she wasn't a good liar, and she had already half envisioned the scene in which she was praising his pictures, but in a strangled, mangled voice.

She sat down on a marble bench. She felt suddenly exhausted, weak with relief. She wanted to crawl under the bench and take a nap.

It was odd that their art, his and hers, took them in such different directions. He was drawn to moments when people showed their strength; she, to moments when they showed their weakness. She wondered if he'd chosen his direction any more than she'd chosen hers.

Isaac was coming her way, but before he could reach her, two people she didn't recognize—a man and a woman, neither of them over five feet tall—intercepted him and engaged him in conversation.

She thought of joining them, but she didn't want to interrupt. The little people looked as if they were praising him, and he seemed to be basking in it.

22

ISAAC WAS SENDING THOUGHT messages to Nora, asking her to save him.

He was trapped by a couple he'd never met before. They'd seen a notice of the show in the paper.

"We're lovers of the arts," the woman told him.

"But more than that," the man said, "we're students of human nature."

They were a tiny, shiny, merry-looking couple—they looked like two wholesome elves. They were telling him, somehow, about her grandfather, who had been a photographer in Latvia.

"He was a brilliant, brilliant man," the woman was saying. "His pictures were more real than life itself."

He was trying to back away, but there was nowhere to go.

Years ago, when he used to exhibit his photographs regularly, strangers would often come to these events and tell him about themselves. It was baffling: you'd think they'd want to find out about *him,* but they never did. At every event at which he was theoretically the center of attention, he'd found himself cornered by some stranger with a story to tell.

Everyone has a story, he thought, and I don't want to hear it.

"He could make the light *speak,*" the woman said. "Even in Latvia."

At any event like this, you wish you could edit the guest list. It wasn't only the elfin couple; there were a lot of people there he could have done without. There was his sister-in-law's brother, David, who'd spent ten minutes telling Isaac how nobody could take pictures like Robert Capa anymore. There were John and Theresa—one of the guys from the news department and his wife—standing in the corner glumly: sallow, sad-sack, perpetual mourners at life's perpetual wake. And there was Louise, the paper's financial manager, looking at all times as if she understood your pain. After twenty years of group therapy, Louise found it impossible to be interested in what people were saying unless they were sharing some sort of inner distress. She was looking at him with eyes filled with googly sympathy, as if she understood that this event was more traumatic for him than anyone else could imagine.

But finally there was Nora, sitting on a bench, relaxed, glowing. She looked, to his eyes, like Greta Garbo, whose face was always shot in a soft, gauzy light. Not, perhaps, as beautiful, but just as elusive. The thing that fascinated him about Nora was that as you glanced at her sitting there in the corner, you knew she was thinking, furiously thinking, and you wanted to know what she was thinking about.

Also, she was wearing a dress. He felt privileged to be the man she was wearing a dress for.

He wanted to be alone with her. A few of his friends were up from Virginia; his brother and sister-in-law were here; even his salesman uncle was here, looking very smart in a pompadour, with his fourth or fifth wife. Isaac was touched that they'd all showed up for his opening, and he was wondering if he could find a graceful way to ditch them.

It wasn't really that he wanted to ditch them; it was just that he wanted to be alone with her.

He had known her for all these years and never gotten enough of her. He wondered whether it was *possible* to get enough of her. He wondered whether she'd remained mysterious, elusive, to her boyfriend, Whoosie. Experience showed that you pretty much get sick of anyone you live with, but he couldn't imagine getting sick of her.

Maybe that's love, he thought: if you can live with someone for years and say *Baby, I'm still not sick of you.*

He wished his sister were here, but she was busy serving God and Guru Nan in Oregon. The only other person missing—the only person important to him—was Renee. He would have liked her to witness his little moment of glory.

The elves were still going at him; he was still pretending to listen while he scanned the room. Miraculously, in the corner—closely examining a photograph of the mayor of Newark tossing a trophy into a cardboard box as he cleaned out his desk on his last day in office—was Cynthia Ellis, the photography critic from the *New York Times.* Isaac tried to reach *her* with a few thought waves—tried to influence her a few feet to her left, toward a photograph he considered stronger. But it was a miracle that she was here at all. He began to write her review in his mind; phrases like "brilliant" and "perhaps the most interesting photographer alive" appeared with a pleasing frequency.

About eight or ten people, friends and family, wanted to take him out to dinner, so, despite the fact that he didn't want to, he went along. When it's your party, you have no rights.

The group drifted out in bunches; he and Nora fell behind the others.

"That was really wonderful," she said.

He didn't quite believe her; he was trying to find the irony in her voice.

"You really liked it?"

"You have your own way of looking at the world. You have your own vision."

They were lagging behind the rest of the group, talking quietly. The big event was over; it had felt like a success. He felt high.

She kept talking about his pictures. This was one of the things he liked about her: she didn't content herself with generalizations; she thought things through.

"Everyone in your pictures seems to be *struggling* toward something. They all seem heroic. Even your nephew."

"My nephew *is* heroic," he said. This didn't mean anything, except that he liked his nephew.

As she went on, he began to believe her. He began to think that maybe these photographs—the ones he'd taken since he'd started to work full-time—expressed a distinctive vision. He began to think that perhaps he'd accomplished something in this latest phase of his career. Perhaps he'd added something to the sum of human something-or-other.

They walked to a Chinese restaurant. He owed his relatives some time, and if he sat with Nora he wouldn't pay attention to them at all, so he sat between his aunt and sister-in-law and Nora sat at the other end of the table. It was all right. Just to have her there was enough. Leaning back in his chair in the loud restaurant, thrillingly exhausted after all the tension of the show, surrounded by family and friends, he allowed himself to feel something like pure satisfaction. He'd finally put up another show, after all these years.

It was true, of course, that he hadn't actually started to take pictures again. And, as happy as he was right now, he didn't exactly feel like he wanted to grab his camera the next morning and spend the day in search of the perfect picture. What he was hoping to do the next morning, really, was stay in bed with Nora.

Nora was talking to his uncle; they looked like they were joking around. He wished he could hear what she was saying.

He was amazed by how comfortable he was feeling, how at peace. Having Nora in the room made everything feel different. The woman he had always loved, the woman whose existence had proved to him that romantic love is not a myth: lo and behold, she was back in his life. He was a lucky man.

23

UNCLE CARL WAS ASTONISHED. He couldn't believe that Isaac was a vegetarian.

"I've never heard of anything so brainless in my life."

"Why is it brainless?" Nora said. "It's healthy."

"It's brainless because we weren't *made* to be vegetarians. We're omnivorous creatures. Our teeth are *made* for eating meat. Our stomachs are made for *digesting* meat. For millions of *years* we've eaten meat. A vegetarian is someone who's trying to deny human nature."

"I don't think Isaac is trying to deny anything," Nora said, loyally.

"Not just *human* nature. *Every* kind of nature. Animals eat animals, and then they get eaten themselves. When I die I'll feed the worms. I have no problem with that. I'm not about to beg the worms not to eat me. That's what nature *is*. That's what *life* is. It's like, it drives me crazy when people say they're against war—they're against any and all war. If you read a little history, you soon find out that most of the technological advances that make your life and mine so pleasant only came about because somebody discovered them when they were looking for a better way to make war. Life is a circle of animals destroying each other, and if you don't see that, then you've got your eyes closed."

Uncle Carl seemed to want to go out and smite all those who tried to step away from the great circle of destruction.

Nora handed him a plate of beef with broccoli. "Have some meat."

He was a large man, and he had a way of leaning over you when he talked. It wasn't menacing; it wasn't harassment. It was just uncomfortable.

His drink arrived—Scotch—and he drank it quickly and signaled the waiter for another. He drank the second more slowly, and grew mellow.

"That nephew of mine has a gift," Uncle Carl said. "He has a special gift."

"I agree," Nora said.

"I'm serious. That boy has a gift. You should take care of him. He could go far—he could go very far if he has a good woman who believes in him."

"I don't really know if I *am* a good woman," Nora said.

Uncle Carl didn't seem to hear this. "Are you two thinking of children?"

"Well..."

"Because that fulfills a man. Men don't always know it before the fact, but it's true. A man does his best work when he has a stake in the future. If Isaac came home at the end of the day to loving children and a wife who stood behind him, there's no telling what he could accomplish."

I should have children, Nora thought, so Isaac can win the Pulitzer Prize.

"You always seemed like a tricky little thing in the old days. I never quite trusted you to take care of him. But you've calmed down. I can see it in your eyes."

"I still am a tricky little thing," she said, but Uncle Carl smiled indulgently, as if he didn't believe her.

"You're artistic too," Carl said. "So you know how hard it is. I remember you. You used to dabble in writing, am I right?"

Her writing had been going so poorly that this remark made her angry at herself rather than at Uncle Carl. If I'd accomplished anything in life, she thought, he wouldn't feel like he had the *right* to be so condescending. She'd been sitting down faithfully with the Gabriel story every day, but it was getting nowhere. Just before her birthday, she'd thought she was on the verge of a breakthrough, but it hadn't come.

"You'll remember what I'm saying, won't you?" Uncle Carl said. He lifted his glass of Scotch to the light and looked up at it. "*I* might not remember this conversation in the morning, but I hope you will."

Nora took her memo pad and a pen from her bag. "Let's see," she said. "*Man needs support of a good woman.* You've said some thought-provoking things tonight, Carl. You've really rocked my world."

Uncle Carl, to his credit, laughed at this.

She noticed that Isaac, at the other end of the table, hadn't touched his food. His sister-in-law was talking to him, and he was trying to act like he was listening, but Nora could see that he wasn't.

She knew, without having to ask, that he'd forgotten to bring his needle and his insulin. He couldn't eat before he had his shot. He must have left them in his car, which was still in the parking lot of the gallery, ten blocks away.

At any other time, she would have stood up and volunteered to get them. This was Isaac's party; he shouldn't have to duck out for twenty minutes to get his medicine.

At any other time, she would have done the right thing, but tonight she felt a twitch of resistance. It was because of

Uncle Carl. After his speech about the importance of standing by your man, she didn't want to get Isaac's insulin.

But you can't let yourself be ruled by other people, and if she didn't do something merely because Uncle Carl would approve of her for doing it, she'd be allowing him to rule her.

"Excuse me," she said to Uncle Carl, and walked over to Isaac and touched him on the arm. "Is it in the car?"

Isaac looked up at her with a puzzled smile, as if he thought she was psychic.

"I think so."

"I'll get it," she said. He started to protest but she put her hands on his shoulders and said, "It's your party. Stay here."

She walked the ten blocks to the gallery. His insulin kit was on the passenger seat. She retrieved it and walked back quickly. It was the first Friday in September, a calm, cool night, and she was happy to be outside.

She got to the restaurant and handed him the kit, and accompanied him to the men's room to help him give himself his shot. He'd been having trouble finding patches of unbruised skin; she ended up giving him the shot herself, in his back.

In the flimsy light of the men's room, he looked pale. "I'm glad you got back so fast," he said. "I was starting to feel a little vasty."

Nora walked him back to the table. Uncle Carl, in conversation with Isaac's friend Eric, was laughing. He had large teeth, constructed for pulverizing animal flesh. He winked at Nora—she didn't know why. She wanted to run off and spend the rest of the night writing, just to avoid being the helpmate that Uncle Carl thought a woman should be. But Isaac needed her, and she stayed where she was.

24

THE NEXT DAY THEY SPENT the afternoon with Isaac's brother and sister-in-law and then went back to Isaac's apartment. Nora was planning to write after dinner while Isaac watched one of those interminable Ken Burns things. The Civil War, baseball, New York City—he somehow made them all seem the same. A cornball narrator, plinky banjos, Doris Kearns Goodwin, and everything slow, slow, slow. After that they were going to watch a movie together. Nora had rented *The Talk of the Town*: Cary Grant, Jean Arthur, Ronald Colman.

It was important to her to write that night. She didn't want to let the Gabriel story float away.

She had the story with her on a floppy disk—160 pages of unconnected scenes. She hadn't brought her laptop: she hadn't turned it off in a month, and she didn't want to risk turning it off and turning it on again. She asked Isaac if she could use his computer.

"Writers are crazy," he said. "But of course you can."

It was a good night to stay in; it was storming. Standing at Isaac's window, Nora thought the storm was beautiful, but Isaac was unhappy, because it meant no one would go to his exhibit. Though the woman from the *Times* had miraculously appeared at the opening, none of the other writers or buyers or gallery owners he'd invited had been there, and he'd been hoping some of them would show up on the second night.

As they were finishing dinner, he got a phone call. When he came back to the kitchen he was beaming.

"Nadine Lyle is in town."

Nadine Lyle was the curator of the photojournalism exhibit at the New York Public Library, the woman who'd selected one of Isaac's old pictures.

"I've never actually met her. She's in the city for the weekend and one of her engagements fell through. She asked if I could come in there and meet her."

"Tonight? But there's a twister out there. You'll never make it back alive."

"I know. But still. I think I should. She'd be a good person to cultivate. She's connected to everybody who's anybody in the photography world, living or dead."

She was surprised to hear him talk like this. She thought of Isaac as more pure than that; she didn't think of him as a networker. It sounded like something Benjamin would say.

The funny thing was that whenever Benjamin talked about networking, it used to send her into a funk of disapproval, yet now, when Isaac was talking about it, it didn't seem like a bad thing.

"I'd love it if you'd come too."

She didn't want to. She wanted to spend the evening concentrating on her story.

"I could really use your support," he said, and this made up her mind for her. If he needed her there, she wanted to be there. She could work later, when they got back.

They drove into the city. It was raining so hard that it was difficult to see. It was like a Hollywood rain. There were stagehands dumping buckets of water from all the rooftops of the world.

They met Nadine Lyle at a restaurant in a hotel in Tribeca. She was at the bar, smoking a thin brown cigarette.

She was an older woman, probably in her late fifties. She kissed Isaac, softly, on both cheeks. There was something sexy about the way she kissed him.

"I'm so happy to meet you," she said. "For weeks I've been trying to picture the man who took that photograph. And here you are."

She had a soft French accent and a kind of insinuating charm. She seemed like an aging seductress whose skills were still intact.

They found a table and ordered drinks—wine for Nadine and Nora, club soda for Isaac. Nadine said she was in New York because one of her artists, a Spanish painter, was having a show at the Whitney. People had been lining up down the block to get in.

"But I don't think most of them will understand his work," she said. "They'd be afraid to. They wouldn't be able to contemplate the meaning of his work and then go back to their lives. It's very dark. Even dangerous."

Nora was trying not to smile at how silly this sounded.

She didn't quite know what this woman *was*. A curator, but also an agent...? She'd have to ask Isaac when they got home.

Nadine and Isaac talked about the photojournalism exhibit.

"Did you know there's going to be a book as well?" Nadine said. "Very lavish. You'll be in it—if you give us your permission—and everyone else who's in the show."

"That's wonderful," Isaac said. "When does it come out?"

"Very soon, we hope. But we're looking for someone to do the text. We almost have a commitment from someone—someone very, very brilliant, and very known. You would be surprised by the name if I told you. But I can't mention it before we're certain."

Phil Mushnick, Nora thought. I bet it's Phil Mushnick. She almost said it, but she stopped herself.

Phil Mushnick was a sportswriter for the *New York Post*. She was feeling hostile toward this woman. She didn't know why. She hoped it wasn't just because she envied her Continental style.

"And you, Isaac Mitchell," Nadine said. "What are you working on now?"

"I've been working on a series of portraits of people after their lives have changed drastically." He said this thoughtfully, slowly. "Cartier-Bresson speaks of capturing his subjects in the decisive moment. I want to photograph people in the moment *after* the decisive moment."

Nora was surprised. She was pretty sure that Isaac hadn't picked up a camera in months.

She'd been puzzled, during these last few months, by the fact that she never saw him take his camera out. It disturbed her. She wasn't sure why she hadn't asked him about it. It was as if she sensed, somehow, that he didn't want to be asked.

What he had just said—Cartier-Bresson, the moment after the decisive moment—struck her as familiar. She wasn't sure, but she had a feeling that she'd heard Isaac say it before, a long time ago.

She hoped it was an old idea of his that he'd never pursued, but that he was intending to pursue now. She hoped it wasn't just a line.

Maybe this is the kind of thing you have to do to make your way through the professional world, she thought. You have to pretend you're in the grip of a grand idea, even when you aren't.

Seeing Isaac play this game made her uncomfortable. But she didn't put much stock in her own discomfort. The standard of integrity, of indifference to worldly success, to which artists, in her opinion, should adhere, was probably, professionally speaking, suicidal.

"And what do you do?" Nadine said to Nora.

"I work in puppet repair," Nora said, before she could stop herself. "Mostly marionettes."

Nora wasn't pleased with herself. This was someone who could be important in Isaac's professional life! She couldn't bring herself to look at him.

"Fascinating," Nadine said. She took a slow, sultry draw on her cigarette, and as she released the smoke she looked at Isaac appreciatively.

"Isaac Mitchell," she said. "I have a favor to ask of you. I want to ask it, but I feel a little shy."

Nora wondered whether this woman had ever felt shy in her life.

"This exhibit, this show, is one of a series. There is going to be a show on the art of portraiture in Washington, at the Folger Library, this winter. I was wondering if I might ask you to take a trip down to Washington and moderate the panel discussion on the opening night. The very best people in the art world will be there. Only the very best. I think you would be perfect."

"I'd love to," Isaac said.

"Wonderful. I am very pleased. I think you will be perfect.

I've only just now met you, but I feel as if I know you well. You are soft-spoken, but you are not soft. You are articulate, but you know when it is best not to speak. You are a presence, but you give other people room, to allow their presence to be felt."

This was all true, Nora thought, and she was impressed that Nadine had seen all this so quickly. But she also thought she was laying it on pretty thick.

"It will be a wonderful event," Nadine said. "We have Richard Avedon, we have Sally Mann, we have others—a very great French photographer, who perhaps you don't know." She smiled sadly. "It was my dream to have Yehuda Landau on this panel, but I can't even discover his telephone number. It's like trying to get the telephone number of God."

"You know," Isaac said, "I might be able to help you with that."

"You can help me get the telephone number of God?"

"I know Yehuda Landau. I studied with him. I won't say we're close, but...we're in touch. I can't give you his phone number, but I can call him for you. I doubt he'll say yes, but I can ask."

Landau was little known outside the photography world, revered within it. He was a sternly private man. He never went to parties or openings; the Guggenheim Museum had staged an exhibit of his work in the early nineties, and until the last minute no one was sure he was even going to show up for that. A mutual friend, a man who'd been Landau's student and Isaac's teacher, had introduced them years ago. Landau and his wife had taken a liking to Isaac, and he still saw them for dinner once or twice a year. Nora had met him once; he was a formidable man.

"Isaac Mitchell. If you can persuade God to take part in our discussion, I shall think of you as a god yourself."

Nadine had to leave; she had another appointment. When Nora and Isaac were alone, Isaac raised his eyebrows.

"Puppet repair."

"I'm sorry," Nora said.

He didn't seem mad. He seemed to think it was kind of funny. He was probably in too good a mood to be mad.

They left the restaurant. The rain was still coming down in clumps.

"Isaac Mitchell," Nora said. "If you can drive us home through this rain, I shall think of you as a god yourself."

They finally decided to go to Nora's place. They drove up Tenth Avenue slowly in the battering rain. It was only ten o'clock, and Nora was happy that she'd still have time to write. It was important for her to know that she could support Isaac and do her work—that she didn't have to sacrifice one for the other.

Isaac went to bed and Nora got ready to write. First she strapped on her Polar Pack. She didn't usually wear it while she was writing, but it helped a little if she wore it for a few minutes just before she got started. Then she spent ten minutes sitting with her eyes closed, letting the day recede. Then she made two cups of coffee with a lot of sugar and a lot of milk, and finally she sat down at the keyboard. She was feeling buoyant and alert; she thought she'd be able to concentrate for three or four hours.

On the table next to her computer she kept an index card with a quote from Henry James: "To live *in* the world of creation—to get into it and stay in it—to frequent it and haunt it—to *think* intensely and fruitfully—to woo combinations into being by a depth and continuity of attention and meditation—this is the only thing."

Yes, she thought. This *is* the only thing.

The phone rang; she let the answering machine take the call. She didn't need any distractions.

She'd forgotten to turn the volume down. It was Billie. All she said was, "Hi, it's me. Call me," but Nora could tell from her voice that she had bad news.

25

I'M REALLY SCARED ABOUT my operation," Billie said.

Nora was sitting in her aunt's hospital room.

"You don't have to be scared. You know how good Dr. Kanter is."

Billie was having surgery. She'd been having stomach pains, and had gone to Dr. Cyclops for a CAT scan—she hadn't mentioned this to Nora because she didn't want to alarm her—which had turned up a malignancy on her gallbladder. The surgeon, Dr. Kanter, was going to remove it and examine the surrounding organs. She had explained to Billie that, luckily, we don't really need the gallbladder: other organs can compensate if it's gone.

"You're right," Billie said. "I like her. Dr. Candy."

She reached over to her night table for her plastic glass of water, but she couldn't reach far enough because of the IV in her arm. "But I have a bad feeling about it."

Up until she said this, she'd seemed as calm as she ever was, but in saying this she seemed to spook herself. "I have a bad feeling," she said again, louder, and she reached out for Nora's hand. "I don't think I'm going to get through this."

"Of course you will. She's just going to take the thing out and you're going to be fine."

"They're going to find something else. They always find something else. They're going to find something bad."

Nora didn't know how to comfort her. What do you say to someone who's sick and might get sicker? Do you offer false comfort? Is that the kind thing to do? The question was academic, because Nora didn't know how to offer false comfort. She didn't say anything, and held on to Billie's hand.

Nora had a feeling of powerful protectiveness, not quite like anything she'd experienced before.

If Nora had believed in reincarnation, she would have found it easy to think that she'd known her aunt in many previous lives. When she asked herself why she loved her aunt so much, there wasn't a reason. Billie was kind, but it wasn't because of her kindness; she was generous, but it wasn't because of her generosity. The love wasn't there because of anything Billie had done. It was just there. Certain people are given into our care, and we have no choice but to care for them.

In a little while a nurse came in pushing a gurney. "Time to get prepped," she said, grinning, with a ghoulish excess of good cheer. She winked at Nora. "If you could just leave us alone for just two minutes, me and your auntie can get to know each other."

Nora was annoyed by her manner, but tried not to be, since this woman was here to help her aunt. She went out into the hall.

After a few minutes the door opened and the nurse wheeled Billie out. Nora walked with them toward the operating room, holding Billie's hand.

Dr. Kanter met them outside the operating room. She was a woman in her early fifties with a manner that was both confident and gentle. Nora had met her two years ago, when Kanter had removed a growth on Billie's spleen, a growth that had turned out to be benign.

"Good morning, my friend," the doctor said to Billie. "Any last questions before we take a look and find out what's going on in there?"

Billie looked up at her with an expression of childlike trustfulness and hope. "Is there any chance it'll be like with the spleen, and it'll be all clear?"

Nora was surprised by this question. Billie didn't seem to realize what was happening to her. She didn't seem to realize that they already knew this new growth was cancerous, and that the only question that remained was whether the cancer had spread.

"No, that won't be a possibility," Dr. Kanter said in a measured voice. "We know there's a malignancy there. We're hopeful we can get it all out. That's what this procedure is about."

Billie nodded, seeming to take it in, but Nora wasn't sure if she really had. She might have been too frightened to understand what her doctor was saying.

Nora let go of Billie's hand and the nurse wheeled her into the operating room.

Billie, Nora thought, had won the jump-rope contest in fifth grade.

A life goes by so quickly! We think of our lives as incredibly complicated and long, composed of many different stages, different eras, when the truth is that a life is but a single note.

Nora found a pay phone in the hall and called Isaac at work.

"I'm glad you called," he said. "I've been trying to reach you. How are you doing?"

"Oh, I don't know. Out on a limb."

He offered to take the rest of the day off and join her at the hospital. Someone else in her situation, she knew, would have been happy for the company. But in difficult moments she usually found it easier to be alone.

"Thank you," she said. "But I'm all right. I just wanted to hear your voice."

Nora went to the waiting room and got some coffee from a vending machine. She knew it would taste terrible, and she could have walked a block south to a diner for a cup of decent coffee, but the masochistic austerity that takes hold of you when you're in a hospital waiting for news about a loved one made her *want* to drink the punishing vending-machine coffee. She looked around idly for something to read, and settled on a copy of *Modern Maturity.*

She couldn't concentrate. Instead she sat in the waiting room trying to make sense of Billie's life. Trying to figure out what her life had added up to. If you looked at one side of the ledger—that she'd wanted children, but she and Nelson hadn't been able to conceive; that ever since Nelson's death, she'd spent most of her free time watching TV; that she was ending up like this, attended only by her niece—it was incredible how little a life could come down to.

Thinking about all this, Nora felt old, because she was old enough to have witnessed the arc of Billie's life. She could remember when Billie was in her thirties: exuberant, full of hope, and lucky—Billie, in the old days, had always seemed lucky; life always seemed to open its doors for her. Nora was old enough to have seen her transformed from the hopeful and high-spirited woman she was in her thirties to the ill and lonely woman she was today.

What was the key? What was the key? Thinking furiously, but with a sense that it wasn't going to get her anywhere, Nora was trying to understand why Billie's life had gone this way, from promise to nothing.

But maybe she was thinking about it in the wrong way. You can't judge the quality of a person's life from the way she ends up. Maybe Billie had lived a successful life—maybe a better life than Nora had. In Billie's years as a pediatric physical therapist, she'd helped a great many children. Nora had once visited her at work and seen the kids clustering around her; they were all in love with her.

Dr. Kanter had said the operation might take up to two hours, after which Billie would spend an hour or two in recovery. And after that, Dr. Kanter had said, she might still be too sedated to talk. Nora thought she should probably go home for a few hours. There was nothing she could do for Billie here. She could get some writing done.

But she didn't want to go home. Even though there was nothing she could do for Billie here, she wanted to stay.

26

DR. KANTER APPROACHED FROM down the hall, and Nora could tell she had bad news, just from the way she walked.

"Well," she said, "your aunt is in recovery. It'll be a few hours before you can speak to her."

"How'd it go?"

"The operation was a success," Kanter said. "We removed the gallbladder. But, as I said, we wanted to take a look around, and I'm afraid the results aren't encouraging. The malignancy has spread quite extensively, it turns out. It seems that her entire liver is compromised."

Nora didn't know anything about the body, but she knew enough to know what this meant.

"You can't really survive without your liver. Can you?"

Dr. Kanter raised her eyebrows in an expression of sympathy, sadness, answerlessness. Her eyes actually appeared to be shot with red. Only women should be doctors, Nora thought.

"Is there anything you can do?" Nora said.

Kanter's expression didn't change.

"How much time do you think she has?" Nora said.

"The variations can be very wide. But I think our main

concern now should be keeping her as comfortable as possible."

Keeping her as comfortable as possible?! But she was *comfortable, up until this morning! She was comfortable as pie! Just last weekend we were planning to go to the zoo! It isn't cancer that's killing her—it's this fucking operation that you insisted on! She was feeling fine before the operation, and now you're talking about keeping her comfortable!*

She was boiling with rage at Kanter, because all of this was Kanter's fault, but she didn't say anything, because she knew it wasn't true.

"Does she have anyone to stay with her?" Dr. Kanter asked.

"No. Yes. I don't know. There's me."

"It might be a good idea to look into the possibility of hospice care. There's a patients' rights office on the first floor where you can get the details. Medicare can pay for an attendant who can care for her at home, or if that becomes impossible for any reason, there's a hospice in the area that I can recommend."

A hospice! For my aunt Billie! For my aunt!

No no no no no no no no no no no no.

The thing about doctors is that they don't stay. They're sorry, but they have to run. Every doctor is a master of the art of backing away. And although Dr. Kanter—perhaps because she was a woman, or perhaps just because she was kind—was more willing than most doctors to explain things in detail and to listen to the concerns of patients and their loved ones, she was still, finally, a doctor, someone who had been trained to withdraw herself emotionally from the plight of the people she was ministering to. It's something you need to learn, Nora thought, because if you don't learn it, the daily exposure to misery will destroy you. Dr. Kanter was moving off even as she was speaking. "Call my office," she said. "They'll give you the number."

Well, this was one doctor who wasn't going to be able to walk away. Nora blocked her path. "A hospice is where you go to die," she said, as if Kanter didn't know this.

"They provide very good care," Dr. Kanter said quietly. "My mother spent the last three weeks of her life there."

Nora, humbled, let her go.

Nora sat down heavily on a hard plastic seat. Her mind wanted to go blank, but she wouldn't let it. She needed to think. She needed to figure out what to do.

First, when Billie got well enough to go home, she needed to go home with her. She needed to take care of her.

But even before that, she needed to find out if she could get someone to stay with her. A nurse. Someone who knew what she was doing. She took her memo pad from her bag.

1. Nurse, she wrote. *2. Hospice.*

She wasn't even sure what a hospice was. She knew it was a place where you brought the terminally ill. But how do they really know when anybody's terminally ill? There's always the possibility of an amazing recovery. Do they give you medical care in a hospice, or do they just give you morphine and let you die?

Mother Teresa used to run a hospice. But the witty and bibulous Christopher Hitchens had criticized Mother Teresa because some of the people she cared for in her hospice could have been cured. He said that her religious ideology made her believe that it was best for them to die and go to heaven. Therefore maybe things weren't so dire with Billie. Maybe she could be cured.

I'm not thinking right, Nora thought. I shouldn't be thinking about Christopher Hitchens at a time like this.

She needed to take a walk. She went downstairs and passed from the air-conditioned lobby into a humid, sweltering day. It was September, but it felt like July. Mankind had destroyed the weather; seasons no longer had meaning.

Walking through the haggard, heavy-bearded air, she ended up in Central Park, at the reservoir. She walked around it slowly, stepping to the margin of the path whenever she heard joggers coming up behind her. Dragonflies hovered just above the water, which had grown a layer of stale green skin.

When she and Billie had been there in the spring, it had been much nicer.

Death moves in on you from a distance, taking things away. The circle of places you even dream of visiting becomes smaller and smaller. She wondered if Billie would ever walk around the reservoir again. She didn't think so. It was as far away as Stonehenge, as far away as the Nile.

Nora made her way back to the hospital. Billie was asleep, breathing in weak, unsteady gasps.

Nora thought about how many years she'd known her aunt—all those years when Billie was healthy—and found it hard to understand why she hadn't done more to treasure their time together.

Treasure it now, she thought. Treasure this.

27

WHEN ISAAC GOT HOME FROM WORK there was a message from Renee on his machine. They were supposed to have dinner that night, and she was calling to confirm. She sounded excited. "I have some great news!" she said. "I can't wait to tell you!"

He wondered what qualified as great news for Renee. Perhaps she'd gone to a party and struck up a friendship with a former Sandinista minister of information. Perhaps she'd secured a new trial for Mumia Abu-Jamal.

He cleaned up his apartment. This last week had been a downer. Nora was despondent about her aunt Billie. Poor Aunt Billie. And—although he felt shabby about worrying about his career while she was going through something so serious—he'd been suffering from a kind of postpartum depression ever since the opening of his exhibit.

He'd been looking forward to it for such a long time—he'd spent a full six months selecting photographs, getting the invitations out—and now it was over. And nothing, absolutely nothing, had come of it. It hadn't been reviewed—not in the *Times,* not even in the *Register.* The two-bit newspaper that he worked for had decided that his show wasn't worthy of review.

There was still a chance that some of the critics from the quarterlies would come by—the pictures would be up for another month—or that some of the high-profile gallery owners he'd invited would see the show and offer him something in the city. But none of these people had come to the opening, and it was hard to imagine any of them making the long journey out to Englewood to look at his pictures without the inducements of wine and cheese.

Well, an hour or two with Renee would cheer him up.

He was so downhearted that he wasn't even having the mixed feelings he usually had when he was about to see her—that queasy intermingling of fatherliness and desire. He was just looking forward to seeing her.

She arrived at his apartment breathless, twenty minutes late. "I'm so sorry I couldn't come to your opening. But I have a good excuse. I have good news." She was smiling mischievously, and for a moment he thought she was about to give him good news about *him*. His show was still the foremost thing in his mind—his show, and what it might do for his career—and he was still in that state where news that's not about yourself seems bafflingly irrelevant.

"The reason I couldn't come was that I was in the city that day, having meetings. Can you believe it? I'm a grown-up now! I go to meetings!"

He smiled at her indulgently and sat down. She was still standing, bouncing on her toes. She looked like a boxer.

"First of all, I was meeting with people from the anti-sweatshop coalition, and the fact-finding tour is really going to happen."

"That's wonderful, Renee. Congratulations." Not exactly his idea of a good time, but her enthusiasm was charming.

She finally sat down. "And then I had another meeting. I think you're going to be proud of me about this one. I was having a meeting with—the *New Yorker*! Your favorite magazine! They're having a special photography issue this winter, and they want to use three of the pictures I took in Chiapas. Can you believe it? It's so crazy I don't even know how to pronounce the words when I tell people. They want to use *three* of my pictures! They want to use three of *my* pictures!"

"The *New Yorker*? Really? That's incredible."

He was happy that his voice hadn't cracked. He wondered whether she could hear any of the things that *he* heard in his voice: envy, disbelief, rage, sorrow, a feeling that she'd betrayed him, a feeling that she'd emasculated him.

He wondered, also, whether she could hear the note of sluggish stupidity. When she'd mentioned the photography issue, he had thought for a moment that she'd shown them some of *his* photographs—that she was telling him that she'd slyly submitted *his* work, and that they wanted to use it.

The *New Yorker*. He'd been sending them photographs, and getting rejections from them, for as long as they'd been running photographs. More than ten years.

"Thanks," she said. "Can you believe it?"

She was glowing. One of the things that was wonderful about Renee was that she was too guileless, too pure, to realize what was happening here—to realize that she'd struck him to the heart.

"Gosh," he said. "We have to celebrate. Can I get you some...decaf tea?"

She smiled at this. Her ultrapure nature—her organic, herbal, free-range nature—was one of their standing jokes.

He went to the kitchen for the tea; he glanced at the

window, and he thought it might be a good idea to put his fist through the glass.

He had always felt sure that Renee would eventually surpass him. He'd felt sure of it because of her zeal for life, her desire to do and see and experience everything. Taking good pictures has very little to do with technique, in the end; it has to do with appetite for life, and he'd always understood that Renee's appetite for life was greater than his own. He'd always known that she would surpass him; he just hadn't thought it would happen so soon.

Renee had just attained a kind of success that he had never come close to, not in twenty years of striving, and never would. He was a known quantity now, and no one was willing to look at his work with a fresh eye. With some of life's rewards, if you don't get them when you're young, you don't get them.

He wanted to kill her. Because *she* was killing *him*. She didn't realize it, but she was killing him. She was diminishing him.

"How was your show?" she called from the other room. She couldn't have said anything more insulting if she'd tried.

"It was nice," he said. Yes, it was nice—he'd been praised by a roomful of old friends, none of whom knew anything about photography. And a woman from Latvia had told him about her grandfather.

He felt his mind working to diminish Renee's achievement. The *New Yorker* was using her pictures because they fit in with a particular article, not because she was a good photographer; they wouldn't be using her again. It was a lucky coincidence. It would look good on her résumé, but it was a one-shot deal.

He ran quickly through his mental file of photographers who'd enjoyed early success and then fizzled out. He was wishing that future on Renee.

But it wasn't working. Renee wasn't going to fizzle out. She was the real thing.

He'd once read an article about how birds lose their plumage when other birds defeat them in the struggle for dominance. He felt himself losing his plumage. If he could take a blood test right this second, he was sure it would show a stark drop in serotonin, dopamine, testosterone, and whatever other chemicals contribute to feelings of confidence, mastery, well-being, vitality, youth.

But you can't be so upset by this! She once called you her mentor! You're her *teacher,* in a way! Your role is to help her! The whole point of working with young people is that you *hope* they'll surpass you! This is what you wanted! At least it's what you claimed to want.

He was making the tea. He'd cramped himself into a corner of the kitchen, hiding from her while all this played out in his mind.

He came back out, bearing two steaming mugs.

"This is just so fantastic, Renee."

What a fucking hypocrite I am. If I was being honest I'd scream at her. I'd throw her out.

But honesty isn't the important thing here, he thought. The important thing isn't what you feel. The important thing, sometimes, is what you appear to feel.

He believed in the authority of the visible. If all Renee saw was his generosity, then his generosity would be real.

When he was in his late twenties, two of his photographs were acquired by the Boston Museum of Fine Arts, and when he told one of his former teachers the good news, the old man had said, "Yes, they've been after me to send them some things, but I've been too busy." At the time Isaac hadn't understood that the old man had no class, that his response had emerged from a stew of peevish envy. He understood it now. And he understood that if he gave Renee anything less than a generous response, it would condemn him, condemn him as a small-souled man, and that a generous response, even if it wasn't sincere, would be enough.

"This is just so wonderful, Renee," he said. "It's fantastic."

"I know!" she said. "It's just so great! I can't believe it!"

The next generation was making its claim, and he hadn't tried to obstruct it. He felt obscurely that this was one of the defining moments of his life.

"Where shall we eat?" he said, wondering if he could possibly eat anything.

He felt as if he'd been enlarged as a man. But that didn't mean he had to enjoy it.

28

NORA TOOK BILLIE HOME in a taxi. Dr. Kanter hadn't told Billie about the seriousness of her condition.

"Maybe we can go for a walk later and get a snack," Billie said on the way home. "I have a yen for some red licorice. There's a candy store on Ninth Avenue that has that kind I like—Peel and Pull."

Nora had cleaned Billie's apartment the day before when she'd stopped by to feed her cats.

"You made it perfect for me," Billie said. "You made it like a palace."

She had a funny cheerfulness. Nora wanted to think that Billie knew how ill she was—that she knew even without being told—and that she was being brave. But it probably wasn't true. Probably when the news was explained to her, she'd fall apart.

Billie looked in her refrigerator. "I have some Boca Burgers, and tomatoes, and buns. Maybe we can have a Boca-fest tonight. And then maybe we can rent a movie."

"That sounds like fun."

"I feel so lucky," Billie said. "I can't believe they just fixed me up in a jiffy. I think I might find out if I can volunteer in the hospital. I like that Dr. Candy."

Billie sat on the couch, and Edwin and Louie hustled up—Dolly lay on her pillow, too weak to move—and in an instant were all over her, licking her and pawing at her. Purring, pushing their paws against her, and pulling them back, each time having to make the effort of disentangling their claws from her shirt. Louie continued flattering her in this manner; Edwin went over to the door and meowed.

Nora let him out into the hall and he went to scratch his back on the banister.

"Maybe we can take a ferry to Hoboken tomorrow, if you're free," Billie said. "I heard on the radio that they set up a temporary amusement park near the river. We could ride the Ferris wheel. We could ride the Wild Mouse."

Nora went to the kitchen, made the veggie burgers, and put together a salad. She brought everything out on a tray and placed it on the coffee table, and they sat side by side on the couch eating dinner and watching the Summer Olympics. "What an adventure," Billie said. "Who would have thought a week ago that I'd be in the hospital yesterday. And who would have thought, yesterday, that today I'd be back home."

During the track-and-field competitions, Nora started to nod off. She woke up to the sight of Billie moving to the bathroom, as quickly as she could move. Nora followed her. Billie was on her knees in front of the toilet bowl. There was vomit in the bowl and on the floor and on her blouse.

"I guess it was a little too soon for a Boca-fest," Billie said.

"Let me help," Nora said. She wetted down a washcloth and cleaned Billie's face.

"Thank you," Billie said.

She helped Billie back to the couch, got her a clean shirt, put the soiled one in the sink and ran water over it and rubbed it down with a bar of soap, and then found a sponge and some paper towels and a container of Ajax and cleaned up the floor.

Billie looked pale and spent. "Maybe I could have some of that sleepy thing," she said.

Dr. Kanter had given her a supply of Tylenol with codeine. Nora brought her a glass of water and she swallowed a pill. She helped Billie into bed, got in beside her, and turned her bedside television on.

They watched a little more of the Olympics. They watched Ping-Pong, and then they watched synchronized swimming.

"I guess it's pretty," Nora said, "but I'm not sure it's a sport."

Nora couldn't tell if Billie was awake. Her nose was barely peeping out from under the blanket.

"You know what sport they're having at the next Olympics?" Billie said sleepily. "Slinky."

Nora put a glass of water on Billie's night table, kissed her on the forehead, and went out to the living room. It was eleven. The home-care worker was supposed to have arrived an hour ago.

When Billie was in the hospital, Nora had called the "extended-care" office and arranged to have someone to stay with her after she got home. Medicare would cover this for fourteen days; after that, they'd have to reapply.

Nora had put in a request for a woman she knew, a soft-voiced grandmother named Joyce who'd worked for her friend Helen's mother when she was ill. Joyce was one of the gentlest people she'd ever met; if Joyce were taking care of Billie, Nora would feel at ease. But she'd found out that afternoon that Joyce was unavailable, taking full-time care of someone else.

The home-care worker finally showed up at 11:30. She was an attractive young woman from Russia; her name was Sofia. She was wearing a short tight skirt with a slit up the side. *She's dressed to kill,* Nora thought, and immediately felt worried.

Nora talked with her for a few minutes and then took the subway uptown.

The phone was ringing when she walked in the door. Something bad had happened to Billie. She moved quickly to the phone.

"Hi," Billie said. "Did I wake you?"

"No. Not at all. I just got back."

"I woke up to go to the bathroom. I just wanted to thank you."

Nora didn't feel as if she deserved to be thanked. She should have still been down there, sleeping on Billie's couch. "How are you feeling?"

"I don't know. I'm feeling a little misty, like parts of me are floating away. But I'm okay. I've got the TV on, and Edwin and Louie are snuggling right next to me."

They spoke for another minute; Nora told Billie that she'd see her the next day, and they said good-bye.

Nora wanted to stay up and write for an hour or two, but she needed to rest for a minute first. She closed her eyes. Her apartment was very quiet; she could hear an occasional car horn, but nothing else. She lay on the couch listening to her own breathing.

She felt so attuned to her aunt, so at one with her, that it seemed, in this quiet, as if she could feel her presence, from blocks and blocks away. Billie was sleeping, breathing wheezily, with difficulty. The medicine and the illness, the painkillers and the pain—her body was a battleground. She was being peeled open and pulled apart. Peel and pull. Nora's own breathing grew more shallow and more rapid, as if it were taking on the rhythms of her aunt's. She tried to calm herself, to make each breath longer and slower and deeper, so she could send healing breaths into her aunt's body, from all these blocks away. She knew it wasn't possible to have the connection she thought the two of them were having—she knew she was connecting only with her own idea of her aunt. And yet she *felt* connected.

It had rained that evening, and after a hot day the night air had turned mild. The windows of her apartment were open, and a breeze was moving softly through the room.

Billie was sleeping, unmoving in her bed, but Nora could feel that within her, in her spirit, something was shifting. She could sense that her aunt was edging closer, hesitantly, toward the hugeness of death. She was like a shy young bride, gathering up the courage to give herself away.

Let it take you peacefully, Billie, let it take you sweetly. I swear it can take you sweetly if you let it.

How did Nora know that it could take you sweetly? She didn't. She merely hoped that it was true.

29

Nora woke at one in the morning and heated up some water. Even though she didn't always have the strength to do it, she believed in the idea of writing through everything, refusing to let any event or emotion interrupt her work. If she felt too sad or too spacy to write, she tried to write nevertheless; she tried to bring her sadness or her spaciness to the keyboard. She wanted to keep faith with that idea tonight. She was feeling sorrowful and tired, and her arm, from the effort of helping Billie up four flights of stairs, was speaking in tongues, but she made two cups of coffee and set them side by side on her card table and started to scroll through the Gabriel story.

Even during this last week, while spending most of her time in the hospital, she'd managed to work a little every night. And her devotion was starting to bear fruit. The story was making sense to her again. Gabriel was on a train, on the way to visit his sister. Nora didn't know why he was visiting her or what would happen when he got there, but she was feeling as if the story was ready to unfurl itself.

She'd barely gotten started when the phone rang. It was Isaac. He never called her this late. Their middle-of-the-night phone calls were strictly one-way.

"What's going on?" she said.

"Oh, I just—I don't know. How's Billie?"

"She's okay. She doesn't know anything yet. She thinks she's fine. At least she says she thinks she's fine. Maybe she's trying to spare my feelings."

"Poor Billie," he said.

Something was going on with him. She knew he was concerned about Billie, but she could tell that wasn't why he'd called.

"What's new with you?" she said.

"Something funny happened to me tonight. Renee—you remember Renee?"

"Sure. 'Too bad you have such a small family.'"

"That's right. Renee from the human family. She dropped by tonight. She told me that some of her pictures were accepted by the *New Yorker.*"

"That's fantastic," Nora said. "You must be proud."

"Yeah. She's got it made. Made in the shade."

She didn't know why, but when he said this, she realized that he was miserable.

"She might be a genius," he said. "A genius with the camera, I mean. The funny thing is that she's not even that devoted. I've met a thousand photographers who know more about the craft of photography, who *care* more about the craft of photography than she does. She just happens to be great at it. It's a gift. You either have it or you don't."

He sighed: a heavy, defeated sigh.

"You either have it or you don't," he said again. "She has it. I don't."

She thought she should say something to comfort him, but she decided not to. She'd always liked his photographs, but she didn't consider herself qualified to judge whether he was truly gifted.

"Life is funny," he said. "It's like, in my twenties, in my early thirties, when I didn't think about anything except taking pictures—during all those years, it was like I was searching for genius. I was doing it as well as I could possibly do it, but I used to think that the one thing I didn't have was that tiny little glint of genius that would have brought everything together. It's like, I don't know anything about cooking, but I'm sure there are complicated sauces, with a lot of ingredients, that don't really taste like much until you add some tiny pinch of one last ingredient. Some spice or something. Maybe just salt. And when you add that last thing, everything else comes together and the whole thing tastes incredible. Am I making any sense?"

"I think so," she said, although she wasn't really sure.

"What I'm trying to say is that I've been searching for genius all my life. And I've finally found it. But it's not mine."

She didn't know what to say. The thought went through her mind that what he was saying was ironic, but she wasn't sure she knew what irony was anymore—not since Alanis Morissette put out that song "Isn't It Ironic?" and all the reviewers pointed out that the things she was referring to as ironic, rain on your wedding day and so on, weren't actually ironic at all.

Probably, she thought, I shouldn't be thinking about Alanis Morissette right now.

Alanis Morissette and Christopher Hitchens.

Together at last.

"But why should I be *sad* about that?" Isaac said. "I've always known that the gift has nothing to do with the person it happens to express itself through. I mean, if you're incredibly gifted, you can't *congratulate* yourself on being gifted—it's just something that happens to you. So I should be happy to have encountered a pure gift. Even if it isn't mine. And the person who has it is someone I really care about. And she's a terrific person. She *is* a terrific person, you know."

"She seemed like it."

"She is. I'm stunned, that's all. And I'm not happy about the fact that—I'm not happy about the fact that I'm not happy. You know? I should just be thrilled for her."

"I don't think you should beat yourself up about it," Nora said. "I think it was Gore Vidal who said, 'I die a little every time a friend succeeds.' Everybody feels that way, to some extent."

Isaac laughed. "That's not bad," he said. "Well, thanks. I just needed to say all this to somebody, and you're the only person I trust enough to say it to."

She admired Isaac for taking the trouble to encourage younger people in the first place. Years ago, after her moment of triumph with *Best American Short Stories,* Nora had taught a writing workshop at Brooklyn College. She'd tried to be a good teacher, tried to help her students cultivate their gifts, but she'd never been able to rid herself of a secret desire to crush them—to guide them, through subtly humiliating assessments of their talents, into careers in dentistry. She had finished out the semester and never applied for a teaching job again. The young will inevitably surpass you, but she had no wish to speed the process along.

It seemed as if the conversation was finished, but they stayed on the phone. They didn't speak. It was comfortable just to listen to Isaac breathe.

She turned off the light and lay back down on the couch. "Isaac?" she said.

It had been a long time since they'd spent a night asleep together on the phone.

Isaac was sleeping, but he was fretful. His breathing was unsteady. His burdened energy, his restlessness...he was turning turning turning around tonight's fresh hurt.

She still wanted to write, but her fatigue was catching up to her. Her second cup of coffee was sitting untouched on the card table, and the first had already worn off.

Anyway, she thought, it might be better not to write tonight. It would be cruel to work on the Gabriel story—to mess around with Isaac's life like that—while he was feeling so wounded. And while he was still on the phone, sleeping, a tiny thing.

She remembered reading that when the frail and neurasthenic poet Alfred de Musset spent his first night with George Sand, he awoke at three in the morning, a few hours after they'd made love, and was astonished to find that she was not beside him in bed, but at her desk, working on her novel with a long quill pen and puffing contemplatively on a hookah. It was this intrepid spirit that made George Sand one of the baddest women of the nineteenth century.

But Nora was too tired to get up and work, too tired to stake a claim to being one of the baddest women of the twenty-first century. She lay on the couch listening to Isaac's breathing.

Oh hell.

She got up, made another two cups of coffee, drank all three, took three Advils for the pain in her arm, sat down, and started to work. She put the phone receiver on the card table so she could hear if Isaac woke up.

She worked past three in the morning, past four. Something was happening. She felt as if she'd finally cracked the code. She finally understood what the story was about.

The story was about the night Isaac met his sister in New Haven to talk her out of moving to the commune.

Isaac's sister, Jenny, had become a follower of a man who called himself Nan, a petulant guru who through the magic of his hands could cure any disease, although—because disease, as he often said, can be a teacher—there were some he chose not to.

Isaac had been sure that Jenny became smitten by Guru Nan only because she found him at a moment when her life was falling apart. She had been engaged and had found out that her fiancé was seeing someone else, and in the depression that followed she stopped going to classes and lost her scholarship at Yale. Isaac had been sure that if he spent an evening with her, he could help her see that it wasn't a good time to be making momentous decisions.

That was just about all Nora knew. She knew that he'd gone up to New Haven, and that the next day, mission not accomplished, he'd come back. She'd asked him what had happened up there, but he'd told her it didn't matter.

Working on the story, Nora felt as if her mind was flooded with light. She had a protagonist she cared about deeply, and, although she knew the main outlines of the event she wanted to write about, she didn't know the specifics, so she was free to invent. She was typing faster than her computer could handle—it kept giving off little beeps.

In the story, Gabriel took a train to New Haven, but it broke down just outside Norwalk, and he got in three hours late, weak from hunger, and it was the height of summer and he felt swoony in the heat, and when he met up with his sister she was with two friends, Yale students, one of whom was so beautiful that he became tongue-tied, the other of whom was so quick and articulate and confident about her future that Gabriel felt slow-witted and old, and when he and his sister were finally alone, he failed to say the things he'd planned to—because he felt so weak and worn and insecure, and because he was afraid that his little sister, whom he had always secretly considered more intelligent than he was, would win any argument that he launched in this depleted state. Instead of thinking about her and what she needed, he could only think about himself and his deficiencies, and he didn't say a word. In the story, he saw her again the next day, at breakfast, just before she was supposed to meet her plane, and she seemed angry and on the verge of tears, and it dimly occurred to him that she was upset because he *hadn't* helped her find reasons not to join the cult, that she'd *wanted* him to, but by this time it was too late, and they ruined their breakfast with a stupid argument about their parents, and they never saw each other again.

After an hour she'd almost forgotten that these details were her own inventions. Or rather, she hadn't forgotten, but she didn't care. If Isaac had woken up and volunteered to tell her what had really happened, she wouldn't have wanted to hear it, because whatever really happened couldn't have been as real as her story.

She knew that this wasn't going to be a story Isaac would like. It concerned one of the saddest nights of his life: a night when he'd failed his sister. And she had an intuition that when she was through with it, it wouldn't be about just this one night. It would radiate out into the main character's life; that one night's failure would seem to illustrate some essential truth about him.

All through the night, her phone was near her, and she

could hear Isaac breathing and moving in his sleep. At five something happened on 108th Street: three or four police cars streaked down the street, their sirens strident and loud. She picked up the phone and pressed the mouthpiece against her breast to shield Isaac from the sound.

If he hadn't called her tonight to share his mixed feelings about Renee's success, the story would never have come together like this. His meditations on his own shortcomings had given her the key.

It occurred to her that this was the breakthrough she'd been seeking for years. It was the first time she'd found the strength to finish a story when she knew it was likely to hurt a man she cared about. It was a breakthrough, yes, but it was one that left her unhappy.

She wrote until 5:30. She brushed her teeth, put on her nightgown, got the phone, and took it into bed with her. She brought it close to her ear. She could hear him breathing, deeply and slowly. It was a trustful sound.

30

BILLIE HAD HER FIRST FALL on her third day home from the hospital. When she called Nora later that morning, she described it almost matter-of-factly.

"I was puttering around in the kitchen—I was reaching for a can of cling peaches—and then all of a sudden I was on the floor and Edwin was licking my face. Scratchy-tongue Edwin. You're a scratchy, scratchy man." Nora could hear Edwin purring, pushing his face against the phone.

"Where was Sofia?"

"She took the morning off. She had to do something with her brother. She just got back."

Nora closed her eyes and tried not to let the anger overcome her.

"I'm really sorry."

"It wasn't so bad," Billie said. "The only scary part was that it was hard to get up."

"What did you do?"

"I just lay there for a while. I think I went to sleep for a few minutes, and then when I woke up I made it to the couch. I slept on the couch with my babies."

Billie was too important to be left with a stranger with a slit skirt. Nora decided to get rid of Sofia and stay with Billie herself. But not for a few days.

The deadline for the *Atlantic*'s short-story contest was coming up. She'd almost forgotten about it, since her writing had been going so slowly, but now that the story had finally come together she thought she had a shot at polishing it and getting it in the mail by the deadline, which was four days away. But she'd need to spend most of her time writing. She could visit Billie in the evenings during these four days, and after that she could stay with her around the clock.

When Nora went down to Billie's that night, she had a talk with Sofia, who nodded smilingly and said that it wouldn't happen again. "Family emergency," she said.

THE NEXT MORNING, BILLIE called at six. Isaac had spent the night at Nora's; she had to climb over him to get to the phone.

"Hi, sweetie. I'm calling from the floor."

"Pardon?"

"I can't seem to get up very good."

"Where's Sofia?"

"I don't know."

"When did you fall?"

"I had to get up to pee at about three."

"You've been on the floor all that time? You should have called me."

"I didn't want to wake you that early. I feel bad about waking you *this* early."

Isaac drove Nora down to Billie's apartment. When Nora let herself in, Billie was still on the floor.

"Isaac's out in the hall," Nora said. She'd asked him to stay outside, because she didn't know if Billie would want him to see her in this state. "Do you mind if he comes in?"

"Not at all. I always liked that boy." She sounded as if Nora had proposed a social visit.

Nora called out to him. He stood in the doorway, awkward and tall. "I'm sorry you're not feeling well." Then he knelt next to Billie, lifted her up, and carried her easily to the couch.

"I feel like royalty," Billie said. "Didn't they used to carry Queen Victoria around?" He set her down gently and she patted his hand. "I'm only sorry I can't entertain you. The last time I saw you we went out for tea and crumpets."

Nora had forgotten. Six years ago, on Billie's birthday, Isaac had taken them out for tea at the Plaza Hotel.

Isaac left to buy some groceries; shortly after he returned, he had to leave for work. He said good-bye to Billie, and Nora walked him to the door. She thought of her story and the way he was pictured in it, and then she put her arms around him and closed her eyes, trying to forget it, trying to put everything except this moment out of her mind.

Nora came back to the living room, where Billie was watching *The View.* "I think we've had enough of Sofia," Nora said.

"She has a sick brother," Billie said. "She's very worried about him. I think that's why she hasn't been taking such good care of me."

When Sofia showed up that afternoon, Nora fired her before she'd had a chance to take off her coat. Then she made a few phone calls and found out that Joyce, the woman she'd requested in the first place, was now available, and could stay with Billie around the clock. She was a woman in her late sixties, a grandmother who had been a schoolteacher in Jamaica until she'd retired and moved to New York to live with her children. Nora knew her to be trustworthy and skilled.

She went into Billie's bedroom to tell her about the new arrangement.

"Joyce'll be here in a couple of hours. You'll like her. I'll show her around the place—you won't have to get out of bed."

"Thank you," Billie said. "You take good care of me."

Nora told herself that since Joyce would be staying with Billie, there was no need for her to move down here. At least not yet. All she needed was three more days to finish her story and put it in the mail.

This arrangement makes sense, Nora thought. There's no harm in waiting another few days.

But experience showed that she wasn't likely to follow through with this plan. She hadn't been able to choose the MacDowell Colony over her aunt, and she doubted she'd be able to choose the story contest.

"I want to cook something for you tonight," Nora said. "What are you in the mood for?"

"You know, when I was in the hospital and they brought the menu, I was thinking I wished I could have Iva's omelet."

Iva's omelet was a family recipe, passed down from Nora's grandmother. After Billie was gone, Nora would be the only person in the world who knew what it was.

"You know," Nora said to Billie, "I think it would be better if Joyce just stayed here in the mornings and afternoons and I took over at night. I think I'll bring my things down here and stay with you for a while."

That was even quicker than Nora had expected.

"It's very nice of you to offer," Billie said. "But I don't understand. You just went through all that trouble to get Joyce."

"I just want to."

Nora couldn't explain that it was because of Iva's omelet.

"It would be a pleasure to have you," Billie said. "It'd be like having a slumber party every day."

Billie was smiling at her—calmly, trustfully.

What a feeling, to have someone's life in your hands!

The strange thing was that it didn't feel strange.

She thought of the afternoon, more than fifteen years ago, when Billie accompanied her to the funeral home after Margaret's death and hadn't been able to go in. She remembered standing near the entrance of the funeral home—how she'd looked back and seen her aunt on the bench, her arms wrapped around her body, shivering, in the full blue ease of early May. Remembering that moment, she felt as if she must have known, even then, when she was still no more than a girl, that she'd be taking care of Billie someday.

31

THIS IS HOW people disappear...

The next day, while Billie was sleeping and Joyce was knitting near her bed, Nora went out to do some errands. First she went to the post office and mailed her story to the *Atlantic.* It was still rough, but she wanted to get it into the mail anyway—she wasn't sure whether she'd be able to write at all while she was staying with Billie, and sending the story out, even in its ragged state, was an affirmation that she was a fiction writer again. After that she went to the supermarket, where she bought soup and juice and tea and toast and frozen yogurt for Billie, and food and toys for the cats. At the video store she rented all three versions of *Little Women*—June Allyson, Katharine Hepburn, and Winona Ryder. They could have a video festival over the weekend.

When Nora got back to the apartment, Joyce gathered up her things and left for the night. As soon as she was alone, Nora knew something was wrong. Edwin and Louie were huddled together oddly near the kitchen door, as if they were trying to create one cat. Nora walked quickly into the bedroom; Billie was in bed, staring at the ceiling.

Nora came in quietly. "Hi," she said.

Billie didn't answer. She didn't move her head. She moved her eyes in Nora's direction, although not all the way.

"How are you feeling?" Nora said.

Billie didn't respond.

Nora pulled a chair up next to the bed. "Do you want some soup?"

Billie shook her head and didn't say anything.

This is how people disappear. Nora had been away less than two hours, but during that time, Billie had moved from one stage of dying into the next.

During the next few days, Billie's strength fluctuated. At her best, she could still talk and go to the bathroom and watch TV. At her worst she wasn't strong enough to lift her head from the pillow. Nora had to lift her head in order to help her drink.

As enfeebled as Billie was, taking care of her wouldn't have been quite so difficult if not for the problem of helping her manage her eliminations.

Joyce was experienced in the use of bedpans, and things went smoothly when she was there. But Nora was new at this. One morning, changing the bedpan, she tipped it over and it spilled onto Billie's sheets. She helped Billie out of bed so she could put new sheets on, and then, when she got her back in, but before she could get the bedpan under her, Billie soiled the sheets again.

Nora helped her back to her easy chair.

"I'm sorry," Billie said.

"There's nothing to be sorry about."

"Well, maybe there is."

Nora put fresh sheets on the bed. "Sometimes I think people just shouldn't have bodies," she said.

"If we didn't have bodies we wouldn't have any fun," Billie said.

Nora thought of getting a wheelchair, but it became one of those things that you keep thinking about doing and never do.

Instead she just tried to make peace with the bedpan, and with the smell of excrement, which had taken over the apartment.

Billie's gums and tongue began to bleed. When Nora brought her something to drink, she would put a straw between Billie's lips, and when she removed it, the straw was always bloody.

One night Billie tried to reassure Nora that things weren't so bad, wanted to show her that she was still capable of smiling, but when she smiled, her teeth were red with blood.

On Billie's torso, on her shoulders, on her neck, boils began to appear. The boils were blue and scaly and their edges were dotted with tiny purple pus-filled sacs. It was as if nature was reclaiming her, inch by inch.

Nora and Isaac had planned to get together one Saturday afternoon while Joyce was staying with Billie. Nora asked him if he'd accompany her to the hospice that Dr. Kanter had told her about. She wanted to see what it was like. She didn't have the competence to take care of Billie anymore.

Isaac picked her up and they drove to the hospice, which was in a quiet part of Queens. It was a crisp October day, and the ride was pleasant, or would have been, if they hadn't been headed out to visit a hospice.

She asked him if he'd heard from anybody about his show—gallery owners or reviewers—and before she finished the sentence she realized it was a bad idea to ask.

"Nope," he said. "It was kind of silly of me to have thought I might."

"It wasn't silly."

He seemed glum, and she thought it was because of her.

"I'm sorry we've been spending so little time together," she said.

"You need to take care of Billie. I understand that."

"Are you sure?"

"Of course I'm sure."

The hospice was called Riverside, though there weren't any rivers nearby. A large and motherly woman named Alice gave them a tour. The halls and the rooms were clean; the nurses seemed attentive and kind.

The place was billed as a "multidimensional care facility"; Alice was vague as to what, if anything, that meant. It seemed to mean that it was part hospice, part nursing home. Which itself seemed to mean that they took in people who weren't necessarily going to die immediately, but who were expected to die soon.

A few times during the day, the thought of her story crossed Nora's mind. She wasn't sure she had the right to be relying on Isaac like this when her story was lying in wait for him, ready to strike.

Near the end of the tour, Alice had to take a phone call; while Nora and Isaac were waiting for her in the hall, an old woman in bed in a private room called out. "Young man? Excuse me? Sir?"

Isaac took one respectful step into the room. "Can I help you?"

"Yes, you can. I'd like you to help get me out of here, young man."

"I'm not sure what you mean."

"I mean I would appreciate it if you would call my father. I'm certain that he doesn't know I'm here."

The woman was at least eighty years old.

She looked at Isaac imploringly. "My daddy wouldn't let me be alone like this," she said.

"If you give me his number, yes, I'll call him for you," Isaac said.

Nora thought that this was probably as kind an answer as he could have given to her. But it didn't seem to calm her. She didn't say anything more, but she continued to look at him pleadingly.

Riverside was affiliated with a hospital, which was across the street. They visited the hospital for a moment; it was quiet and clean.

They found a coffee shop nearby. They each ordered something, although neither of them was hungry. They just needed a place to sit down.

Isaac asked her what she was thinking.

"I was thinking it's good they have a hospital across the street. Maybe she'll get better, and then they'll transfer her to the hospital, and eventually she'll be able to come home again."

Isaac smiled at her sadly. It was as if he was trying to read her, trying to determine whether she was strong enough to bear up under the sadness of Billie's death.

He accompanied her back to Billie's. Nora talked to Joyce for a minute, then looked in on Billie. She was awake and alert, watching figure skating on TV. Nora asked her if she'd like to say hello to Isaac.

"Of course," she said. "He's a man who carries a girl very nicely."

Nora brought him into the bedroom.

"How are you?" he asked.

"I haven't been too peachy. But Nora is making things nicer for me."

"Is there anything I can do for you?"

"Just take care of her, while she's taking care of me."

Isaac didn't want to tire her out. He kissed Billie on the cheek and said good-bye.

Nora saw him to the door.

"I could stay here with you if you'd like," he said.

She knew that Isaac wanted to be here, wanted to help her; she knew that it was frustrating for him that she wasn't *allowing* him to help her more. But she was about to have a talk with Billie that wouldn't be easy for either of them, and she wanted to be alone with her. She put her arms around him and whispered into his shirt, "I'm sorry."

After Isaac left, Nora rejoined Billie, who asked her what she'd done that day.

Without using the word hospice, Nora told her that she'd visited the place that Kanter had told her about, a place where people could take better care of her.

"That's what you did today?" Billie seemed frightened. "That doesn't seem very romantic."

"It wasn't."

"You think I need a place like that?"

The question was meant sincerely. Nora didn't say anything. She just took Billie's hand.

"I don't want to go," Billie said.

"You don't have to. Not if you don't want to."

"Is it clean?"

"It is. It's very clean."

"Did the food look okay?

"I didn't see the food. They showed me a menu, though. It looked pretty good. But I can bring you anything you want."

"Were they nice there? Do you think people make friends there?"

"They seemed nice," Nora said. "The ones I met."

Billie watched another minute of the figure skating.

"I'll miss you," she said. "You've been a very jolly housemate."

"You'll still see me every day."

Even though she herself had set it all in motion, Nora was disturbed by how easy this was turning out to be, how meekly Billie was accepting this fate. She didn't want her to be so easily defeated.

Edwin was at the bedroom door, meowing.

"What about my sweeties?" Billie said. "Will I be able to take them with me?"

"I don't think so," Nora said. "But maybe I can sneak them in for visits. I'll carry them in a picnic basket."

This, of course, was pure fantasy, but Billie seemed to believe it. "That would be fun," she said. "But I'm not sure Dolly's well enough to travel." She put her head back on the pillow. "It'll be hard to say good-bye."

32

SIX DAYS LATER, NORA CALLED Riverside, and they sent someone to pick Billie up. Billie had been continuing to slip away.

The man from the hospice brought a gurney up to Billie's apartment. Nora helped him shift her to the gurney from the bed. He was a large man in his late fifties who looked like he should have been working down at the docks. Nora was surprised by the carefulness with which he handled Billie when he moved her. He had the air somehow of someone doing penance for a lifetime of mistakes.

Nora followed him as he wheeled her out of the apartment. It was one of Billie's bad days. As they went through the living room, near the front door, Billie seemed to rouse herself—it was hardly perceptible—and turn her head slightly for a last look at her little lovelies. Dolly was in her corner, dozing, but Edwin and Louie were nowhere to be seen.

Even though Nora had told them that Billie lived in a fourth-floor walk-up, the man had come by himself, so she had to help him move Billie downstairs. By the time they reached the sidewalk Nora's arm hurt so much that she was trying not to cry.

Nora rode in the front seat. They crossed the Triborough Bridge, passing a sign that said "Explore Beautiful Queens!" It was a rainy day, but the sun, somehow, was shining brightly, and the greenery bordering the highway seemed to be glowing unnaturally, radioactive.

At Riverside, Billie was given a room on the first floor. A high wide window looked out on a garden. There was another bed in the room; the woman in it was sleeping.

Nora spent the afternoon sitting next to Billie's bed as Billie slept. It was hard to see how she could sleep through her own breathing: each breath was a long loud shudder. Nora was less than a foot away, close enough to lean over and kiss her without leaving her chair, and yet there was nothing she could do to protect her. Soon she would be gone.

33

NORA TOOK THE SUBWAY BACK to Manhattan. She was supposed to meet Isaac later that evening and accompany him to the opening of the photojournalism show, but once she got home, she couldn't bring herself to go out again. She knew it was important to him, but she couldn't face a party that night. She left a message on his answering machine, apologizing and apologizing, and told him that if he wanted to come over later, she'd love to see him. She didn't say anything about Billie. She didn't want to talk about it on his machine.

She put on an ice pack and then went back to work on the Gabriel story. Though she'd sent out a version to the *Atlantic*, she didn't consider it finished.

After she'd been working on the story for an hour, she realized that she might finally be done. She printed out a copy and read it slowly.

She was always surprised by the way she could go over a story a hundred times on the computer screen, convinced she knew it in its every nuance, and then see new problems when she printed it out. The story *wasn't* done. But it was very close. The changes she wanted to make were all minor: providing a better sense of what Jenny looked like; showing that Gabriel was in some way intimidated by his sister's sexuality; describing Gabriel's soft white chewed-up nails. (Isaac had stopped biting his nails, but Gabriel hadn't.) She could finish the story with another hour or two of work.

The phone rang; she answered, but no one was there.

She picked the story up again and wondered whether she really needed to finish it. It wasn't as if she was going to *do* anything with it. Isaac had been having such a rough time. The kindest thing to do would be to spare him the sight of what she'd written. He didn't need to see it; no one did. She'd managed to write it, instead of clamping down on her imagination: that was the important thing.

She went to the closet door and opened it and sat on the floor. There were three cardboard boxes against the wall. One of them contained the five stories she'd published. The second contained stories that she'd tried to publish, but hadn't been able to, at least so far. There were eight stories in that box.

She leaned over and dragged out the third box, which was heavy, filled with paper. It contained stories that she'd never finished, or stories that she'd finished but had decided not to send out into the world. A few were simply misfires, stories that had never found the right shape, but most were things that she hadn't wanted to show to anyone because of the unhappiness they might cause. There was a folder full of notes for the story about Benjamin that she'd never finished, that she'd barely even begun. There was "Problems of the Middle Game," the unfinished story about Daryl and the death of his ambitions to be a chess champion. There was "What She Wasn't," about her old friend Sally Burke. There was a group of connected stories about her high school friend Helen. They were about Helen's family, about the way her father's mental illness had twisted their family life when Helen was young. There was the story about Isaac that she'd begun years ago and never completed. It seemed there was a story, finished or unfinished, about everyone who'd touched her life.

Maybe it was only because of what she'd been through earlier in the day, but she felt sick. It made her sick to think of putting the Gabriel story into the box—burying it as she'd buried all these others, and moving on to a new story that she'd probably bury as well.

She didn't want to do that anymore. If that was what it meant to be good to Isaac, then she couldn't be good to him anymore. She'd have to finish this story, and then she'd have to ask him to read it.

She pushed the box back against the wall and closed the closet door. Then she stood up and tossed the story back onto the card table.

If anyone had been watching her—say, from an apartment in the next building—this would have seemed to be an insignificant moment. It would have seemed to be simply a woman dropping some paper onto a table. But it was more than that.

34

Isaac was chewing on stuffed grape leaves. Mealy, mushy, slick, slimy, sour. Nora was late.

He was in a diner on Forty-second Street. The waitress was a gorgeous dark-eyed Arab girl. He watched her as she leaned over a table, stretching to retrieve someone's plate. She was probably still in her teens.

When a man reaches a certain age, there are no more innocent pleasures. You see an attractive woman down the block, your senses leap, and as she draws closer and you see her more clearly, you suddenly feel like a child molester.

Nora was more than half an hour late. He tried to make himself feel worried. Billie had taken a turn for the worse. Nora herself was sick. He didn't want to believe that she'd simply forgotten about the reception.

If this had happened a month ago, he just would have called her and said, "Where the hell are you? We've got a date." But he couldn't do that tonight. He was still feeling demoralized—because of the failure of his show, because Renee's success had highlighted the limits of his talent. He was feeling weak, meek, mouseified.

And for another reason. Two weeks ago, he'd left a phone message for Nadine Lyle, telling her that he'd spoken to Yehuda Landau, and that, unfortunately but not surprisingly,

Landau had no interest in taking part in the panel discussion in Washington.

He'd expected to get a call from Nadine in response—one of her flattering phone calls, in which she'd thank him for trying and find a few fresh reasons to tell him she thought of him as a god. But she didn't call; instead, she sent him an e-mail, informing him that, because of a regrettable mix-up, one of the other conference organizers had asked someone else to moderate the discussion, so she had to withdraw her invitation to Isaac. But, she assured him, there was another panel that she hoped he'd moderate, "also filled with people who are very prestigious, though perhaps not as known"—people, in fact, whom even he, who had been in this world for two decades, had never heard of. She was offering him a place at the kiddie table.

So he ended up thinking that he'd been had. She'd probably always known that Landau was a friend of his. She'd probably asked him to take part in the discussion in D.C., he thought, only because she hoped he'd deliver Landau. Maybe that was the only reason she'd selected one of his pictures for the show in the first place.

This was probably paranoid. He wouldn't be thinking like this if he weren't feeling so demoralized.

It was time to go. He went to the pay phone near the men's room and called Nora. She answered. Obviously, she'd forgotten about their date.

He didn't say anything.

He remembered the night she'd called him and he'd recognized her silence. She didn't recognize his. He hung up.

Isaac walked east toward the library. It was a cold night in October, the first night that year that truly felt like fall. There was an end-of-everything feeling in the air.

When he got to the library, the reception was already in full swing. The room was dotted with photojournalists, each of whom was in the midst of a little cluster of friends. Photojournalists: a curious tribe. The most successful, the most famous of them were those who had traveled to the world's danger spots. Some of them did it out of political conviction, some out of a sense of journalistic calling, some because it seemed one of the best ways, one of the only ways, for a photographer to become a celebrity. They went into it for many different reasons, but all of them shared a certain style. They all seemed like swashbucklers. Most of them smoked, as if they believed they'd soon meet with violent ends and therefore didn't give a damn about cancer. None of them went so far as to wear safari jackets, but they all *seemed* to be in safari jackets just the same. There were about twenty of them in the room, and there wasn't one of them who couldn't have been a big-game hunter in another life.

The first thing he did, of course, was look for his picture. The photographs were arranged in groups that made no sense to him. "Witnesses," "Visionaries," "Redeemers," "Mourners," "Avengers." How can a photojournalist be an avenger? The tragedy of photojournalism is that you can't avenge anything. You can only watch.

His own photograph was of an elderly victim of the Tuskegee Experiment—in which the government had secretly left untreated a group of syphilitic black men, in order to study the long-term effects of the disease—confronting one of the bureaucrats who'd dreamed it up. He looked through Witnesses and Mourners, and his picture was in neither group. It must have been lumped in with the Redeemers somehow.

But it wasn't among the Redeemers, or the Avengers, or the Visionaries. Or at least he couldn't find it. I must have walked right by myself, he thought. He noticed a table with a stack of brochures about the exhibit, picked one up, and scanned the list of photographers. His name wasn't there.

He leaned against a wall and tried to breathe normally.

A tall and embarrassed-looking young woman in a vest came by, bearing a tray of fried zucchini sticks. As she held it out to him she said something that sounded like, "You look like the one person here who isn't verifying the mumps." He thought of asking her to repeat herself, but he was so disconsolate that he couldn't form the words. He smiled and nodded, hoping that this added up to an appropriate response, and he felt old. This is what old deaf men do: they smile and nod at everything.

He looked around the room for Nadine, but he couldn't see her. Finally he caught sight of her underling, a jolly-bearded man named Freddy. Isaac took another moment to collect himself, and then bore down on him. He was glad to be so tall, glad that he could use his height to intimidate people when he chose to.

"What's the deal here, Freddy? Where's my picture?"

Freddy looked stricken with concern; he had the same expression Isaac's grandmother used to have when Isaac had a fever. "Oh gosh. Oh my gosh. You were supposed to get a fax. There were space problems, and we had to cut about ten pictures out of the show. Don't worry, though—you're still going to be in the book. And the book's the thing that lasts."

"Freddy, that's bad." He put his hands on Freddy's shoulders and for a moment considered picking him up and letting him dangle in the air. But then he remembered that Freddy had nothing to do with the decision, so he let him alone, and Freddy slipped away.

A few minutes ago, he'd been excited about mingling with

the people in the room, but now he felt he didn't belong here. Over the years he'd met a fair number of these people, but though some of them passed their eyes over him, none gave any sign of recognition. It wasn't that they were snubbing him: they didn't remember him. He wasn't important enough to snub.

Nathaniel McCall, who'd made a name for himself with his photographs of the aftermath of ethnic cleansing in Bosnia, was heading Isaac's way. He was a large man with long and lovingly tended hair. For reasons Isaac had never been able to fathom, McCall had always disliked him.

"Hello old man," McCall said. He had somehow acquired an English accent over the last few years. "Wouldn't have expected to see you here. Are you still with—what is it? The *Bergen Bugle*?"

The insult was like a chess move you couldn't parry. The name of the paper was the *North Jersey Register*, so if Isaac were to correct him, he'd merely be humiliating himself a second time.

If you can't parry an attack, launch one of your own. "How are you, Nathaniel? Still carrying around that curling iron?"

Nathaniel, a legendary fop, had traveled to North Korea for *Newsweek* at a time when relations with the United States were particularly tense, and when the border guards had come upon a portable hair dryer in his luggage, its vague resemblance to a gun had given them a (completely spurious) excuse to detain him for two days.

"I'm serious, Isaac. I've often wondered about you. I'm really curious as to why you decided to hide your light under a bushel."

Isaac began to search for a comeback, but then decided that it wasn't worth it. McCall must not have gotten the news that I'm not even worth being hostile to anymore, Isaac thought. He patted him on the arm and walked away.

He ended up at the bar and ordered his usual: club soda. He liked to order club soda rather than, say, Coke, because it seemed more romantic. A man who orders a club soda, one must assume, is an alcoholic, waging a lonely war against his demons. He'd never quite been an alcoholic, but he wasn't above playing the lonely tragic haunted alcoholic card—as feeble as it was, since no one was watching.

Someone was waving to him. Earl, his former assistant, Renee's semi-boyfriend. Earl was here.

He was wearing overalls and a Nike cap. He looked like a country bumpkin, gawking at the city slickers, all agog. He looked as if he was astounded to be in a room where there was free food.

"Wow," he said to Isaac. "Great party."

Isaac had invited Renee and Earl to the show a few weeks ago. He'd invited Earl only because he wanted Renee to come, and if you asked one you had to ask both. He'd thought—this was before Renee got her *New Yorker* news—that she'd be impressed. He'd had a fond picture of Nora and Renee standing next to him, bearing witness to his success, bearing witness to the fact that he was good enough to play with the big kids. Which, it had turned out, he wasn't.

"Renee asked me to tell you she's sorry she couldn't be here. She's leaving for Indonesia on Sunday and she has a lot of packing to do." He tugged on his cap, looking like Huntz Hall in the old Bowery Boys movies, except that Huntz Hall used to wear a beanie. "Man," he said. "This is great."

Isaac felt embarrassed to be standing here with him. Where was Nora? Where was Renee? How had he ended up like this—squiring around a coarse twenty-three-year-old boy at a social function where you're supposed to have an interesting woman on your arm?

Isaac was actually glad that Nora and Renee weren't here to witness his evening of defeat. But he would have liked it if Earl wasn't here either.

Isaac finished his club soda, excused himself, and went to the men's room. When he returned, Earl had a drink in his hand and was chumming around in a little cluster of young people. He'd already made friends. Isaac felt relieved, because Earl was off his hands, but also strangely angry: insulted, because Earl had already found some other grown-ups, assuredly more successful than Isaac, to latch on to.

Someone had made a joke, and Earl was laughing, with a high, horselike laugh. Maybe later he'll bark like a dog for them, Isaac thought, and felt ashamed of himself.

Another young woman came around with a tray; she looked arch and remote.

"What are those?" Isaac said, grinning, trying to flirt, although "What are those?" wasn't much of a line.

"Stuffed mushrooms," she said. "They're superb." And then, before he could take one, she moved on.

She was probably heading over to McCall—hurrying, so the mushrooms wouldn't cool off before he could taste them.

Earl seemed to be at home around the "superb" hors d'oeuvres and the inflated reputations. No, Isaac thought, that idea was not only unkind, it was inaccurate. Even if some of these photographers weren't as good as their reputations, the fact was that they'd stuck with it, as he hadn't. They deserved their success.

He finally spotted Nadine, but he didn't approach her. She

was talking with a man he didn't recognize, a broodingly unshaven man in his twenties. Although he looked quite grave, she was laughing at something he'd said. She threw her head back, baring her throat in a gesture of animal invitation.

Susan Becker, an editor from the *Boston Globe,* came up to say hello, and she and Isaac small-talked for a few minutes. Isaac had always liked her; she reminded him of his sister.

Susan was unhappy because three people who worked for her were leaving: two to have babies, one to travel the world. "If you hear of anybody good who needs a job, let me know."

"Do they have to have experience?"

"Young, old. Doesn't matter. They have to be competent, and they have to be reliable. No flakes. But that's about it."

The job would be perfect for Earl. The *Globe* would be a great place to start off. And he could handle it. He was a talented, hardworking, responsible young man.

When Isaac was in his twenties, he'd once said to his sister that every time he'd gotten a break in life, it was because one old Jewish guy or another had helped him out. "What'll I do when they're all gone?" "By that time," his sister had said, "you'll *be* the old Jewish guy."

Glancing over Susan's shoulder, Isaac could see that Earl was still having a fine time, and he realized that he didn't feel like doing him a favor.

"If I think of anybody, I'll let you know," he said.

There are times when you know what you should do, but you don't do it. During the two years it took him to quit smoking, almost every time he picked up a cigarette he would think, "This is wrong," and then he would light it.

The opening, the public part of the event, was coming to an end; the dinner, which was invitation-only, was beginning.

People were beginning to drift off toward the dining room. Isaac didn't want to go in. He thought he'd just give the ticket to Earl.

"Well, buddy," he said, "I've got to get going a little early. Why don't you take this." He gave him the ticket.

"Really?" Earl said.

"Really."

"I can't believe this. You're awesome!"

The poor kid had no way of knowing that Isaac had screwed him. Would never know.

"You're a true mentor," Earl said.

Isaac shook his hand, leaning backward to ward off a possible hug.

After he left the building, walking past one of the great stone lions, he thought that he'd not only let Earl down, he'd let himself down. He had obeyed his baser instincts.

If Earl had been a young woman, would Isaac have done the same thing? If he'd been an attractive young woman...?

He remembered how, a few weeks ago, he'd forced himself to behave generously toward Renee—forced himself to appear delighted by her success—and how, at the end of that evening, he'd felt a little more human.

He turned around and went up to the dining room, found Earl, found Susan Becker, and introduced them. "Here's your man," Isaac said, clapping Earl on the back with a false heartiness.

Leaving the building for the second time, he didn't feel better. He felt worse. He would have felt better if he'd hurt someone. Nadine, Freddy, McCall, Earl, Susan. Almost anyone.

35

HE FOUND A PAY PHONE on the corner, called his answering machine, and got Nora's message. She'd remembered the exhibit after all; she'd just been too tired to attend it. He didn't know if that made him feel better or worse.

She'd invited him over. He took the subway to the Upper West Side—his car was in the shop. Nora's doorman, Arthur, greeted him by name, and Isaac had to be personable.

When he got out of the elevator, Nora had her door open. She was leaning against the doorjamb, looking welcoming but tired.

"Hi," she said. "I'm really sorry about the library thing. I'm glad you came."

He nodded. Somehow her calling it "the library thing" made him angrier.

"How was it? What did I miss?"

"You missed some superb mushrooms."

"How was Nadine? Did she spend the whole night flirting with you?"

"Nadine. Yes. Nadine and I are thick as thieves."

The upright bass he'd picked up for his nephew was still in the corner—he kept forgetting to take it to his brother's, though he lived only about fifteen blocks away. Against the wall, sitting on its little card table, Nora's computer was on. She had a

Star Trek screensaver: silver stars slipping slowly through space. To the right of the computer was a stack of printed pages. He thought of Nora at her computer, thoughtfully replacing a semicolon with a comma while he waited for her at the diner, his mouth full of mushy wet grape leaves.

"You been writing?"

"Yeah." She swept her hand in the air in a gesture that seemed to indicate the poetic difficulty of writing.

She'd been too tired to join him at what they both thought would be a special occasion for him, but she hadn't been too tired to write.

"You know, I haven't read anything of yours in a long time," he said.

"I know," she said. "I know."

"Why don't you let me read what you're writing?" *Let me see what was so much more important than coming to the reception with me.*

"It's funny you should ask. I was just thinking I'd like you to read it." She didn't look as though she'd been thinking this; in fact she looked as if the idea made her ill.

He was oddly disappointed. It was as if he'd wanted her to say no, so he could have another reason to be angry with her.

"Great," he said. He walked toward the card table.

"I didn't mean *now.*"

"Why not? If not now, when?"

"If not now, later. It'll be weird being in the same room while you're reading it. I'll wonder what you're thinking about every sentence."

"I'm sure I'll be loving every sentence."

He didn't know what he was after. He wanted the story to be great or terrible. If it was great, he could punish himself with the reflection that Nora, like Renee, was artistically out of his league—the thought of how untalented he was. If it was terrible, he could be angry with her for staying home to write instead of keeping her date with him.

He picked up the story and sat on the couch.

"I can't sit here while you're reading," she said. "I'm too nervous. I have to take a walk."

"Okay." He looked down at the story and then looked up at her again. She seemed to have more to say. "Yes?"

"I need you to keep in mind that it's a story. And I need you to keep an open mind. I know you're going to have your reactions, but I hope you won't make up your mind what you think about it until we talk."

"Fine. Of course." He was beginning to wonder what he'd gotten into.

She picked up her wallet. "I'll be at the bookstore. I'll see you in half an hour."

She left, and he read the first paragraph of her story. It was about him.

He read the story slowly. When he read the first page, he was flattered. She was describing his appearance, and she evidently thought he didn't look bad. She'd always *told* him she thought he was handsome, but you can never be sure.

When he got to the third and fourth and fifth pages, he was touched. She was writing about him and his sister. She'd never met Jenny, but she'd captured her on the page. He was touched that Nora had listened so well; he was touched that she cared enough about him to put him at the center of a story.

When he came to the middle of the story, he started to feel uneasy.

When he had finished the story, he felt stunned. Stunned and unloved and alone.

The story was about the trip he took to New Haven to

reason with Jenny about her decision to join the cult. Nothing in the story took place the way things had actually happened. The train had never broken down; the friends of Jenny's who'd cowed Isaac into silence didn't exist. But at the same time, Nora's intuitions were uncanny. His failure of nerve hadn't taken the form it took in the story, but he *had* had a failure of nerve. And he *had* let Jenny down.

He closed his eyes and thought about the way it had really happened—the argument about the cheeseburger, the lost keys. The way things had really happened was so undramatic that a year from now he'd probably remember Nora's version more vividly than his own.

The most horrible thing was not the account of the visit, but what Nora seemed to be saying about it. She seemed to see his failure with Jenny as an emblem of his entire life. She had taken his life and shown it in the worst possible light.

If she was so eerily accurate about what had happened that night—about the feel of it, if not the facts—could she be wrong about his life, wrong about who he was?

Over the past few months, although she'd never mentioned it, Nora must have noticed that he wasn't taking pictures anymore. She'd stopped asking him about his plans for future work; it had certainly been a long time since she'd called him anything like a "touchstone." But since she'd never said anything, he had allowed himself to believe that maybe, just maybe, she hadn't realized that he wasn't a practicing artist anymore, that maybe she still respected him.

The story made it clear that she didn't. The person in the story, "Gabriel," was a man who, in the end, lacked strength and conviction. He'd had both when he was young, but he'd let them leak away.

This was what she'd been working on for the last few months, while he thought they'd been falling unbreakably in love. This was why she hadn't joined him at the reception. While Nadine was ignoring him and McCall was insulting him, Nora had been injuring him in a much more intimate way.

He'd never believed that she could write a hurtful story about him. And he'd underestimated her power to wound him. He hadn't read *1984* since high school, but he'd never forgotten the part about Room 101: how the torturers had a way of fitting their torture to each victim, finding precisely the assault that would make each person crack. Nora, he now thought, or the demon that resided inside her—the goblin, as she called it—had the power to ferret out that one thing you feared might be true about yourself, the thing you hoped nobody else had noticed.

He heard the key in the lock. Very softly, Nora pushed open the door. She had an expression of nervousness and concern, and maybe a tiny sliver of hope.

"Did you read it?"

"Oh yes."

"Are you upset?"

"Oh yes."

"Isaac—you need to know that this isn't what I think of you. This is just what happens when I write. I see things one way, and the stories see them all another way. It's something I can't control. The difference between you and Gabriel is that Gabriel *ends* there. I know your life didn't end there."

The more she apologized, the worse he felt. He didn't believe her. The voice you could hear in her story was her truest voice.

If he had read it at another time, it might not have hurt so much. But tonight it was unendurable. For more than a month now, the world had been letting him know that he just wasn't good enough. Up until now he'd been learning that he wasn't good enough as an artist, but Nora's story was telling him that he wasn't good enough as a man.

In her story, Gabriel, too timid to say what he wanted to say to his sister, had thought that his shortcomings as a man and an artist grew from the same root. *You need to have a little wildness in you, which is the one thing I don't have*: those were the words that Nora had put in Gabriel's head.

Her computer was sitting placidly on her card table, waiting for her to turn her unique form of attention to someone else.

Whenever you visited her, Nora's computer was on. She never turned the fucking thing off. You'd be having what you thought was an intimate conversation, but all the while it would be sitting there humming away, so you could never forget that it was her work Nora was committed to, not you.

He felt like smashing it.

He walked over to the window. He could see the river, sleek and dark, and, beyond it, the lights of New Jersey, blinking with a provincial ardor.

She smiled at him sadly. "Would you jump off this roof for me?" she said. As she'd said to him years ago. It was as if she was asking him to sacrifice himself for her in a new way: asking him to forgive her for writing about him without charity.

What was she alive for? What was the point of her? She moved through the world doing her little acts of saintly care—giving blood on her birthday, moving in with her aunt—but then at night she'd go home to her computer and shit on the people she claimed to love.

He was getting angrier and angrier.

Isaac was a careful man, even on the rare occasions when he lost control: he prepared to lose control before he lost it. He knew that Nora's window didn't overlook the sidewalk or the street but the roof of a smaller building. Now he glanced outside to make sure the roof was empty.

"Probably not," he said. "But I'd *throw* things off the roof for you."

He picked up her story from the couch where he'd laid it, stepped quickly to the window, and tossed it, underhand, like a bride tossing a bouquet. Before he let go, he imagined that the pages would flutter gracefully, one by one, through the night sky, but instead they went straight down in a clump.

"Okay," Nora said. "I deserve that."

"You know, Nora, I might have a little more wildness in me than you think." He picked up the computer and pulled the plug out of the wall.

"Come on. Put that down." She moved toward him.

"You've been complaining about this thing for months. Why don't I help you out?" He headed back toward the window. He was feeling a jolt of macho joy, as if he were about to make a monster slam dunk. Pseudo-macho joy, since the path to the basket was blocked only by Nora. She moved in front of the window, putting out her hands to try to stop him from raising the laptop over his head, and for a moment he thought they were going to knock each other out the window, that they would die that way, and in the next moment he thought he'd drop the computer and embrace her and they'd make love, and then he just leaned over her and lobbed it, in a soft, heavy arc, into the night.

There was a silence, and then they heard it, faintly, breaking. The sound wasn't as satisfying as he would have liked.

"Jesus Christ. You could have killed somebody."

He didn't tell her that she was wrong, that he knew there was nobody down there. He wanted her to think that he'd been, for once, reckless.

She was standing there with an expression of childlike disbelief. She looked terribly tired; she looked like a frail, unhappy creature, and it struck him that although she was younger than he was, he wouldn't be at all surprised if he outlasted her. He wouldn't be surprised if he someday had to endure a world in which there was no Nora.

He wondered why she was so tired, and then remembered that she'd been spending all her days and nights at Billie's, and thought guiltily that he hadn't even asked after Billie.

Looking at her, so tired, so small, he wanted to take everything back, he wanted to tell her he loved her. He opened his arms and took a step toward her. She backed away. She looked like an animal who'd been placed in a cage with a dangerous larger animal.

It was amazing that this could happen. That after everything, the two of them could reach a point where if he took a step toward her she responded with instinctive animal fear.

"Oh God," he said.

He didn't know what else to say, so without saying anything else, he left.

36

IN THE CROWDED SUBWAY CAR, he wondered how he could have been so stupid. Not because of what he'd just done, but because he'd let her back into his life in the first place. And because he'd been longing for her for all these years. After that miserable afternoon five years ago, he should have known they had no future.

Five years ago, on the day of the abortion, a freezing day with a splattery intermittent rain, he had heaved himself, heavily bundled, into the cab, feeling pale and ill. Beside him, she was oddly bright and chipper, gossiping away about people they knew, and he couldn't understand how she could be taking it so lightly. He understood that she might *not* be taking it lightly—that this might be her way of masking how gravely she was taking it. But he wasn't sure.

The cabbie was insane; he hunched himself over the steering wheel and jerked wildly through the traffic.

Isaac tapped the partition. "Can you go a little slower?"

"Don't be afraid," the cabbie had said. "There is no fear. In Lebanon we fought the tanks with only droomsticks."

Isaac assumed he meant broomsticks, but he wasn't interested enough to inquire. Nostalgia mixed with racism: he had a spasm of longing for the mythical New York cabbie of the

1950s—a guy with a Brooklyn accent, who knew every street in all five boroughs, who drove like a mensch, and who dispensed wise homilies along the way. If only they'd had that kind of cabbie, Isaac thought, they'd never end up at the abortion clinic: they'd be on the way back to Nora's apartment by now, cheerfully swapping ideas about what to name the baby.

Nora, on the cab ride, which he felt as a ride to their doom, or the doom of someone they were meant to bring into the world together, was chirping away brightly about nothing. He would never forget the stupidity of the things she was talking about. A block away from the clinic, she was talking about how she wished that screwdrivers weren't her favorite drink, because they were really only a summer drink rather than something you could drink year-round—he couldn't believe that she was talking about such shit at a moment like this. He remembered thinking that maybe he didn't really *get* her: maybe her magnificence was just his delusion, something he only thought he saw. He wanted to believe that she was concealing herself, hiding out from him in the thickets of the trivial; he couldn't believe that this side of her was genuine.

He got out of the cab with her, though she'd told him that she didn't want him to accompany her into the clinic. He couldn't stop himself from making one more attempt to change her mind.

"Think about it," he'd said. "We could bring a new person into existence."

The remark didn't have the intended effect. "I just want to bring myself into existence," she'd said. "That seems like enough work for this lifetime.'

He didn't want to think about this anymore. He took the subway to Port Authority and waited there for a bus to New Jersey. Nora was probably at her card table, writing by hand, beginning a new story, about a forty-year-old man who throws temper tantrums.

37

After he left she sat there for a long time. She couldn't blame him for being mad.

She wondered if there was any way she could make it up to him. She didn't know if there was.

Maybe I'm a wicked person, she thought.

She still couldn't believe he'd done that with the computer. At least she had everything backed up. Ever since the time Helen's son had zapped one of her stories out of existence, she'd saved everything compulsively onto floppy disks.

She found a copy of the version that she'd submitted to the contest a few weeks earlier. It was different from the version Isaac had read, but close enough. She went through it slowly, lingering over the lines that must have hurt him. She was appalled by her own cluelessness: how had she *expected* him to react?

After a few more minutes, without quite realizing what was happening, she stopped thinking about Isaac and became absorbed in the problems of the story. There were still those passages that she needed to add. She got out a pen and a yellow legal pad and started working on a description of Gabriel's badly bitten nails and his doomed, deluded hope that he'd someday find the strength of character to stop biting them.

38

IT WAS TEN O'CLOCK WHEN he got back to New Jersey. He stopped off at a liquor store and bought a bottle of Irish whiskey—because, he thought as he took it down from the shelf, I am a fucking phony, and in the days when I used to drink I always used to drink Irish whiskey, pretending that I liked it more than Scotch whiskey, which tastes the same.

When he got home he poured himself a tall glass and drank it quickly, and poured himself another tall glass and drank it quickly, and then turned on the TV.

The phone rang. Nora. It had to be Nora. She was calling to say that she'd also been writing another story during these last few months, a story that showed his strength of character...

The machine answered it before he could. It was Renee. She was saying something about how she was leaving for her fact-finding tour on Sunday and she was hoping they could meet somewhere for one last cup of herbal tea and also she wanted to give him back his Kertész book and she thought he might have been home tonight but how silly of her because it was a Friday, and come to think of it he must still be at the reception and she hoped he was having a great time—and so on and so on. He didn't pick up.

Renee. Renee was the hope for the world.

Renee was at least as dedicated as Nora was, and she would almost certainly be more successful. She was more successful already. And she was also more humane. Nora's art was an art of caricature; Renee's was an art of conscience.

Renee was the future. The future! He lifted his glass in a toast to the future.

He would do better than that. He would toast the future in person. Renee was home. He tried to call her, but he kept getting a busy signal. She was a no-frills kind of girl: no call waiting, no voice mail. The last busy signal in America.

Well, he could drop by. He could do the pop in. Renee lived only two towns away; several times he'd dropped her off after work. Maneuvering himself drunkenly up from the couch, he found his keys and put on a jacket. Then he remembered that he didn't have his car—but this was actually a good thing, because he was too drunk to drive. He decided to take his bicycle. He thought of putting on his helmet, but he decided not to, in order to spite Nora. Because she obviously thought of him as the kind of man who would never ride a bike without a helmet.

He hated the fact that he was thinking about Nora even now. Forget her. Think about Renee.

He thought about how nice it would be to get close to her—her youth, her hopefulness, her newly blossoming beauty.

He reached her apartment and stood outside. She lived on the first floor in a garden apartment complex. Her lights were on.

He saw her. She was moving around in her kitchen. He couldn't see what she was doing.

You could walk in and change everyone's life. You could walk in and tell her you love her.

She was the future. Let her live. Let her live.

He stood on the lawn, his hands in his pockets against the cold. The night was alive; columns of crackly leaves were spiraling and swirling all around him.

There was a voice in his head saying: Come on, man, your relationship with her is the only purely good thing in your life. Don't fuck it up.

He wished he were a reckless man who would go in there and fuck up everyone's life or else a saint who wouldn't even consider it, but here he was, standing outside Renee's window, Mr. In-Between, thinking that he wanted to hold her, thinking that she was the future, thinking that this was insane, she was someone else's future, not his.

He rang her doorbell. She came to the door.

"Hi," he said.

"Hi." He could see ten different emotions and questions passing across her face. Her wonderfully expressive face. "Are you okay?"

"I don't know," he said.

"How was the reception?"

"The reception was fabu." He tried to remember if that was a word that young people used. He'd had an assistant who'd used it a lot, but that was five years ago. "I saw your friend Earl. He says howdy."

She asked him to come in. He kept a distance from her, hoping she wouldn't realize how drunk he was.

"Sit down. Sit down. Can I help you? I mean, can I get you anything? Can I get you a beer?"

"You shouldn't have beer on the premises, young lady. You're not old enough. I'll have to report you to the authorities." A lame jest, but maybe it was his subconscious trying to restore order, trying to place an obstacle between them, trying to prevent him from doing anything stupid.

"I actually am," she said. "I turned twenty-one this summer, you know." He was surprised she was that young. He'd thought she was twenty-three.

She peered into her refrigerator. "Bass Ale or Rheingold?"

"Rheingold?" he said. "I didn't think they still made Rheingold."

"It's a very manly beer," she said. "I must have known you were coming."

He didn't know what that meant. Was she insulting him? He tended to feel insecure about his manliness. One woman he'd gone out with had told him he was womanly. She'd meant it as a compliment, supposedly, but it hadn't made him happy at all.

But he tried to tell himself that Renee had just been making a harmless, meaningless joke.

"What's going on?" she said. "You look a little down."

She was concerned about him. Bless her darling heart.

She brought out two beers and sat next to him on the couch. She was wearing shorts and a short-sleeved shirt, unbuttoned, over a leotard. She sat facing him, in some sort of modified lotus thing, so that both of her knees were almost touching his thigh. It was impossible to tell whether she knew she was being provocative. She might have been too innocent to know, too trusting even to imagine that he was thinking of her with desire.

He was moved by this, he was touched by this, leave leave leave leave leave! Get out of here! Don't curse her with your life! She trusts you! Don't fuck it up!

These thoughts were going through his mind, but with such sloshing slipshod sloppiness that he couldn't focus on them. And at the same time another current of thought was guiding him in a different direction. She's *here,* man! You're in her *house*! Look at the way she's leaning toward you! She wants you! She's of age! What are these inane scruples? What are you, a Victorian? Even the Victorians didn't really act like Victorians! You just read a book review about that! Kiss her, man! She's kissable! She *wants* to be kissed!

He felt like a cartoon character, with a little angel perched on one shoulder and a little devil on the other.

Talk to her first. Talk, then kiss. Tell her about your disappointment that your show didn't lead to anything. Tell her that you're a tiny bit envious of her success. Tell her that you hope she has the success you never had.

"Have you ever felt that life is just...what am I talking about? I can't ask you if you've ever felt the way a forty-something-year-old man feels."

"Of course you can," she said. "Don't be silly. We all feel the same things."

We all feel the same things. She said it herself. She wants me to kiss her.

No she doesn't. She's too innocent to be thinking that at all.

"Did you ever think you took a wrong turn somewhere, and you can't go back?" He wasn't sure what he was talking about, except that he was mad at himself for having given so many of his years to the worship of Nora.

"That's a terrible way to think," Renee said. "I don't believe it. No matter how many wrong turns you make, you can always go in a new direction. As long as you're alive."

"Maybe it finally gets too late."

"I don't believe that," she said. "If I believed that, I wouldn't want to keep living. And I do want to keep living. Passionately."

Passionately. You can enter another universe, just by leaning forward. You move from one moral universe into another, just like that.

I can't kiss her. I can't do it. I shouldn't do it.

You need to have a little wildness in you, which is the one thing I don't have.

To hell with Nora. She was wrong about him. He'd prove she was wrong.

Renee was sitting next to him, and there was an invitation in her eyes, he was sure of it, and he leaned forward and kissed her.

As soon as he kissed her, as drunk as he was, he could tell that this wasn't what she'd wanted. She was returning his kiss, but he could tell that she didn't want to.

She was kissing him to be polite.

They brought their lips apart and he opened his eyes and she was looking at him with . . . he didn't know what it was, but it wasn't happiness, so to blot out the sight of it he kissed her again. He pulled her toward him; he had never realized how delicate she was. Birdlike bones. Her mouth was communicating nothing now. Deadness.

Having started, he didn't know how to stop. He had made the mistake, and now he couldn't take it back; all he could do was keep kissing her, in the hope that some combination of kisses would unlock her desire.

Somehow he was pinning her against the back of the couch. He hadn't meant to; it wasn't passion, it was more like a drunken lurch. He remembered Ellen Barkin and Al Pacino in *Sea of Love,* the way they'd hurled each other against walls, that's how hot for each other they were. This did not resemble that.

She put her hand on his chest. He had known her for almost a year, had noticed many times the expressiveness of her hands, and now she was resting one hand familiarly on his chest. "Excuse me," she said. She went to the bathroom.

He leaned back on the couch. What's going on here? He wondered if she was putting her diaphragm in. Jesus. His head was spinning. He looked at her CD rack. Bands he'd never heard of. The Palace Brothers. Death Cab for Cutie. Modest Mouse. *What am I doing here?*

He picked up a book from the end table. Marguerite Duras. For someone who was so politically committed, Renee had unusually avant-garde tastes in literature. He wished there were something easier to read—*Entertainment Weekly* or something. But she wouldn't have *Entertainment Weekly.* She was too serious for that. He opened the book, read a few sentences, couldn't follow. Looked at the title. *The Malady of Death.* What the hell did that mean? Death is a bit more than a malady, I should think. He was proud of himself for mentally employing formulations such as "I should think" when he was drunk and waiting for his twenty-one-year-old lover to come out of the bathroom.

Lover? The word didn't fit. Renee was his spiritual daughter, his protected one, his dear one—what was he thinking? He needed to tell her this was all wrong.

He sat there with a growing headache, looking through Marguerite Duras.

Five pages passed, and then ten. He kept waiting to hear water running in the bathroom, but he couldn't hear anything.

He thought of asking her if she was all right, but he didn't want to be intrusive. Maybe she had a stomach virus.

Finally he went up to the bathroom door.

"Renee?"

No answer.

He knocked on the door.

No answer.

He tried the knob. The door was locked.

There was a rustling sound; a piece of paper was emerging from beneath the door. It was a page of a book. *The Cultural Turn,* by Fredric Jameson. At the top of the page, in Renee's tiny, splintery handwriting, were the words "PLEASE GO HOME."

He felt stupid. He didn't know what to say.

He stood there for another minute. For lack of anything better to do, he read a sentence from the book. "This grand moment of Theory (which some claim now also to have ended) in fact confirmed Hegel's premonitions by taking as its central theme the dynamics of representation itself: one cannot imagine a classical Hegelian supersession of art by philosophy otherwise than by just such a return of consciousness (and self-consciousness) back on the figuration and the figural dynamics that constitute the aesthetic, in order to dissolve those into the broad daylight and transparency of praxis itself."

What the fuck?

He heard the sound of a page being torn, and then another page made its way under the door.

On this one, Renee had simply written "PLEASE."

He thought that maybe he would stand there all night, and she could keep passing him notes telling him to go away, and he would read the notes, and then he would read the page of Fredric Jameson, and in the morning he would be able to discuss postmodernism.

That probably wasn't the best idea.

"Sorry," he said. He wasn't sure if he'd said it loud enough for her to hear. He thought of writing *her* a note—two could play the old mark-up-Fredric-Jameson game. But then he thought he should just leave. "I'm sorry, Renee," he said, louder, but she didn't say anything back.

He went outside and got on his bicycle and set off toward home. He'd humiliated himself, and he'd humiliated her too. He was sure she would have liked to think of herself as someone who could have handled a situation like that with more poise. He'd forced her to reveal a side of herself that was just a scared kid.

Or maybe he'd only humiliated himself.

He was sailing through the cool night streets. The front wheel of his bicycle seemed a little off-kilter. He thought he should get off the bike and check the wheel to see if it needed air. Just give it a squeeze. You could probably tell if it needed air just by tapping it with your foot. He was going down a slight incline; he took his left foot off the pedal and gave the tire a slight tap, and only as he was doing this did it occur to him that this would make the bicycle twist out from under him. He was riding his bike, and then his bike was riding him, and then he was lying in the road, and something had happened to his face.

He managed to make it over to the sidewalk, dragging the bike. His face was reverberating. It hurt so much that he couldn't tell which parts of it he'd hurt.

There was blood all over the sidewalk. His nose was bleeding; his mouth was bleeding. He hoped he hadn't lost any teeth.

Isaac's grandmother, who had died many years ago, had suffered terribly from her ill-fitting dentures, and once, when he was eight or nine, she had solemnly, even desperately, told him to take good care of his teeth. That was the only piece of advice she'd ever given him, or the only one he remembered. Drunk, stunned, splayed out on the sidewalk, Isaac reflected remorsefully that he'd let his poor grandmother down.

He examined his bicycle. It seemed to be in one piece. He needed to get to an emergency room. No—that wasn't a good idea. They'd arrest him for drunk driving.

It took him a moment to reason this out and to realize that you don't get arrested for drunkenly driving a bicycle.

He picked up his bicycle—it still worked—and wobbled toward home. He could go to the hospital tomorrow. He didn't care that he was in pain, or that he might have messed up his face. What he cared about was that he'd messed things up with Renee.

With another young woman, the mistake might not mean much. It might mean everything with Renee. He knew that he occupied some paternal place in her mind. He'd always known it, but that hadn't prevented him from fucking things up. She'd looked up to him, she'd trusted him—much more than he deserved.

She was a funny combination of moralism and vulnerability—maybe not such an unusual combination, actually—and he could easily imagine her deciding never to see him again.

When he was a kid there was a damp little boy down the block named Ross, who, whenever he made an error on the baseball field, would start pleading for a do-over. Isaac used to have contempt for him: he didn't believe in do-overs. But he wished with all his heart that he could ask for a do-over now.

If he could erase the last hour, then the thirty years ahead would be different for both him and Renee. The next thirty years could become again what they were always supposed to be: a time in which they would cultivate a trusting, lasting friendship. That was impossible now.

It was amazing, the way thirty years can be irrevocably altered by one bonehead move.

39

NORA WENT OUT TO RIVERSIDE every evening. Billie was rarely strong enough to talk for more than a few minutes. With the strength she had, she'd tell Nora what she'd dreamed the night before. One night she dreamed that Fiorello LaGuardia was the mayor again and that he was building beautiful homes for the poor. Another night she dreamed that the whole city had become a park, with no cars, no factories, just land for everyone to picnic in. Her dreams were getting larger as she herself was dwindling away.

Listening to one of Billie's dreams one day, Nora thought that maybe the point of life was to send one dream into the mind of the universe. Everything else in your life is incidental to the dreaming of that dream, but you can't know which one it is.

Billie's skin lesions had grotesquely blossomed: the boils had given birth to baby boils. Until recently her face had remained untouched, but now they'd spread there too. One of the boils, large and swollen, was just below her left eye, so that the eye could barely open; another was spreading over her lips. They were painful, so that everything she did was an ordeal.

Nora had brought Billie's cats uptown, to her own place. She wasn't happy about it—the cleanliness of cats was a big myth, and she knew they'd inevitably stink up her apartment. But there was nothing else to be done.

She bought a Polaroid camera and every day before she left for Riverside, she took pictures of the cats to give to Billie.

One night when Nora came home, Dolly wasn't breathing. Louie and Edwin were off in the other room, unconcerned. Nora called an animal hospital on Broadway and they confirmed that they disposed of dead animals. She tried to brush Dolly's fur one last time, but it was hard work—her coat was matted and gnarled. Although it made no sense, she felt as if she was hurting her, and put the brush away. Then she put her in a plastic shopping bag and carried her to the animal hospital. She could feel her little body through the bag, sliding around formlessly, a mess of bones.

She wished she hadn't inaugurated the tradition of bringing pictures to Billie. When she went to Riverside the next day she showed Billie pictures of Edwin and Louie. Billie looked up, and Nora nodded. Very slowly, Billie reached out to her night table, where the previous days' pictures were stacked, and she found a picture of Dolly. She ran her finger over it slowly. "She used to be so glamorous," she said.

BILLIE WAS SHARING A ROOM with an old Frenchwoman named Juliette. Skin cancer had eaten away at the left side of Juliette's face. She looked as if an animal had attacked her and chewed all the way down to the bone. But she was inexplicably cheerful, and she usually had enough strength to talk. One day when Billie was sleeping, Juliette propped herself up in bed and asked, "Is that your mother?" It sounded more like "muzzer."

"My aunt."

"She's a courageous woman."

"Why do you say so?"

"She was in great pain last night. I could see that. But she didn't complain."

Nora thought she should make conversation with this woman, as long as she was there.

"Have you been here long?" Nora said. She couldn't think of anything else to say.

Juliette managed a small laugh. "I don't think anyone stays here very long."

LATER THAT DAY BILLIE OPENED her eyes for a little while; she even tried to sit up.

"I'm not having much fun," she said, in a dry, cracked voice.

"I know," Nora said. "I wish there was something I could do to make it easier."

NO ONE BUT NORA VISITED Billie; no one at all visited Juliette.

While Billie slept, struggling miserably for each breath, Nora talked to Juliette. Juliette told her her life story. She had worked as a teacher at the High School for Performing Arts in Manhattan after coming to New York in the 1940s and marrying a man from the Bronx. Her husband had been a college teacher—"a professor," she said proudly—and had died twenty years ago.

Billie's one love had also died decades ago. Within the city, Nora thought, there's another city, a city of old women living alone.

"Oscar and I were democratic socialists. We spent our life

fighting for a dream." Juliette waved her hand weakly, indicating Nora-didn't-know-what. "It doesn't look like we did very well. But it's still a good dream, you know."

"Are you trying to recruit me for the cause?"

This made Juliette smile. "No. I don't know. Maybe I am."

ONE AFTERNOON BILLIE WOKE suddenly, with a worried expression. She didn't move or speak, but she looked as though she was thinking intensely. Nora asked her if she needed anything, but she didn't respond.

"Did you feed Dolly today?" she finally said.

Nora didn't know if Billie had forgotten that Dolly died, or if she hadn't understood it in the first place.

Nora didn't say anything; she just smiled.

"It has to be the gourmet tuna fish," Billie said.

40

BILLIE HAD BEEN PUT ON A morphine drip, and she slept about twenty hours a day now. When she was sleeping, Nora talked to Juliette; when Billie and Juliette were both sleeping, Nora sometimes left the room and talked to other patients. Coming here day after day, she got to know them. There was Mr. Arnold, a man in his nineties, who kept telling her the same story about the college football exploits of his son. There was Mr. Ursino, in the last stage of esophageal cancer, who told her, in a croaking voice, that he had no regrets, because a life without cigars wouldn't have been worth living. Sometimes he begged Nora to smuggle some in for him. "Anything. It doesn't have to be my Cubans. I'm not proud anymore. Just get me a pack of Tiparillos." Nora couldn't bring him cigars, but she could sit with him and listen to him talk about how much he loved them. That, she hoped, was something.

One by one, each in his own way. A man named Mr. Allan, with pancreatic cancer, talked nonstop about how badly he'd been "fucked" in life. His wife, his kids, his bosses: everyone had fucked him; everyone, he told Nora, had fucked him up the ass. She wanted to leave the room, but she made herself stay. She thought she might be helping him by letting him talk.

"Listen," he said to her, "I have one last wish." He smiled

at her with a touching air of hopefulness. He motioned with his index finger; she moved her chair a little closer, and he gathered up his strength to bring his mouth toward her ear. "Here it is," he said. "Before I go, I'd love to piss all over your face, you ugly bitch."

Nora left the room. She tried to find some compassion in herself for this man, and couldn't.

She didn't encounter anyone else like Mr. Allan. Most of the patients at Riverside, if they were strong enough and lucid enough to talk, were grateful to have someone to talk to. A few of them, men and women, were strangely flirtatious, as if they thought that if they could prove themselves attractive to a young person, then death wouldn't come for them yet.

Every evening, when she entered Billie's room, Nora was brought close to tears of gratitude, fierce wild gratitude, to see that she was still alive. This gratitude didn't surprise her. What surprised her were the feelings that came over her even with people she didn't know. Talking to the other patients here, people she'd just met, she felt overwhelmingly, shockingly *aware* of them, in some way she couldn't define. It was as though whatever animated each of them, whatever made each of them unique, whatever it was that would shortly vanish, leaving each of them a vacant house of flesh—it was as though that animating principle, call it the soul, was rising up, trying to cast itself into her, trying to leap from the dying body and onto safe and welcoming terrain, just as she herself had leaped off that boat last spring and out of her old life.

At home, at night, in bed, she could hear them, she could hear their voices: not only Billie's, but Juliette's; not only Juliette's, but even Mr. Allan's. Two days after her encounter with him, he'd died, and now that he was dead she could see that his sick last wish was a fucked-up manifestation, from a man who didn't know any better, of the same thing she found holy in Billie, the same thing she found holy in Juliette. Juliette, with her hope of passing on the legacy of humanist socialism to someone young; Billie, with her extraordinary kindheartedness, her concern about whether her beloved cats were being cared for: both were trying to make a bequest of what was special in themselves, trying to make sure it wouldn't be lost. Mr. Allan evidently had little to pass on but the desire to avenge his humiliations and the desire to humiliate. Billie and Juliette had something else: the capacity for tenderness, the capacity for care.

One evening Billie had much more strength than usual. She was speaking easily, as she hadn't in a while.

"Can you make me a promise?" she said.

"Anything."

"My birthday is coming next month. I want you to do something nice for me."

"I'd love to."

"This is what I'd like. If I'm not here, don't sit around feeling sad. Go dancing with that nice Isaac. That would make me happy."

Nora hadn't told her about what had happened with Isaac.

"I'm going to be with you," Nora said. "You'll be here."

Billie put her hand on Nora's.

"I know. But if I'm not."

BILLIE FELL ASLEEP SHORTLY after this. Nora sat at her bedside, wanting time to stop. Then, very gently, trying not to wake her, she lay down beside her on the narrow bed.

Nora put her arm around her. She didn't actually touch her, because Billie was so sore that every touch was painful; instead, she held her arm just above her in the air, cradling her without contact. Nora was lying on her right side; it was her left arm, her damaged arm, that was holding Billie in this way.

The lights in the hallway went off and then on again—visiting hours were over—but Nora didn't want to leave her aunt alone just yet, and she lay beside her, with her arm around her awkwardly, for a few minutes more.

41

ISAAC HAD BEEN INVITED to give a talk at Rutgers about photojournalism in the computer age. He came home from work to take a shower before driving down to New Brunswick. There was a message on his answering machine. It was from Nora. They hadn't spoken since the night he'd read her story.

She was sobbing. She was calling to tell him that Billie had died.

"I wasn't even there. I came in yesterday afternoon and her bed was empty. I should have been there. I should have been holding her hand."

He called her, got her machine, and left a message telling her how sorry he was. He was relieved to get her machine.

He'd never known Billie well, but he'd gathered a strong impression of her from Nora's stories. Not from her stories, really, but from the feeling in Nora's voice when she told them.

Good-bye, Billie.

The thought flickered across his mind that maybe he and Nora would get back together now. Maybe taking care of Billie had sapped her spirit in some way, which had led her to write that cruel story about him, and now that Billie was gone...

This line of thought made no sense, and he didn't pursue it.

He went to the bathroom and shaved. He had to shave very carefully, because his face still hurt. He'd broken his nose and his left cheekbone when he fell from his bike. He still didn't quite recognize himself in the mirror.

He took a shower, lay dripping on the bed, turned on the TV, and watched a few minutes of *Gladiator*.

The three stages of mourning, he thought: Gee, that's too bad; what's in it for me?; what's on TV?

Not a good way to live.

He got out of bed, turned the television off, sat down in a hard wooden chair, and spent a minute commemorating, in silence, the life of this woman whom he had never really known.

He looked at the bed, the quilt damp and slightly disturbed where he'd been lying. He thought of taking a picture of the empty bed, a picture that would serve as a record of his attempt to make a gesture of decency. Because he'd sat up; because he'd turned off the TV. He was just about to get a camera when he saw the clock and realized he had to get going. It didn't matter anyway. Even if he took the picture, no one would understand what it meant.

42

NORA SPENT MOST OF THE NEXT month alone. She wrote, she did her freelance work, she read.

Billie's death was like an ache that traveled from one part of her body to another. Nora would wake up every day and feel it in a new place.

She missed Isaac, but she didn't call him.

She missed many things about him, but more than anything else, she missed *thinking* with him. She missed the way his mind worked. Her thoughts kept running out to meet his thoughts, but his thoughts weren't there.

She kept thinking she saw him on the street, but it always turned out to be somebody else. Once, when Nora was about ten years old and Billie's husband was still alive, Nora had asked Billie how she knew she loved him, and Billie said that even after fifteen years, she still felt excited when she saw him on the street.

But Nora had no intention of calling Isaac again. They were through. She was reconciled—happily reconciled—to the thought of being alone. On Thanksgiving Day she wrote in the morning, read in the afternoon, had Chinese food delivered to her apartment, and ate at her coffee table while she watched *North by Northwest*. It was a good day.

She'd had friends who, after romantic disappointments, had declared that they were swearing off men for good. Nora had always marveled at their powers of self-delusion, and of course all of them had gotten hooked up again in due time. Her own case, she thought, was different. She'd known from an early age what it meant to be alone. And if being alone was the price she had to pay in order to write freely, she was prepared to pay it.

She still wasn't happy that her stories hurt people, but she wasn't worrying about it anymore. She didn't need to worry about hurting Benjamin; she didn't need to worry about hurting Isaac. She didn't need to stifle her own talents to avoid wounding anyone. She didn't need to take care of anyone, ever again.

Them lady poets must not marry, pal.

But if you don't have anyone in your life, who will you write stories about? You won't have anyone's secrets to spill.

She concluded that it didn't matter. She probably had years of stories in her, stories she'd stopped herself from writing because she was afraid of where they'd lead. Or maybe she'd learn to live entirely in her imagination. Balzac had believed so completely in his characters that on his deathbed he'd called out for Bianchon, a doctor who existed only in his novels. That seemed like a noble death for a writer. Maybe she could create a world in her imagination, a world large enough for her to live in. Maybe she'd call out on her deathbed for her own Bianchon.

But not yet. Since finishing the Gabriel story, she'd been sitting at her card table every day, trying to begin something new. She was writing disconnected scenes about characters who were still unformed; she was still straining to see them in the dark. A story had yet to emerge. But she had the dreadful sense that however long it took to emerge, she already knew what it would be. She could sense the activity of the part of her imagination that guided her fiction; she could feel it stirring. She pictured it as something inhuman: a cunning lump, huddled somewhere in the gray of her brain. It was slowly settling on its next victim, sending out its long tentacles into every corner of her mind, searching, searching, searching, with a horrifying patience, for the person Nora loved more purely than she loved anyone else. The next story was going to be about Billie. Nora had always held Billie in the warmest part of her soul, but now she would be removed for a while, taken to a colder region, and examined there.

She wished she could shield Billie from what was coming, but she knew it was no use. She also knew that whatever came out, she wouldn't love her any less.

ON THE MONDAY AFTER Thanksgiving, Nora got a call from a social worker at Riverside. Juliette had died the day before, and in going through her things a nurse had found a sealed envelope with Nora's name on it. Juliette had left her something. The social worker offered to send it to her, but Nora decided to pick it up herself. She felt sorry that she'd never returned there after Billie died, never returned to visit Juliette. The trip out there in the subway didn't seem precisely like an act of penance—it was too small a sacrifice—but at least it was an acknowledgment that she had something to do penance for.

When she got there they told her that the envelope was across the street, in the hospital's lost-and-found office. She crossed the street and picked it up. There was no note inside the envelope. The only thing in it was a necklace. A silver chain, a single pearl.

Walking back toward the elevator, she glanced down a long corridor and saw colorful drawings on the walls, children's drawings in crayon. She heard the sound of a child's laughter. At the end of the corridor she saw a sign that said Tyler Children's Center. She walked down the hallway, following the line of drawings, and pushed through the double doors and went in. The gift from Juliette had made her melancholy; she needed, just for a moment, to be close to children's laughter.

She was in a cramped waiting room. There were four or five families here. Parents were scattered randomly, sagging people on sagging couches, in various stages of exhaustion and denial, with their children, who were in various stages of bone-stuntedness and brain-stuntedness. The girl whose laughter Nora had heard was sitting on the floor, putting brightly colored plastic mice into her mouth. She was probably ten or eleven years old. She was unnaturally puffy, and hairy in the wrong places: little tufts sprouted from her cheeks and chin. Her mother kept leaning over and wearily extracting toy after toy from her mouth.

Across the room, a meek-looking mother was sitting with her son, a boy of about seven or eight. He was bald, and he had several long scars on his skull. The scars must have come from brain operations, but they were so thick and long and jagged that they didn't look like the results of a procedure that involved exactness and care. He looked as if some waggish uncle while carving the Christmas turkey had decided to slice up a few sections of his head.

From down the hall Nora could hear an infant crying out, in pain, or in fear, or both. It sounded like a girl's voice. She was howling, howling, howling.

The thickness of the misery in this room made Nora weak. She went to the water fountain, and she was disturbed to discover that she had a clear line of sight into the room where the infant girl was howling. She was probably about a year old. She looked beautiful, but Nora only caught a glimpse of her, because there were so many people surrounding her. A nurse was holding down her arms and a woman who must have been her mother was holding down her legs while a doctor was attempting to fit an intravenous tube into her neck. A man who must have been her father was leaning against the wall with his hands in his pockets, weeping. The girl was crying out, "Dada dada dada!" Nora couldn't tell if she was calling for her father—she was so young that she probably wasn't; this was probably a sound that had no meaning except that she was in pain—but, seeing her father crying in the corner, it was easy to imagine that he felt as if she was begging him to make this stop, and that he was crying because he couldn't.

Nora thought she'd never witnessed anything more horrible than this: strangers inflicting pain on an infant who was too young to understand that they were trying to help her, and too young to understand why her parents were allowing this to happen.

The sight of someone this innocent being subjected to such pain was overwhelming. During her visits to the hospice, Nora had felt as if she had seen the depths of human suffering. But now she understood that she hadn't seen a thing. The hospice was filled with people in their seventies and eighties and nineties; it was sad, but it was comprehensible. There was nothing comprehensible about this.

She didn't know anything about this family. She didn't know what the beautiful child was being treated for; she didn't know why the mother looked so capable while the father was standing uselessly in the corner, weeping. What she knew was that following the sound of laughter in search of spiritual refreshment, she had once again encountered only suffering—suffering, and the effort to relieve it. And she knew that this was going to be her life: wherever she turned, the suffering world would be upon her.

She didn't know if she had stumbled onto a fact about existence or merely a fact about herself. Life isn't just suffering; she knew this. Life is also joy and creation and procreation. Yes, we're a community of suffering, but we're a community of ecstasy as well.

She knew this, but at the moment she couldn't feel it. At the moment it seemed to her that at the deepest level, what unites us is that we are creatures who suffer.

The father came out of the room for a moment. He bent down at the water fountain.

Nora went up to him and held out the necklace.

"This is for your little girl," she said.

He didn't seem to want to take it. She took another step forward, and he drew back, almost as if he was afraid of her, but she pressed the necklace into his hand, and his grief made him too sluggish to do anything but accept it. She quickly walked back into the waiting room, and he didn't follow.

She still felt weak, and she sat down on a couch. After a little while a nurse approached her—a hip-looking modern girl, with a very weird haircut and a very sweet face. She looked a little like Isaac's Renee, but a few years older and a few years calmer.

"I'm not sure we have you listed on our appointment schedule," she said. She had a singing voice. She looked down at her clipboard. "What's your child's name?"

Nora looked at the nurse's kind face, and felt the force of her youth—she couldn't have been out of her twenties, and she was radiant with good health—and she thought that she must be a remarkable woman. She spent her days caring for children, many of whom were so young that they didn't even realize she was trying to care for them, so young that they responded to any attempts to care for them by screaming.

Nora remembered Isaac's uncle Carl, with his theory that we're all bound in an eternal circle, animals destroying animals who have destroyed animals. But there are other circles.

She thought of her own desire to stop taking care of anyone, and she saw how hollow it was. It was like a dream of stripping away a part of her own nature.

The nurse glanced up from her clipboard, with a small soft smile that said she wanted to be of help.

"I'm sorry," she said. "Who's your child?"

Nora had never had an experience of déjà vu—not until now. She had the sense that she'd encountered this young woman before, a long time ago, although that couldn't have been true. She had a confused rush of feeling, and before she could assess the words that were coming to her lips—she would have rejected them if she'd had time to think—she answered.

"You are," she said.

The nurse looked at her with puzzled concern. "Are you all right?" she said.

"I'm sorry," Nora said. "I kind of wandered in here."

43

NORA RAN HER HAND ACROSS the window and wiped away the wet. She wanted to see the lights of the city as her bus crossed the George Washington Bridge. She was on her way to see Isaac.

He didn't know she was coming. She'd been calling him for over a week without reaching him. She hadn't left any messages; she wanted to talk to him face to face.

It was early on a Friday night. She didn't know if he'd be home, but she thought she'd give it a try. She thought she'd try him at his apartment, and, if he wasn't there, at his darkroom.

She walked from the bus stop. It was raining, but very lightly. She waited until someone was leaving his building and slipped into the lobby before the front door closed. She didn't want to ask him to buzz her up, because she was afraid that he wouldn't.

And she didn't want him to be able to prepare himself. If he wasn't expecting her, then the look on his face when he saw her would tell her everything she needed to know.

But when Isaac opened the door, Nora didn't even notice his expression. She was too shocked. His cheek was all mashed and caved in.

"You should see the other guy," he said.

"You're not serious. Are you? Were you in a fight?"

He didn't say anything. She saw that he wasn't going to tell her.

"Hi," she said.

He still had his hand on the doorknob.

"Aren't you going to invite me in?"

"Of course," he said, and stepped back.

She walked into the living room. As she passed him, she tried to feel the air around his body—not merely to breathe it in, but to sample it in some way that was larger and harder to define. It felt unresponsive, unremarkable, flat. He wasn't happy to see her. Which shouldn't have been a surprise.

She felt her courage draining away. The sight of his caved-in cheek had alarmed her. She was reminded of his fragility, and she was afraid that if they did get back together—which was, after all, what she was here for—she would hurt him again.

She considered just making idiotic small talk for a while and then slinking back home. But no. That wasn't the way.

She took off her jacket and sat on his couch. She'd cheated a little by wearing a dress and putting on a perfume that she knew he liked. She wanted to meet him soul to soul, but it never hurt to wear a dress.

"I've been calling you a lot," she said.

"Really? I haven't gotten any messages."

"I haven't left any."

She expected him to offer her something to drink; merely out of habit, he'd make an effort to be sociable. He didn't. He just sat across from her, looking uncomfortable, with his hands on his knees.

"Nora?"

"Yes?"

"Why are you here?"

She thought of making operatic declarations, telling him everything that had gone through her mind over the past two weeks. Telling him about her visit to the pediatric ward, where the cries of the beautiful child whose name she would never know had shown her that freeing herself from the needs of others was a naïve ambition, that the feeling of connection was rooted just as deeply within her as the need to create. Telling him that if she couldn't remain lashed to her desk—if she didn't want to—then she wanted to be with him. Because it was in his presence that she felt most alive. If her fate was to spend her life struggling, doing battle with some man in the effort to preserve her autonomy, then he was the man she wanted to do battle with.

But she didn't say any of this. She didn't want to make a speech.

"I'm here for two reasons. I wanted to remind you that you left that bass in my apartment. If you want it, you should pick it up. Or ask your brother to come get it. I would have brought it with me, but it's bigger than I am."

"Thanks for reminding me. I'm sorry it's taking up space. I have to be in the city tomorrow afternoon. I'll stop by and get it, if you're going to be around."

"Thank you."

"What's the other reason?"

"Billie asked me for something before she died, and I need your help with it. She said that for her birthday, she wanted me to go dancing with the person I'm sweet on. And her birthday's coming up."

"And I'm the person you're sweet on?"

She'd expected him to smile, but he wasn't smiling.

"Yes. You are."

"Even though I don't have wildness in me?"

"Isaac. I've told you many times what it's like for me. You always seemed to understand it when I told you what it was like to write about other people. I borrowed from you for the story, but that isn't you. I borrowed a side of you. I borrowed one of your ribs. But that isn't you."

"Did you ever finish it, by the way?"

"Yes. I did."

"What are you planning to do with it?"

This was a question she'd been hoping he wouldn't ask. But he'd asked it, and she had to tell him the truth.

"It's getting published."

"*Boulevard*?" Three of the five stories she'd published had been published in *Boulevard*.

"No. This one's getting published in the *Atlantic*." The version of the story that she'd sent them, as ragged as she'd thought it was, had won the contest.

He didn't say anything. He was trying to take this in. "Congratulations," he finally said, but he didn't look happy.

He stood up. "I'm afraid you came at a bad time. I'm meeting some people for dinner, and I was already late when you got here. I'd give you a ride to the bus stop but my car's in the shop."

"Still?"

"It's been in and out for the past month."

"That's okay. It's pretty out here. I like the walk." She put her jacket back on.

He was already at the door, holding it open, but she didn't want to go tamely home. "What about the dancing?" she said.

A faint smile—as angry as he obviously still was, he couldn't help but smile at her persistence.

"I don't know. I really don't know. When's her birthday?"

"Next Saturday."

"Well, like I say, I'm going to be in the city tomorrow, and I'll come by and pick up the bass. I guess I'll let you know."

Nora walked to the bus stop in the light faint rain, wondering what he'd decide. She couldn't guess. She didn't know if *she* would want to get back with herself if she were him.

But she hoped he would. He'd once told her that she had to respect her demon. She hoped he'd remember this, even now that the demon, the goblin, her unforgiving inner eye, had turned its gaze on him.

Love me, love my goblin, she thought. But she didn't know if it was possible.

She got on the bus, wondering if this was the last time she would ever make this trip. She was looking forward to the rest of the night with a mixture of pleasure and sorrow. Pleasure, because she'd be spending the night writing; sorrow, because she'd be continuing to expose Billie to the coldness of her imagination.

She wished she could tell Isaac that she was going to change for him, but she couldn't.

44

After Nora left, Isaac gave himself an insulin shot, and then went out to join a few friends for dinner. The restaurant was within walking distance; the rain was so light he didn't bother to open his umbrella. During the meal he didn't think about Nora. He thought about her as he walked home.

It was a no-brainer. He wasn't even going to be around next weekend. He'd be in Washington, moderating the panel discussion at the Folger Library. He'd decided to accept the sop Nadine Lyle had thrown him—the place at the kiddie table. Even though he wouldn't be on the panel with Avedon and Mann and the other hotshots, the conference was an opportunity he didn't want to miss. He'd be meeting a lot of influential people: photographers, editors, agents. If he ever wanted to get back into the picture-taking life, he'd be a fool to pass it by.

He walked slowly through the calm streets. He was glad he'd moved out here. It was a blessed retreat from the city. He knew he could never go back.

He was trying to understand Nora. How she could write what she wrote about him and still say that she was—what did she say? Sweet on him.

He supposed he could half understand it. In the weeks since he'd read her story, he'd thought about it a lot, and he'd come to a conclusion that surprised him. Nora was wrong about her writing. She'd always said that her stories had no compassion, but that wasn't quite accurate. Her portrait of him was a perfect rendering of the person he was afraid he might be. She'd intuited some of his worst fears about himself and written a story based on the premise that they were true. To write about him with such damning finality, as if he would never rise above his limitations—that, it was true, could be called cruel. But to go so deeply into his inner life that she could unearth his most intimate fears about himself—that was a large act of sympathetic imagination. She wasn't like a Diane Arbus, whose camera turned her subjects into freaks, but like a Bill Brandt, who plunged his subjects into harsh shadow and harsh light, and revealed them as no one had revealed them before.

What the hell am I defending her for?

When he got back home, it was only ten o'clock. He turned on the ball game, and then he turned it off. He went to the window and looked out at the city. There was a huge body of fog coming in from the north, making its stately way down the river. The city kept fading out and reappearing.

The photographs from his show, although it had ended weeks earlier, were still in their frames, stacked against the wall.

Maybe he had no right to be disappointed that his show had come to nothing. If your devotion to something can be measured by how much you're willing to give up for it, he wasn't sure how devoted he was. He used to be devoted, but he hadn't been in a long time. So what did he expect? It was as if he wanted the rewards without having made the sacrifices.

He wasn't even sure *why* he wanted to go to Washington—*why* he was still dreaming of reviving his career.

Sometimes he thought it was because he missed taking pictures, but that couldn't be it. If he missed taking pictures that much, he'd just start taking them again.

Sometimes he thought that what he really missed was the belief that there was an overarching meaning in his life. This was something he'd had since he was a boy, first because he was dedicating himself to God, then because he was dedicating himself to taking pictures: a thread that tied one day to the next, a bright thread of meaning that took the loose purposelessness of everyday life and gave it form and value and direction. He didn't have that anymore.

But maybe photography could no longer provide that. Maybe it was time to admit that he was happier doing what he did now—going to work and doing a job and coming home—than he'd been when he was taking pictures, and that the thing that was missing from his life now, the bright thread of meaning, wasn't art, it was love, love and family. Maybe the trip to Washington would be a trip in the wrong direction.

For years he'd been in the habit of thinking that because he wasn't taking photographs single-mindedly anymore, he'd let himself down. But maybe he'd been wrong. Maybe the ability to change course—to admit to himself that his old vocation didn't nourish him enough anymore—was a sign of sanity and strength.

But even if all that was true, it didn't mean he should let Nora back into his life. He now had firsthand knowledge of what it was like to get the Nora treatment, what it was like to be the subject—the target, really—of one of her stories. It was painful to know that her story would soon be running in the *Atlantic*, that thousands of readers would soon have the opportunity to read about his flaws.

Now that she'd broken through, now that she'd learned to

write as freely as she needed to, even at the expense of someone she loved, what he'd have to look forward to, if they made a life together, was a succession of decades in which everything he did would be documented with a merciless eye. Was he up for that? Forty years, perhaps, of being loved in daily life and lacerated in her stories?

And would she ever want children? And if she did, what kind of a mother would she be? How would a child enjoy being the beneficiary of the Nora treatment?

He didn't blame her for the way she was. She had a kind of integrity that he still, after everything, found exhilarating. He respected it, but that didn't mean he had to endure it.

ON THE NEXT MORNING, a Saturday, he left his apartment at noon and took a bus into the city. Two of his colleagues from the paper were getting married in a synagogue in the West Village. They were both in their late twenties; standing before the rabbi, they looked radiant and nervous, and very young.

After the ceremony, he went uptown. Nora's apartment was more than ninety blocks away, but he decided to walk. He needed time to figure out what he wanted to say to her.

It was the seventh of December. At five in the evening, it was already dark. And it was chilly. He hadn't dressed warmly enough. He had counted on global warming, but for one night, at least, global warming hadn't come through.

At a street corner in midtown he bought a bag of chestnuts from an old woman with a heated cart. She had long, stiff, stark-white hair; she was twisted low to the ground with age. As he was paying her, he was oddly aware that the same transaction—a man buying roasted chestnuts from a woman on a frigid late-autumn evening—might have taken place, on this same corner, a hundred years ago, and might take place here a hundred years in the future.

When he reached Central Park, he stopped at Wollman Rink to watch the skaters. There were young couples, lithe and confident; there were fathers and mothers teaching children who looked as if they'd never been on the ice before. The wedding must have put Isaac in a sentimental mood, because all of them, all of them, struck him as beautiful.

Finally he stood outside Nora's building. He couldn't tell which of the windows was hers: her apartment was too high up. It didn't matter. He knew what she was doing. She was sitting at her card table, in front of her computer—a new computer—working on a new story, a story that would turn out to be a sort of letter bomb addressed to someone she loved.

Arthur, the doorman, let him in, and Isaac took the elevator to the fifteenth floor. Nora opened her door. She looked as if she hadn't slept. She looked wary, guarded: he might have come just to pick up the bass.

But he knew her so well that he could see what she was thinking. She was trying not to show it, because she didn't know what he was going to say to her, but he could tell that she was hoping for the best.